A GI

BOOK FOUR OF THE GARDEN GIRLS SERIES

JEMMA FROST

Copyright © 2023 by Jemma Frost

All rights reserved.

No part of this publication may be reproduced, distributed, or transmitted in any form or by any means, including photocopying, recording, or other electronic or mechanical methods, without the prior written permission of the publisher, except as permitted by U.S. copyright law. For permission requests, contact authorjemmafrost@gmail.com.

The story, all names, characters, and incidents portrayed in this production are fictitious. No identification with actual persons (living or deceased), places, buildings, and products is intended or should be inferred.

Book Cover by The Arrowed Heart

Special Thanks

Our Garden Girls journey is coming to an end, but I can't close this chapter without thanking some very special readers!

Candy: You were my first beta reader way back with *Charming Dr. Forrester* and your encouraging words truly impacted my author journey and gave me hope I could do this. You can't imagine how many times I've said, "Thank goodness for Candy!" during particularly tough writing times.

Jenna: We're so similar, sometimes it amazes me that we connected! I'm so grateful for your insights and beautiful encouragement whether in beta reading or in your poetic reviews. You've been with me almost from the beginning, and I can't express how much I look forward to hearing from you. You're truly a kind and wonderful reader and person!

Jordan, Nicole, & Melinda: Thank you for all of your wisdom and advice on my stories. I swear you discover things I never even considered, and I'm always so impressed. You make my books better, and I can't thank you enough for your time and generosity!

I wish I could thank everyone personally, but to those not mentioned (readers/reviewers/editors etc.… THANK YOU! I can't do what I do without you!

Now, on to our grand finale with Caraway!

PROLOGUE

HAMPSHIRE, ENGLAND 1860

Screams of laughter drifted over the meadow as Caraway Taylor fought her way through the tall grass. Her sisters had decided it was time for a break from their lessons, which meant gallivanting outside like a trio of reckless hoydens. Lifting her skirts above the ground to avoid dirt, she lamented being the one to end their fun... *again*.

As the eldest, Caraway's responsibility was to ensure they finished their schoolwork and chores, especially since their parents were more focused on their research than them. Mr. and Mrs. Taylor loved their daughters but tended towards a more laissez-faire type of upbringing as they barely remembered to take care of themselves. Which is why it fell to Caraway to keep the household running smoothly.

Spying the three girls running wildly through the waves of grass, she almost called out their names before noticing the two boys chasing them. The lanky youth with a shock of copper hair resembled his father, the Earl of Trent, and the Taylors' neighbor for years. The earl's estate butted up against the back of her family's small property before continuing on for miles.

Owen Lennox had become something of a brother to her over the years as they were similarly aged and in regular contact trying to wrangle her sisters. Though, even Owen had a rebellious streak. Unlike Caraway.

Upon closer inspection of the group, she didn't recognize the second boy—his floppy brown curls shielding part of his face with its unruliness. He stood slightly shorter than Owen but just as fit.

"Cara!" Hazel, the youngest Taylor, waved enthusiastically as she ran towards her. "Come join us. We're playing tag, and Owen brought his friend, Miles Brandon. He's Lord Bellow's son."

Grabbing her hand in a sweaty grip, Hazel pulled her directly toward the stranger. "This is our sister Caraway."

Embarrassed, she dipped her head and dropped into a curtsy. One of these days she'd have to teach Hazel that such an introduction wasn't proper, but at twelve years old, she still held onto childish precociousness with no regard to etiquette.

Bowing, the boy extended his hand for Caraway's. With his mouth hovering over the back of her ungloved hand, his mischievous eyes peeked up at her. "Pleasure to meet you, miss. Miles Brandon, at your service."

A hot blush bloomed on her skin which she tried to attribute to the blazing sun instead of this boy's nearness. It felt scandalous having him so close. He could almost graze his lips on her bare skin!

The thought sent her usually practical self flying into a whirlwind of fantastical ideas such as letting him kiss her cheek or hold her hand. Acts she'd never done before—displays of affection she'd never had any yearning for until now.

"We've missed you, Caraway." Owen broke in as he pounded the back of Brandon's shoulder, causing him to jerk away from her. "I need your help. Your sister is refusing to take turns in our game."

"Girls don't chase boys, Owen," Lily spouted from the side, the heavy breaths falling from her a testament to her previous exertion. Iris trailed behind, quiet in her approach. Out of the four girls, she kept to herself the most. Despite being raised as their sister from a baby, Caraway wondered if the fact that she was their abandoned cousin weighed on her.

Turning her attention back to Owen and Lily, she rolled her eyes heavenward, knowing where this was headed. They needed to get into a good row every day before settling into their teasing taunts. It was obvious to everyone how much the pair liked each other despite the disparity in their social classes—Owen being of noble blood, heir to an earldom, whereas the Taylor sisters were simple country folk born to a professor and botanist. While they managed to get by, the grants her father received from various universities for his work hardly qualified them for the upper echelons of society.

"They do when you're playing tag, and I've caught you three times now," Owen argued, crossing his arms in a belligerent stance, clearly digging in for a fight. Sweat darkened the auburn hair at his temples as his eyes narrowed, daring Lily to refute his claim.

Leaving them to their tiff, Caraway asked Brandon, "Will you be staying in Hampshire long?" Walking arm in arm with Hazel and Iris, she led their small group away from the raised voices of Owen and Lily.

"I'll be here for the entire summer. The Lennoxes graciously invited me to stay once my parents decided to extend their trip on the Continent. The earl and my father are old chums, and it's their wish for Owen and me to form the same bond." He held his hands behind his back in a contemplative gesture, evoking the sense of someone older than his tender years.

"Is that why you didn't join your parents?" Hazel asked. "The Continent sounds like such fun! Think of all the history and stories to be told." Her eyes lit up as her imagination ran wild with possibilities. She was the dreamer of the family, always creating entertaining tales and drawing elaborate scenes to go along with them.

"Hazel, it's not polite to intrude on Mr. Brandon's privacy. Surely, spending the summer with a peer is preferable rather than traveling to events where you'd most likely be left out due to your age."

"Thank you, and it's Miles, please," the boy in question replied, a smile tilting his lips. "And you're correct. I wouldn't have had nearly as much fun staying in random hotels and conversing with various old people as I am here." He made a face that made them laugh. "I much prefer the present company." Piercing eyes met hers, giving a distinct feeling that he meant her alone—not her sisters collectively.

Ducking her head at the implication, Caraway bit her lip in shyness. How did one react to his possible flirting? Especially with Hazel and Iris hanging about.

As if understanding her sister's dilemma, Hazel pointed out a floating butterfly crossing their path. "Look, Iris! That's the monarch butterfly I was telling you about in my story. Let's follow it and see where it lands. This will be great information for my book!" Pulling Iris away, the girls ran after the flying insect, leaving the two of them alone.

Sweeping her hand over the tall grass, Caraway stole glances at Miles. He was quite an attractive young man even with flying curls and ruffled clothing.

Suddenly, a gust of wind whipped by them, attempting to blow her bonnet right off her head, and she quickly plopped a hand across the top to hold it in place until the breeze passed.

"Have you known Owen long, then?" she inquired, feeling silly with her hand on her head.

But he just stepped closer before responding, "Since we were in leading strings, though it's only recently that we've become better acquainted. Forced proximity and all as roommates at Eton." His words trailed off as he lifted a hand towards her face.

Wondering at his intentions, she froze like the Trent Estate's lake in winter. "Would you mind... That is, let me..." He caught a stray curl that had blown free of its pins and tucked it behind her ear. The slight caress of the delicate lobe sent a tingle of awareness down her body before they separated.

"Thank you," she murmured, unsure of what to do. While her sisters bore varying degrees of beauty even as children, Caraway knew she was more brains than beauty. Whenever they visited the village, comments would be made about Hazel's lustrous hair or Iris's unusual grey eyes. When it came to her turn for compliments, it usually revolved around her practical nature and how mature she acted for her age.

Never before had such sentiments bothered her.

But now in the presence of this attractive boy, she wished she had some experience—knew how to use her looks to her advantage. The boys in the village hardly spoke with her, instead captivated by other more traditionally pretty girls. Oh, how she loathed her inexperience and appeal to the opposite sex at that moment.

Trying to remember tactics used by some of the interactions she'd seen, Caraway reached out a hand to touch his arm in conjunction with her gratitude. Instead, she ended up swatting him in the chest when he turned away from her to continue walking.

"I'm so sorry!" The humiliation made her want to sink into the field, hidden from sight. "I didn't mean to hit you."

Laughing, he shook his head. "Don't worry. I hardly felt a thing... Will you be coming out soon?" The change of topic eased her embarrassment.

"No, I have a few more years before my parents will allow me to have a Season." Which she'd been fine with previously. At fifteen, she knew she wasn't ready to marry. She was needed at home to take care of her sisters and parents.

"Really? You seem older to me." A charming grin brightened his face. She didn't know how to take his comment—whether he wanted her to be older or not.

"People say that about me a lot, actually. I think as the eldest child you're automatically placed in a role of authority or maturity or else the younger siblings would run wild. Although, I'll admit they still do that sometimes."

"You don't say," he teased as they saw Hazel and Iris hike their skirts up to catch another flying creature while Lily and Owen continued to argue, standing chest to chest.

Sighing at the tableau before her, she shrugged. She could only do so much. "Some days are easier than others."

"I can't imagine being in your shoes. I'm the youngest of three sons—the opposite of your dilemma," he explained deprecatingly, snapping off the top of a grass blade. Obviously, this was a sore subject for him.

"Sometimes I dream of what it would be like without siblings running around, and while the quiet would be nice for a time, I fear it would be terribly lonely."

"At times," he agreed. "Though it can be lonely with two older brothers who choose their friends over you."

"Or three younger sisters who require supervision rather than another playmate."

They shared a look of commiseration before continuing to walk amiably while Caraway glanced back at her sisters every so often to ensure their safety. It looked as if Owen and her sister had settled their squabble as they were now teamed together and running after Hazel and Iris.

Miles followed her gaze to the rambunctious group. "Do you care to join them?"

She wanted to refuse but couldn't think of a reasonable excuse why they shouldn't return without seeming desperate for his undivided attention. Sighing, Caraway nodded, and they backtracked through the narrow path they wove through the field, the indentation of their steps clear markers.

"You two are a team, and you're it!" Lily yelled, her hands cupped around her mouth. Before they knew it, everyone scattered to avoid being touched by either Caraway or Miles.

Strategizing, she pointed to Hazel and Lily. "Why don't you run after them? They're the fastest. I'll take Iris and Owen." Saluting her with a hand to his forehead and a click of his heels, Miles ran after his sprinting prey.

Spying Iris attempting to duck and hide beneath the eye line of the grass, Caraway darted through the tall stalks, within an arm's reach before her sister skittered away. They played for another half hour before the setting sun reminded Caraway they needed to return home before dark.

Placing two fingers between her lips in a practiced gesture, a high-pitched whistle resounded through the field bringing everyone to a halt. "It's time for us to go home. We need to make sure supper is ready for Mama and Papa."

Their morning routine consisted of gathering vegetables and herbs from the garden in preparation for the day's meals, then at suppertime chopping them for some sort of stew or side dish. They would have a late start tonight due to her oversight of how late it was getting. Though with Miles paying so much attention to her, she could hardly be faulted for being a little scatterbrained.

"Allow us to walk you home," Miles offered, coming to her side and extending his arm. A rush of nervousness slammed into her, combining with the adrenaline from their game. The mixture created a pleasant buzzing along her nerve endings as she looped her arm through his, resting a hand on his bicep. Glancing around, she tried to see if anyone noticed the improper action, but everyone was occupied with their own conversations.

An unconscious squeeze of his arm revealed the sinewy muscle beneath his thin shirt eliciting more butterflies in her stomach.

What's come over me?

No wonder the girls in town always seemed silly around boys if these were the feelings they were experiencing.

The journey passed too quickly as the Taylor cottage rose into view surrounded by lush gardens and trees. It formed an idyllic scene that brought a comforting peace to Caraway—she loved their cozy home.

At the latched gate leading to the front door, Miles stepped closer to whisper, "I hope to see you again soon," before moving away and echoing Owen's louder sentiments of farewell.

Waving goodbye to the boys, the four girls traipsed up the stone walkway chattering about their new acquaintance and the sudden hunger that seemed to have appeared out of nowhere.

The rest of the night, through dinner and listening to their parents' afternoon findings, Caraway floated in a dreamlike haze, imagining seeing Miles again—having picnics by the pond or exploring the village shops. Who knew what the summer would bring?

And later as she lay in bed next to a snoring Lily, for the first time she allowed herself to dream. To fantasize about a life with the curly-haired boy next door who struggled with loneliness as she did at times.

How maybe they could be each other's cure.

Right before sleep claimed Caraway for the night, one last thought flitted like a wisp of fog through her mind and heart—one that permeated her dreams with scenes of charming smiles and gentle affection—*was this what love felt like?*

CHAPTER ONE

HAMPSHIRE, ENGLAND 1874

The cottage was too quiet.

Caraway Taylor sat at the kitchen table studying the empty chairs around her and remembered a time when they were filled with her sisters, Mama, and Papa. Now they remained dormant.

The sole disruption to her breakfast came from two birds twittering about on the windowsill. Not from her bickering sisters. Or her father's pencil scratching across a page of notes before he forgot whatever thought cluttered his mind.

Silence.

Loneliness.

Those were Caraway's companions.

"They don't have to be," she scolded herself, clearing the used dishes from the table before grabbing her bonnet hanging near the front door. "You have a sister, a brother-in-law, and an adorable nephew to keep you company."

Trekking toward Lily's home, Caraway muttered more reminders of the plethora of people in her life—a family who cared for her—yet it wasn't enough to fill the empty hole in her heart that widened by the day. Somehow, she needed to figure out a way to change her current circumstances or risk wasting away in Hampshire as the spinster aunt.

Years ago, she'd voiced her envy over Hazel's bravery to leave Hampshire and chase her dreams in Manchester. Her youngest sister had always known what she wanted from life—to become an author. Caraway wasn't as fortunate.

Her only purpose in life had been to steer Iris, Lily, and Hazel away from trouble. To raise them as their parents focused on studying all sorts of flora and fauna. Mr. and Mrs. Taylor were good people and good parents. Caraway loved them. But they could also be scatterbrained and absent, lost in their own world.

Thankfully, those traits didn't seem to impact her younger sisters. They held fond memories of their parents as did Caraway, though she also recalled the couple's faults, at times begrudging the freedom they enjoyed because Caraway took care of her siblings.

And now you have no one.

Hazel, Lily, and Iris were taken care of—all married now—and didn't need their spinster sister hanging around while they built their new lives.

"Which leaves me adrift in an unending sea of dismay."

"Beg your pardon, miss?" The Trent butler caught the end of her bitter musings after answering her knock on the door. She wasn't usually prone to melancholia or pitying herself, but something must be in the air today because Caraway couldn't shake the dark cloud roosting on her shoulders.

"It's nothing. Is Her Ladyship available?" *Her Ladyship.* Caraway couldn't resist the amusement twitching at the corner of her lips. Lily wasn't quite the proper lady a countess should be. She could be cantankerous, ornery, stubborn—all the descriptors of a woman who acted without thought to consequences or propriety—but Owen adored her, probably even more for her forthcoming nature.

"Yes, the family's lounging in the Blue Room. Follow me, please."

They ambled down the familiar marble hall until a murmur of voices drifted from a room on the right. The butler announced Caraway's name and then discreetly bowed out, leaving her alone with Lily, Owen, and her nephew Benjamin.

"Cara, we weren't expecting you this morning. Is everything alright?" Lily asked while father and son played on the floor at her feet, stacking wooden blocks before knocking them down. It was a cozy scene, and one she immediately regretted interrupting because of her own lack of husband and child.

"Everything's fine," she said, choosing to sit in an armchair across from her sister. "I just felt like visiting, but if you'd prefer no company, I can—"

"Nonsense. You're always welcome." Owen tossed a block in her lap which sent Benjamin toddling in her direction. Lifting the little boy into her arms, she ignored the pinch of longing in her belly.

Being surrounded by family is supposed to improve my mood, not blacken it even more.

"In fact, you're right on time to hear the news. Brandon's going to Manchester."

Caraway glanced up at Owen's declaration while Lily paused in her embroidery. "Why?" his wife asked, her nose wrinkling in distaste. Lily loved living in Hampshire, the picturesque countryside her home. The few times she'd visited Iris and Hazel in London and Manchester had been torturous, people-filled, and dirty. She didn't understand the types of people who preferred crowded city life to the wide-open spaces of the country.

"Apparently, he spoke with Travers last month and expressed an interest in investing in his new venture." Owen joined Lily on the settee, and Caraway watched him place a soft kiss on her temple as he settled beside her. Averting her eyes, she tried to quell the gnawing jealousy unbecoming of an older sister.

"Miles Brandon is willingly offering to enter trade?" Skepticism dripped from Lily's tone, and Caraway couldn't help but agree with her assessment.

Brandon was the third son of a respectable noble family. As such, he gallivanted about town free to do as he pleased, which seemed focused on general rabblerousing with his friends. The man wore ostentatious colors and kept himself perfectly coiffed at all times. Toiling in Manchester over the construction of a modernized textile factory didn't fit his personality.

Perhaps he's tired of frivolity.

The possibility excited Caraway. Ever since Brandon had returned with Owen from the Continent four years ago, she'd struggled to douse her affections for the man. No matter what Lily told her of his previous exploits, Caraway's heart wouldn't be swayed.

A hopeless crush had plagued her since their first meeting. Realistic in most circumstances, Caraway allowed herself this one fantasy—a romantic dream of capturing his attention despite the many women in his life. Had nurtured it for years. Even when she'd stayed in London at eighteen while her father taught at King's College, she'd held onto Brandon.

In retrospect, that might not have been the smartest idea—to close herself off to potential suitors when Caraway had no concrete reason to. But as the months wore on, and hardly a man approached her at luncheons or musicales, the illusion of Brandon provided comfort and a much-needed shield to protect her from dwelling on the reasons why most of the men preferred the lithe, blonde beauties over her plump, brunette self.

Surrounded by appropriately aged young men on the King's College campus, Caraway had failed to garner anyone's attention. It added another layer of pain and assurance to the truth that she was the plain but responsible Taylor girl when all she'd wanted was to be seen as beautiful and interesting for once in her life.

Perhaps I should visit Hazel.

It would be the perfect cover for following Brandon to Manchester and finally doing something with her life. Nothing would change for Caraway if she remained sequestered in Hampshire. That much was clear.

But in Manchester, she could show Brandon how suitable she'd be as his wife. Be more outgoing at parties and be more forthright with her own intentions towards him.

She knew she didn't offer much in the way of looks or pedigree, although having an earl for a brother-in-law certainly lent her a bit more status. And Owen had set up an account and dowry for her should she marry. So, Caraway had something to offer a future husband—a husband she hoped would be Brandon.

"What a coincidence! Yesterday, I thought it might be nice to see Hazel and Jonathan," she announced, trying not to display too much eagerness. Sweat lined her palms as she adjusted her grip on Benjamin, who'd decided to tug her curls falling from their pins.

"Yes, quite a coincidence," Lily's dry voice agreed. An indecipherable look passed between her and Owen, but Caraway pretended not to understand their disapproval. It was her life, after all. They were already living their happily-ever-after. Was it too much to ask to manufacture her own?

"Have you written Hazel to see if this would be a good time?"

"I've started one in my room. I suppose I should finish it, so it can go out with the post this afternoon." Caraway gently lowered her nephew to the ground before standing up, covertly drying her hands on her skirts as she straightened them out. Hazel wouldn't refuse her request; she extended an open invitation in every letter.

"I'm sure she'll be excited to have you. And little Callum will be over the moon." The mention of the little boy Hazel and Jonathan were fostering made Caraway smile. Though the couple didn't have children of their own, their home never lacked the presence of a child in need due to their influence in Devil's Haven, a rookery located in Manchester.

Lily set her unfinished doily aside. "You can bring the socks I've knitted for him!" She hurried from the room, calling for a maid to help her gather the gifts, while Benjamin raced after his mama.

"Callum will love them." Owen's wry tone stopped Caraway as she moved to follow Lily—she had her own packing to start—and they shared a look of bemusement, both knowing that Lily's knitting skills weren't exactly up to snuff.

"Since he's four years old, I'm sure he will. Now, I must be off myself. I'll let you know my travel arrangements once they're finalized."

"Cara," Owen called, and she paused again, glancing back in question. "Please be careful. Brandon is..." He ran a hand through his auburn hair and sighed. "Well, he's Brandon, and I don't want you getting hurt."

I'm already hurt, she wanted to say. Every day she woke with a pain that wouldn't abate. With a fear that this was all she'd ever know—the life of a spinster rather than one as a loved woman, a cherished wife.

Frankly, it was slowly killing her from the inside out.

"Thank you, Owen, but don't worry about me. I'm a grown woman. I'll be fine." With a wave of farewell, she left him behind, his shoulders drooping at her refusal to heed his warning. But she couldn't abandon this course.

Not now that she'd gathered enough courage to act on her feelings.

I'll be brave like Hazel.

Confident like Lily.

Sweet-natured like Iris.

And Miles Brandon won't be able to help but fall in love with me.

CHAPTER TWO

MANCHESTER, ENGLAND 1874

Gentlemen maintained memberships at clubs and gyms for their physical pursuits. However, Silas Riverton never felt compelled to join one of those establishments when it came to bare-knuckle boxing. He craved the rough and tumble ways of Devil's Haven men like the one he faced now. Status meant nothing, and Silas preferred it that way. He didn't have to worry about hurting some nobleman's pride or tempering his own volatile leanings.

Dodging a right hook, Silas shook the sweat out of his eyes. The salt stung, but he welcomed the pain. It made him feel alive. Rushing forward, he landed two quick punches, bringing his opponent to his knees.

"Get up," he ordered. *I'm not done yet.*

Cheers rose from the opposite corner of the ring as the stocky man staggered to his feet—one fist smearing blood across his cheek while the other covered his abdomen, and Silas's eyes narrowed at the obvious weakness. Victory was close. Like a savage beast stalking the forest, he sensed his opponent's impending loss and reveled in it.

The rusty smell of blood permeated the air around them as shouted bets rang throughout the dim warehouse.

Technically, the building should be condemned, but some enterprising men had decided to run this boxing operation, along with other illicit gambling endeavors, within its dilapidated walls, instead. Travers had brought him here a few months ago after learning of Silas's pugilistic interests.

It became the perfect outlet for his energy.

Taught from a young age to master his emotions—to, in fact, have none at all, Silas found himself able to survive the cold life his father created by relying on two things whenever emotions boiled too close to the surface.

Boxing and bedsport.

Case in point, today had been particularly frustrating with machines breaking down and Horace Cannon visiting Ashley Mills. A fellow factory owner, the man never failed to rile Silas's temper, which he kept strictly in check during their meetings. But once the clock struck six, his destination was obvious—the place simply known as The Warehouse.

Because this evening his needs ran rougher than a woman could satisfy—no matter how coarse. And she was *always* coarse. Experienced. Jaded like him.

Never a lady. One who might expect more from him than he had to give.

A determined roar broke through Silas's musings as his opponent tried to stage a final attack, but he sidestepped the swing. Charging forward with an uppercut to the man's already bloodied chin, Silas's fist hit its mark and knocked out his opponent. Whoops of triumph bellowed behind him while audible grumbles from losing betters were scattered throughout the crowd.

"Looks like you need this." A boxing judge offered Silas a cup of watered-down ale as he exited the ring.

"Thanks."

Ignoring the brackish flavor, he guzzled the much-needed liquid and grabbed his discarded shirt to do a cursory sweep over his chest and arms before donning it. Sweat slicked his body, and the cotton absorbed some of it, though his trousers clung uncomfortably. As an abandoned warehouse, a bathing room was hardly available, but Silas didn't mind. The cooling perspiration reminded him how hard he'd fought and evaporated the last of his tension.

He nodded goodbye to several acquaintances he'd made since coming to The Warehouse and stepped onto a dark street minutes later. Gaslights barely lit the road, most of them left unlit in this part of town. It wasn't prudent to be strolling alone in Devil's Haven, but he refused to bring his carriage here.

The well-built conveyance would be a beacon for thieves. Besides, he enjoyed the walk home. It gave him time to consider everything that needed to be accomplished the next day. Like another meeting with Travers about his plan for a modern textile mill, which would fill the majority of Silas's afternoon.

Jonathan Travers intrigued him. Until a few years ago, he'd been part of the Cobblewallers gang that ruled Devil's Haven. Now after marrying and opening an affordable boarding house, he'd become a respected member of the community. A man intent on bettering it with state-of-the-art factory plans.

Silas admired the younger man's ambition. It would serve him well in this business. And it's why he agreed to mentor Travers as well as invest in the endeavor. Part of Silas liked the idea of aiding the man's efforts since he hadn't received the same sort of help when he'd built Ashley Mills.

In a way, he was righting a wrong—even if the responsible party never knew the truth.

CHAPTER THREE

Caraway longed for a cup of chamomile tea and a rejuvenating nap to rid herself of the pounding headache that cropped up somewhere between Birmingham and Stafford on her journey to Hazel's home. As train rides go, she supposed it was smooth enough, but the monumental task ahead of her—attempting to engage Brandon's affections—weighed heavily on her mind. Unpinning her grey satin hat provided some relief, though removing the multitude of pins holding her mass of curls in place would have been ideal.

Sighing in resignation, Caraway studied the parlor she'd been directed to upon arriving at the Travers home. It was a stark contrast to their previous lodgings in Devil's Haven. The boardinghouse Jonathan spent years renovating had been convenient for a time, living amongst his tenants, but she was happy when he and her sister decided to move to a safer part of town.

They still ran the boardinghouse and school Hazel started but the separation between their professional and personal lives could only harbor good things for their family. Including the ability to foster Devil's Haven orphans.

Figurines lined the fireplace mantel while frames of country landscapes were artfully placed around the room.

It seemed Hazel hadn't completely left her country roots behind. Tracing a finger down the delicate face of a maiden figurine, tendrils of disappointment slipped through Caraway again.

She was glad her sisters had all found love. Marrying in startling fashion, one in quick succession of the other. It comforted her to know they would always be taken care of and would no longer have to worry about money or shelter. However, it stung that, as the oldest, she remained unwed. And likely to stay that way as a spinster of thirty.

Heat suffused her cheeks in embarrassment, and she swallowed hard as tears formed. Glancing at her image in the mirror on the opposite wall, Caraway lamented the plain, plump woman reflected back to her. She was the shortest and the roundest of her sisters. Did she really think she could make Brandon fall in love with her?

Stop being such a ninny! You've come to try. To take charge of your life. It's too late to turn back now.

Straightening her spine, Caraway gave herself a determined nod in the mirror before continuing her foray around the room. Muted voices drifted through the solid oak door marking an adjoining room to the parlor, and curiosity drew her closer. She placed a hand on the brass knob, but before she could decide whether to interrupt the speakers or not, the door swung open from the other side.

"Oh, I beg your pardon." A deep male voice punctured Caraway's surprise as she staggered forward. "I didn't realize anyone else was here."

The man before her stood tall and intimidating in his black necktie, vest, and coat. There was no peek of brightness in his attire, causing Caraway to think of Mr. Gunner, the undertaker from home. Always doom and gloom with death hanging about him, and although this man was missing the sunken wrinkles of Mr. Gunner, the abundant silver in his hair lent him the same air of maturity.

"No, I apologize. I shouldn't have been loitering in a doorway. I heard someone speaking and curiosity got the best of me." Caraway smiled sheepishly, meeting his dark eyes before looking away and finding Jonathan behind him. "Jonathan, how lovely to see you!"

"Always a pleasure, Cara." He welcomed her with a grin. "Is my wife making you wait too long? You're already trying to escape?"

"Hardly... I'm sure Hazel's busy with Callum."

"Ah, yes, wrangling the little hellion can be a difficult task." His bemused tone belied any frustration when it came to raising the young boy—an orphan after his mother perished from pneumonia. Remembering they weren't alone, Jonathan introduced Caraway to the stranger, who'd been observing their little reunion. "Mr. Silas Riverton, let me introduce you to one of my lovely sisters-in-law, Miss Caraway Taylor. She'll be visiting us for a time. We'll have to expound on the benefits of living in the North compared to the rolling countryside of Hampshire while she's here."

"A pleasure, Miss Taylor." Mr. Riverton bowed though his gaze remained on her. "I'll endeavor to ensure you are availed of every pleasure Manchester has to offer."

Caraway blushed as his tone implied a double meaning to the innocuous statement. Of course, she was imagining any innuendo on his part. Men didn't flirt with her. The man was only being polite, and she needed to rest before further ridiculous imaginings occurred.

"Thank you, sir." Their eyes held for a moment longer before he excused himself and left. Releasing a labored breath, Caraway turned back to Jonathan, whose speculative gaze escaped her notice.

"Darling, you're here! I'm sorry for the wait. Callum refused to take his nap, so Nanny finally had to step in." Hazel swept into the room with all the cheerfulness Caraway was used to from her little sister. Being the youngest of four daughters, she'd grown up as the baby of the family, doted upon. Rarely did something dampen her perpetually bright spirits.

Caraway waved her hand in a dismissive gesture. "No need to apologize. It gave me a few moments to see Jonathan."

"And meet Mr. Riverton," Jonathan added as his wife sidled up to his side. He dropped a brief kiss on her forehead, the love between them evident.

"Oh, Mr. Riverton, what an imposing fellow—always so serious." Hazel gave a mock frown. "It's no wonder he's still unmarried. He frightens all the young debutantes."

"I doubt it matters to him," Jonathan interjected. "He doesn't seem interested in marriage."

Hazel shrugged then twined her arm through Caraway's to drag her back into the parlor. "No matter! Enough about him, I want to hear from you, Cara. Tell us about your trip. Was it dreadful?"

They settled into a comfortable conversation in the parlor where tea and cakes were served, and Caraway filled them in on her uneventful ride to Manchester while sharing the latest family tidbits from Hampshire.

Her headache ebbed to a dull pinch at her temple with each sip of tea as she relaxed into an overstuffed armchair, grateful for Hazel's ramblings now that she'd done her duty and relayed family news. One of the best things about Hazel, though it could also switch to the worst, was her ability to carry a conversation.

All Caraway had to do was sit and listen while her youngest sister yammered on about Callum and his new fascination for carrots over peas. It's not that she didn't value the information, but frankly, the child's diet failed to eclipse her fatigue.

"I think it's time we let your sister rest, sunshine."

Blinking awake, Caraway flushed. "I'm sorry. I didn't mean to doze off. You were saying?"

Hazel chuckled. "Jonathan's right. Let me show you to your room, so you can rest. We have plenty of time to catch up later."

Yes, plenty of time to chat and plenty of time to formulate a plan to capture Brandon's attention.

As Caraway followed her sister upstairs to her bedroom, it occurred to her that it was too bad Brandon hadn't been visiting today rather than Riverton. Though, perhaps it was for the best considering her current state of ruffled traveling gown and bleary eyes. She must've looked positively peaked to Riverton.

Count your blessings it wasn't Brandon, after all.

CHAPTER FOUR

The cobbled streets teemed with people rushing home for the evening, and Silas weaved his way through the crowds as he walked back to Ashley Mills. His meeting with Travers had gone better than expected considering the man was an ex-gang member with no previous mill experience.

However, the younger man understood business and that was the most important quality to have when it came to starting a company. Travers's factory aimed at creating safe conditions for its employees would be quite the feat, and Silas wasn't so greedy as to refuse to offer help when asked.

Competition was good for the economy.

He hadn't expected to meet Travers's sister-in-law, though. She'd surprised him. Short and curvy, a delightful handful, her dark brown curls were barely restrained and begged to be released from their pins. Images of it draped across her bare shoulders like a rising Venus raced through his mind. Her blue eyes deepened to navy by a desire beckoning him closer.

A rough laugh scraped his throat. Nothing good could come from those thoughts. He'd met enough women to know they weren't interested in a bachelor factory-owner, no matter how much they enjoyed spending his money. It didn't make up for working in trade or his lack of title and charming demeanor.

Besides, his tastes ran decidedly to a baser level than any good English rose would want to satisfy. Too bad the knowledge refused to stop his blood from heating in arousal at the thought of *that* particular English rose trying.

Entering his home located across from the mill, Silas handed his hat over to his butler Giles and headed toward his private study. Divesting himself of any more useless thinking, he sat down at his large mahogany desk to focus on the paperwork that had piled up while he was away. Work never ceased to stop it seemed.

He ate his dinner as he reviewed and signed off on new contracts, bills of sale, and the like, then afterward, continued to work late into the night. With no wife or children—no family— to draw his attention, it only made sense to fill his time with items of importance.

Hours later, Silas glanced at the clock to see it was past midnight. Rubbing his strained eyes, he leaned back in his chair, observing the stark room. The fire had long ago flamed out, leaving his desk lamp as the only light in the room. One item adorned the walls: a copy of his deed to Ashley Mills. The day he'd officially taken ownership of his own business, no thanks to his father.

No, Elias Riverton could never be accused of spoiling his son. On Silas's eighteenth birthday, his father had sent him packing, telling him it was time to be a man and make something of himself. Elias would not be offering any monetary or emotional support just as he had received none from his own father.

Emotions were a weakness. No self-respecting businessman let himself be governed by them let alone admitted to having any. The lesson had been hammered into Silas from a young age.

Scoffing at the maudlin turn he'd taken, he closed his eyes, determined to clear his mind for a second before continuing his work.

It was dawn before Silas realized he'd spent the night in the study instead of his bed... again.

A FEW DAYS LATER, SILAS was running late for his appointment with Travers because a previous meeting with distributors had run longer than expected. *Damn inconvenient.* Time equaled money, and punctuality was key. He hated feeling like a dog chasing a cat when his entire schedule got pushed. It was a never-ending game of catch-up.

Quickening his pace after exiting the carriage, the Travers butler greeted him before directing Silas toward the study down the hall. Travers was already in conversation with a young man by the window, both of them sipping from glasses filled with amber liquid. The stranger wasn't familiar, and he hadn't been notified of a guest attending the meeting.

"Ah, Riverton, I'd like to introduce Miles Brandon, a friend of my brother-in-law Owen. He just arrived from Hampshire." Travers gestured to Brandon who wore bright green velvet. Such ostentatious attire seemed out of place in the muted tones of the study.

It harkened back to decades earlier when vibrant colors were fashionable for men rather than the neutral tones currently popular. Obviously, Brandon thought himself a bit of a dandy and didn't care who knew it.

Shaking the smooth hand offered to him, Silas dipped his chin in greeting. "Good to meet you."

Handing a glass to Silas, Travers continued, "Brandon will be our fourth investor, taking a more visible role rather than being a silent partner like Calloway. He's decided he's interested in the cotton business, and I thought he could learn alongside me during our meetings, if you're agreeable?"

Bewilderment filtered through Silas at the unexpected news. He hadn't realized Travers had been looking for another investor since they had enough capital between the three of them to fund the venture. Though with the downturn in the economy lately, he supposed it couldn't hurt having another person share the burden of starting a new company—as long as he wasn't dead weight.

Silas looked the dandy up and down, examining his manicured hands which probably had never seen work in this lifetime, and the expensive decorative clothing not meant to withstand any type of physical exertion. He doubted they'd be receiving much more than cash from this type of man unless a brilliant analytical mind hid behind the outward trappings of frivolity.

"Of course, we can always use more manpower."

"Excellent!" Travers slapped a hardy pat on Silas's back before moving to his desk, and they shifted gears to review the architect's plans sent earlier that morning. Brandon stayed silent most of the meeting which Silas appreciated—maybe the young man *did* want to learn.

CHAPTER FIVE

Spending time with Hazel and her family brought Caraway untold joy. She enjoyed morning walks with her sister and playing with Callum in the afternoon when Hazel taught classes in Devil's Haven. However, tonight she could officially start her plan of getting Miles Brandon to notice her as more than his friend's sister-in-law.

The Travers were hosting a small get-together, and when she learned of the event, she'd sought an inconspicuous way to mention inviting Brandon. Imagine her surprise when Hazel shared that Brandon had just met with Travers and Riverton because he was joining their venture, thus he was already invited. It seemed like fate, a nebulous thing Caraway hadn't given much thought to before, but now wondered if she'd been destined to pursue Brandon, after all.

The true test will be this evening when you see him again.

Caraway studied herself in the vanity mirror as a maid arranged her hair in an intricate design with artful curls trailing down the back. Tonight, she must be outgoing, and vivacious—the opposite of her reserved nature. One of her best dresses completed her ensemble, a periwinkle blue velvet whose ruching and pleats disguised some of her roundness while the color enhanced her eyes.

Voices floated into the room as guests arrived, and a cold sweat broke over Caraway's skin as she dried clammy palms on her dress. One of those voices might belong to Brandon, whom she hadn't seen in months. The fluttering of butterflies in her stomach reminded her of that fact.

Calm down.

Brandon needed a confident wife—a serene woman who could handle herself in any situation. If she couldn't survive a small gathering of Hazel and Jonathan's friends, what hope did she have of proving herself a worthy partner?

"All done, miss." The maid stepped back to admire her handiwork, and Caraway had to admit she'd done a lovely job. It was no easy feat to tame her wild curls, but the girl had managed to use their untamable nature to her advantage.

"Thank you, Maude, that will be all."

Inhaling a steadying breath, Caraway steeled her courage and headed downstairs. Everyone was gathered in the salon which glittered from above with chandelier crystals. The women shone like jewels in colorful dresses while the men stood as a neutral canvas in their blacks, navies, and beiges.

Like a beacon of light, Hazel stood at the center of attention. Accompanied by her handsome husband, the couple was surrounded by the austere Riverton, a lithe raven-haired woman, and Brandon. Tension released then doubled as Caraway's relief that he came morphed into fear of actually following through with her plan. Lifting her chin a fraction higher and holding her shoulders back, she tried to appear graceful and calm while approaching the group.

"There you are! We were just telling Mr. Brandon how glad we were to hear he was in town. And he's introduced us to his friend Miss Emily Bradshaw." Hazel stepped aside to make room for Caraway in their circle, forcing her to stand next to Riverton, who loomed over her shoulder like a somber scarecrow.

A delicious-smelling scarecrow.

But that was neither here nor there.

"Yes, I was delighted to receive an invitation to tonight's festivities. It's good to see you, dear Miss Taylor." Brandon bowed his head slightly in her direction, causing a blush to appear at the endearment.

Caraway's lips tipped up in a slight smile. "You, too, Mr. Brandon. We are all most happy for your presence," she said, shyly meeting Brandon's light grey eyes.

"Indeed." The inflection in Jonathan's tone implied something other than pleasure, but she dismissed the thought. What grudge could her brother-in-law have against the man?

Changing the subject, Jonathan continued, "Riverton has agreed to include Brandon in our consultations about the textile factory. With the latest mechanical innovations, business is booming, and we're hoping to be at the forefront of success."

"How exciting! Does this mean you'll be staying in Manchester for a while, Mr. Brandon?"

"Naturally. I plan to stay as long as necessary. Hopefully, you don't tire of me." His charming smile brought another rush of scarlet to her cheeks.

She had known him for over a decade and hadn't tired of him yet. She doubted she would start now. And this helped her plan immensely. Close proximity was just the thing she needed to give Brandon the opportunity to reciprocate her feelings.

Whenever he visited Hampshire, it was for short stays dominated by hunting with Owen. Rarely did the two of them have cause to spend long hours together.

But now he'd be visiting the Travers home—*her* home for the time being—discussing business. The possibilities were endless for them to bump into each other and strike up a conversation.

"It's time for us to lead the way to dinner, sunshine," Jonathan said, nodding toward the servant who'd signaled him in the doorway.

Disappointed at having their conversation cut short, Caraway maintained a serene facade, though a frown of regret threatened to form.

You'll have another opportunity soon.

Jonathan took Hazel's arm, and they slowly made their way through the crowd to the dining room. Brandon turned to Caraway, and a flurry of nerves sparked in her veins at the thought of him escorting her. The feel of his strong arm under her hand was an exciting prospect, but before he could speak, another male voice interjected, "Miss Taylor, would you allow me to escort you inside."

Riverton offered his arm, effectively shutting down any objection she might have had. Of course, it would have been incredibly rude to refuse him, but frustration seethed inside her belly.

Pasting on a resigned smile, Caraway accepted his arm but couldn't resist leaving Brandon with a promise. "We'll chat over dinner. Perhaps about your travels?"

It was a simple but bold statement, and she gave herself a mental pat on the back for voicing it. It was a small step in the right direction of being more sociable and helping him see her as a woman, not a girl he'd known for years.

Smells of the first course of roast beef wafted through the dining room where a long table showcased dishes of all sorts. The Travers spared no expense when it came to entertaining. Silver candelabras stood tall and polished, beacons of light across the table. Pride swelled in Caraway's chest at the evidence of how far her youngest sister had come. How far Jonathan had come.

Two people determined to help the unfortunate citizens of Devil's Haven by creating a school, a boarding house, and now a safer working establishment. Through investments of Jonathan's previously ill-gotten gains and royalties from Hazel's children's books, the couple had obviously done well for themselves. Even Peter, Jonathan's younger brother, attended Eton, a prestigious school that would've been out of reach a few years ago.

As luck would have it, Caraway's name card sat between Riverton and Brandon's. *Thank you, Hazel.* While she'd never expressly mentioned her feelings for Brandon, over the years her sisters had guessed at her emotions—Lily especially as she was Brandon's most vocal critic. But Owen remained friends with the man, so if he maintained a relationship, how terrible could Brandon truly be?

"Mrs. Travers tells me you also have a sister in London. How does Manchester compare to the excitement of Town?" Riverton leaned closer as he spoke, his clean scent mixed with a pine aroma. Oddly, it reminded her of home in this industrial city.

"London has its charms, but I much prefer Manchester's smaller feel—despite its rather less than ideal locale."

"Yes, we do experience harsher winters than I'm sure you're used to in the South. I'm surprised you're not disappointed more by the considerably fewer opportunities for entertainment."

Her nose wrinkled in disagreement. "Oh, Manchester has plenty—more than I'm used to coming from a small village. But those things don't matter much to me anyway."

In her childhood home, her sisters used to provide a plethora of distractions. Hazel created outlandish stories which they acted out inside or in the neighboring woods. They'd even built a makeshift shelter out of branches as part of their stage. Caraway sighed remembering such happier times. Now, they were all grown up and separated by circumstances and marriages.

These days her amusement relied on visits to the Trent Estate or reading alone at home. *Goodness, I already sound like the proverbial spinster aunt.* The unwelcome realization prompted a large gulp of her wine.

"What *does* matter to you?"

Shaken from the dismal thought, Caraway met Riverton's imploring dark eyes. Something hot flickered between them, confusing her. His question seemed innocuous, a natural progression from their conversation, yet an undercurrent of deeper meaning washed through her. His gaze held hers, searching beyond the surface to a place inside she kept carefully walled up and guarded.

A GENTLEMAN NEVER SURRENDERS 39

Licking her lips, Caraway swallowed another splash of wine in an attempt to rid herself of a suddenly dry throat. The action drew his attention lower to focus on the undulation of her throat—breaking the strange spell threading between them before casting an even stronger hold on her.

A gentleman shouldn't stare at a woman like this.

A gentlewoman shouldn't find her breathing stuttering at his obvious interest. Shouldn't wonder what his own lips would feel like against hers. *Scratchy*, she thought, trying to recall herself to the party. His beard would be scratchy.

But the longer Caraway stared, the more curious she got until she almost reached up to test the growth for herself.

Thankfully, a throat cleared next to her. Startled, Caraway jerked back, unaware of the way her body had unconsciously shifted more toward Riverton. She noted the tightening of his mouth into a frown before readjusting to focus on Brandon.

"I apologize. What did you say?"

Here was the man she was supposed to be thinking of. The one she should be having scandalous moments with. Not some northern factory owner who was certainly too old for her. *Old may be a bit harsh.* He wasn't exactly decrepit. But definitely more mature than she'd like. She needed someone her age who was lighthearted and could break her out of her reserved shell.

Someone like Brandon who still looked at her expectantly.

Annoyed with her failure to concentrate, Caraway tried to piece together the few words she thought she'd heard from him. "Yes, the roast duck looks delightful. It's your favorite, right?"

Relieved to see him nod and go on, she took a calming breath and sat a little straighter. Time to be serious and show Brandon what an engaging partner she could be. Prove her worthiness as a potential wife.

An inkling of fear crept in, whispering doubt over making him fall for a version of herself that wasn't real, but she quashed it. Brandon knew the real her. Now he needed to see that she could play the game and be wifely material.

CHAPTER SIX

Silas shifted to speak with the woman sitting to his right, but his frustrated expression warned her of his foul mood, and she immediately excused herself to continue chatting with her neighbor. The tablecloth bounced with the movement of his rapidly tapping foot under the table as he stabbed at the course in front of him.

The anger heating his blood made no sense. Women, or anyone, really never garnered such demonstrative a reaction from him.

Because Silas Riverton always kept his cool. It was a known fact.

But Brandon had interrupted them, his slick demeanor rubbing Silas the wrong way from the first time they'd met, despite his efforts to remain congenial and unbiased toward the man. Though even before the disruption, Silas's conversation with Miss Taylor and the inappropriate urges it summoned irked him as well.

What possessed him to engage with her so intently? He knew she was out of his league—that she wasn't someone he should be toying with. Yet, he couldn't resist probing her, trying to see who she really was underneath the perfect lady facade.

Why? He had no goddamn clue.

Better figure it out soon and crush the improper yearning before you find yourself inextricably tangled with the woman.

Unfortunately, Silas's traitorous body and mind did not "figure it out," and a week later he stood frozen at the sight of Miss Taylor and little Callum playing on the floor of the parlor. He'd never seen her so lighthearted and relaxed during his visits to the Travers home.

Her cheeks were flushed red from exertion despite the freedom of wearing no corset—a fact his body became instantly aware of as his cock refused to ignore the sight of her gently swaying unbound breasts.

For fuck's sake. Silas warred with himself. Sweat broke out on his forehead while his lungs worked double time, desperate to draw in her scent like a damn hound. A man of forty-five should not so easily be affected, and Silas cursed his inability to control himself.

Training his gaze on the boy as a distraction, the blonde toddler seemed to be enjoying himself, babbling as he haphazardly waved his hands, and an unfamiliar sense of regret pierced Silas's chest. Domestic scenes like this had never been allowed in his father's home. All of his nannies had been strict old crones more likely to spank him with a switch than to show any kindness.

Once upon a time, he would've been starved for some of the softness exuding from Miss Taylor for the child. But he'd lived his entire life without it now, and he didn't see anything changing.

Finally, she glanced up, jolting in surprise at his perusal—no doubt uncomfortable with being caught so unawares. "Mr. Riverton, I didn't hear you come in. We've been a bit distracted, haven't we?"

The boy lifted his chubby arms for Miss Taylor to pick him up. He rested naturally on her hip while his arms wrapped around her neck. Lowering her head, she nodded toward Silas. "Won't you say hello to our guest, Callum?"

Overcome by shyness, the child buried his head against her neck. What Silas wouldn't give to be in that same position. Breathing her in, tasting the delicate skin where her neck and shoulder met, biting just hard enough so everyone would know she belonged... Silas slammed the door on those wayward fantasies.

Trying to concentrate, he caught Miss Taylor's words of apology.

"It's fine. I'm a stranger to him," he paused before continuing, "And how are you, Miss Taylor?"

"I'm well, thank you. We've visited a few of the city's sights, and we were accompanied by Mr. Brandon to the park on Tuesday."

Silas gritted his teeth at the mention of the man. They'd met a couple of more times at Ashley Mills as he walked Travers and Brandon through his operation, and the dandy grated on Silas's nerves with his air of superiority. He knew nothing of the manufacturing business yet contradicted every bit of advice Silas offered—like he knew better because he was "an Oxford man" as he was so fond of saying. An educated man himself, Silas knew there was more to learn than what books provided—practical knowledge that came from experience which Silas had and shared.

"He regaled us with interesting tales of his time abroad."

It didn't help Silas's feelings toward Brandon either when Miss Taylor was so obviously enamored with the man. He'd first noticed it at the Travers's party last week and now this.

"Yes, I'm sure he was very entertaining," Silas tried to stop a note of sarcasm but figured he'd failed by the sharp glance she shot him.

"Along with being an enlightening and charming companion," she defended. Shifting her weight due to the child still hanging onto her like a monkey, Miss Taylor dismissed him. "I believe we'll head to the nursery. We won't keep you from your meeting."

She hurried forward only to stop in front of him. This close he could see the lighter blue flecks in her eyes. Wondering at her abrupt halt, her annoyed words interrupted his musings. "You're blocking the door."

Chastened and irritated with himself for being so caught up in her, Silas stepped aside and watched as she ascended the staircase. Everything about this woman drew him in, and that was a problem he couldn't afford. Emotions had no place in life, so the pretty, little Venus needed to get out of his head.

"Riverton, there you are. I've been waiting for you. Why are you just standing there?" Travers entered the room from the back.

"No reason that bears repeating. Let's go over your projections." *Because I sure as hell am not going to divulge my lustful fascination for your sister-in-law.*

CHAPTER SEVEN

Hazel sat at the writing desk in her personal retiring room while Caraway stared out the window overlooking the street after putting Callum down for a nap. It was another rainy day, but at least the rain would wash away the muck in the streets and the smoky smell that seemed to inhabit the city.

Her mind drifted as Hazel continued through her correspondence until a curious question broke the quiet. "What do you think of Mr. Riverton, Cara?"

"What? Why would you ask that?" Surely, she hadn't noticed the peculiar conversation they had at the dinner party or Caraway's strange reaction to the man. Or witnessed the intense way Riverton had watched Caraway downstairs with Callum.

The man was entirely inappropriate. And clearly disliked Brandon, which honestly should be her first clue to stop these infernal... well, she wasn't quite sure how to label what she felt. Caraway couldn't be *attracted* to the man. Her affections were solely for Brandon.

"Oh, no reason... I thought you two seemed to be getting along at the dinner party."

"Hardly," Caraway refuted. "We barely spoke. I spent the majority of the time speaking with Brandon."

"Right, right," Hazel conceded. "But he *is* an interesting man and a very eligible bachelor. Jonathan likes him tremendously."

"Yes, I suppose he's likable and obviously available, but I don't see what that has to do with me." Acting dumb felt foreign to Caraway. She was the oldest sister, the one with all the answers. Except for when it came to Riverton.

"I just thought you two might be compatible is all." Hazel shrugged her shoulders innocently.

As if Cara wanted her little sister to play matchmaker.

"The man is much too old for me. Too somber. Too—"

Hazel rolled her eyes at the dramatics. "It's true he's fifteen years your senior. But he's not so old as to not be able to perform his husbandly duties." Her eyebrows waggled suggestively.

"Hazel May!" Caraway's mouth dropped open at the insinuation. "That is not appropriate talk for a young lady."

Hazel waved away her concern. "Oh, la! I'm a married woman now. I'm allowed to speak of such things. Allowed a few freedoms."

Caraway shook her head, knowing her sister would do whatever she pleased—proper or not. The girl had moved to Manchester with nothing but a hazy plan of becoming a published author at twenty-three years of age. Nothing fazed her indomitable spirit.

"Well, no matter. It's a moot point because I've set my cap on someone else."

"Oh, really?" Hazel pretended surprise and paused in opening another letter. "And let me guess: it wouldn't happen to be Mr. Miles Brandon, would it?"

"So, what if it is?" Caraway challenged. With the declaration said aloud, she knew it gave Hazel free rein to voice her opinion—one learned from Lily, no doubt.

"He's known you for years and hasn't declared any marriage-minded intentions, has he? I'm worried you'll be disappointed."

It stung that her own sister didn't think she had enough allure to attract a man of Brandon's caliber. But Caraway shoved the hurt down and chose to focus on defending her feelings.

"He just needs time to see me in a different light. He's only ever known me as the mother hen to you three hooligans out in the fields and such. He needs to see me as a proper lady who can run his household and make him happy."

"Mhmm... Sounds like he *needs* to do a lot," Hazel's skeptical murmuring didn't deter Caraway. So, what if her sister didn't agree? She was the eldest, therefore the wisest, even if that sounded petulant in her own head.

When Caraway didn't respond, Hazel sighed. "Well, good luck with your plan, I guess. You'll have another chance to reel Brandon in at tea this afternoon. The men are staying for refreshments after their meeting."

The information buoyed her determination. Most of the time, Riverton and Brandon left straightaway, and she hadn't been able to talk to Brandon as freely as she'd expected upon learning of his regular visits to the Travers home. However, tea presented the perfect opportunity to engage him in conversation.

Except Riverton would be there, too.

She didn't understand why the reminder caused her belly to tighten in anticipation.

"WE CAN START BUILDING in the spring. Demolition should be complete and ready for us to break ground by then," Travers added as he began rolling up the architect's plans for the factory.

"That will work." Silas considered their timeline. "Planting will occur then, so by the time the mill's done, harvesting will be taking place. You can open the factory with the next crop of cotton."

"Capital plan!" Cigar smoke wafted over from Brandon. He'd stayed seated while Silas and Travers had perused the newest building plans. To be honest, he wasn't that much help in these meetings at all, but since he'd invested in the company, they tolerated him.

Brandon had clearly never worked in his life. Why he'd decided to change that streak, Silas had no idea. He, on the other hand, had been raised in a factory. He knew hard work from a very young age because his father made sure of it.

Following the men into the parlor, he saw Mrs. Travers and her sister sitting with a tea tray and cakes.

"Ah, the men have decided to grace us with their presence," Mrs. Travers teased. "Please join us for tea." Her hand motioned for them to take seats. Comfortable chairs and a settee spanned the room, everything outfitted in blue velvet.

Silas watched as Brandon placed himself beside Miss Taylor on the settee—watched as a pretty blush bloomed on her skin at his proximity and forced himself to swallow a sound of annoyance. What did he care if Miss Taylor preferred a man like Brandon?

"Did you have a successful meeting?" Mrs. Travers asked the group after pouring tea for everyone.

"Yes, very beneficial. We discussed the current timeline for completion," Travers answered his wife.

Their union was unusual. Most husbands never confided business information with their wives, and most wives were perfectly content with that arrangement. However, the Travers enjoyed bucking tradition, and he often heard them discussing all manner of things usually left out of polite conversation.

They continued in that vein until talk turned to Mrs. Travers's latest children's book. As she became animated at the prospect of describing the story, Silas noticed Miss Taylor lean toward Brandon.

"Would you like another cup of tea," she asked, all solicitousness.

"That would be fine. Thank you, Miss Taylor. This clime has left me feeling out of sorts, and more hot tea is just what I need."

Silas resisted the urge to scoff at such blatant pandering. But Miss Taylor thought nothing of it, becoming the epitome of womanly concern.

Setting a refilled cup in front of Brandon, she exclaimed, "Oh, no. Are you feeling feverish?" Concern crinkled her eyebrows as she brought her ungloved hand to rest on his cheek. "You don't feel overly warm, thank goodness."

Silas's lungs struggled to take an even breath while his hand tightened around the delicate handle of his own teacup. Her palm stayed on Brandon's cheek as their eyes connected. An almost imperceptible shudder ran through Miss Taylor at the contact. Needing to escape the suddenly stifling room before he released the aggression filling him, Silas jumped to his feet.

"I think I'll take my leave now. I've been gone from the mill too long already."

Everyone voiced their farewells as Silas gathered his coat and hat. Agitation quickened his gait, betraying the swirling annoyance in his belly as he walked back to Ashley Mills.

Lightning imbued his muscles, thunder crackled with every step he took away from Miss Taylor and Brandon. This was an untenable situation.

He needed to return to The Warehouse. *Or find a woman to fuck*.

Because he shouldn't give a rat's ass about the couple.

CHAPTER EIGHT

The smoky card room housed several tables of men playing vingt-et-un during the Gibbons Ball the next evening. Silas preferred to use his money wisely instead of squandering it on gambling, but a lot of business occurred over these types of games. Thus, he found himself seated at a table with Lord Brooks, Mr. Nettles, and Mr. Cannon.

The latter sat on the Mill Owners Board with Silas. Mr. Cannon had built one of the first mills in Manchester forty years ago and clung to the old ways of doing business. His balding head sported tufts of white hair around his ears while the remaining hair grew from his chin, the beard long and wiry.

"I hear young Travers plans to build his own factory in the Dixon District," Nettles drawled as he tapped the table for another card. "You've been spending a lot of time with him lately, Riverton. What's going on there?"

"I'm sure you know as much as I do, Nettles, as everything's been filed with the appropriate offices." Silas knew spies ran amuck throughout the city, keeping owners apprised of business news from competitors. He and Travers figured it would only be a matter of time before someone approached them about their plans.

"Come now," Cannon butted in. "Surely, you can share more than what those forms tell us. We're all friends here." He laughed in feigned camaraderie, but Silas saw the narrowing of Cannon's eyes: his interest went further than just friendly conversation.

"That may be, but I like to enjoy my card game. Talking about business matters hardly encourages such," Silas argued, adding a twist of his lips into a brief smile. Best not to refuse too harshly and cause offense. He laid down his cards as their game ended and another one began.

"Too bad. I've heard rumors of some opposition against your friend's venture."

Training his features into a neutral expression, Silas took the bait. "Oh?" This was the first time he'd heard of it. Why anyone would object to an infusion of work in the area was beyond him.

"Seems Travers means to install some newfangled machines meant to decrease an employees work time yet still pay the same wages. Doesn't sit well with some: paying comparable wages for less work."

"God forbid, people actually have time for their families," Silas mumbled under his breath. Cannon was of an older generation that worked his employees past a reasonable hour, only to have them return a few hours later for another sixteen-hour shift.

"What was that?" Cannon cocked his head to the side, his hearing on the left not as good as it once was in his old age.

"I don't see how what Travers does with his own company is anyone else's business." His fist clenched under the table. People needed to mind their own damn business. If the Cannons of the world had their way, nothing would ever improve.

"Settle down, Riverton, old fellow. It's only a concerned observation," Lord Brooks interjected. The younger man shifted the conversation to a horse he was thinking of purchasing, and Silas was grateful for the change of topic though frustration flared through him.

Once their game finished, he excused himself and made his way to the ballroom to relay this new information to his partner. Travers stood by his wife and sister-in-law on the outskirts of the crowd.

Silas observed Miss Taylor as he maneuvered through groups of colorfully dressed women and the more austere-dressed men. Her curls lay gathered at the back of her head while a few ringlets drifted to her shoulders. His eyes followed the strands as they rested on top of her pale breasts. The golden dress she wore revealed much more of her than he'd seen at their previous meetings: modest necklines giving the hint of cleavage. Now she appeared to be overflowing from the decolletage.

As he neared their group, he dragged his eyes upward to meet Travers's curious gaze, an eyebrow raised, but Silas refused to feel embarrassment at being caught ogling Travers's sister-in-law. The man needed to keep a tighter leash on the woman if he didn't want men visually devouring her assets.

"Travers, Mrs. Travers, Miss Taylor," Silas greeted each of them with a slight bow. "I wonder if I may have a word." He gestured to the side, creating a bit of space between them and the women. "Horace Cannon just informed me of possible trouble concerning our plans for the mill. Apparently, there's been some disagreement with our wage policy and modern equipment."

Travers shook his head in amusement. "Old goats can't stand progress. We'll see if anything comes of their talk. For now, we'll continue on. Not much we can do about gossip."

Silas agreed. Let them wag their tongues in private. He had more important things to tend to... like Miss Taylor.

He knew he should resist becoming any more enamored of her than he already was, but a secret part of him had been making itself known lately—trying to reason that he couldn't be alone forever. Someday he'd have to take a wife if only to have an heir to leave his business to. He wouldn't be like his father, forcing his child to sink or swim without him. No, he'd teach his child how the business was run, and when the time came would hand it over. Of course, he wouldn't push it onto him if his passion lay elsewhere... Silas yanked his thoughts to a halt.

What the fuck? He was already imagining their hypothetical children? He inhaled deep breaths to ground himself in reality—a reality he seemed to have lost.

Gathering himself, Silas refocused in time to hear Travers mutter, "Brace yourself."

With that warning, they rejoined the women just as Brandon approached with a familiar raven-haired woman in tow.

"Good evening, ladies and gentlemen." He tilted his head in the semblance of a bow. "You might remember Miss

A GENTLEMAN NEVER SURRENDERS 55

Bradshaw? Her father is the owner of Bradshaw Soaps, Mr. Richard Bradshaw."

Everyone greeted her accordingly. She was young, nineteen or twenty perhaps, with jewel-covered hair glinting in the candlelight. Diamonds studded her body, creating a blinding spectacle.

Silas noticed Miss Taylor studying the woman as well, furrows forming around her mouth and eyes as they tightened. Clearly, she disapproved of this competitor for Brandon's affection.

Though in his mind, there was no competition.

Caraway's womanly body and personality far outshone this delicate piece of fluff. Of course, his opinion didn't matter, and Brandon was too ignorant to realize the prize he could have if he just opened his eyes to Caraway.

Miss Taylor.

"Did you mention how long you're in town for, Miss Bradshaw?" Mrs. Travers asked the young woman.

"Father decided to bring me along while he works with his manufacturer. So, we're here indefinitely," she replied, her voice light and airy.

"Lovely! You must come visit us. Cara and I would love the company."

Silas doubted that, judging by the worried look on the aforementioned lady's face.

"I'm sure you'll be seeing quite a bit of Miss Bradshaw," Brandon's sly words dripped with obvious meaning. "I've asked Mr. Bradshaw his permission to court his daughter. After our meeting in London earlier this year, I knew it was fate that brought her back into my life, and I couldn't miss this chance to make my feelings known."

The girl blushed demurely at the charming declaration. The rest of the group was not so pleased—shock may have described it better. Horror, if one was to study Miss Taylor.

"Why, we had no idea you'd been pining over someone, Brandon!" Mrs. Travers lightly hit him with her fan. Or perhaps not too lightly judging by the way Brandon discreetly rubbed the spot. "You've kept this secret well hidden." She glanced at her sister, reading her distress as sympathy filled her eyes.

"A man must have a few secrets, Mrs. Travers."

The notes of a waltz billowed from the back of the room where the orchestra was set up. "If you'll excuse us, I believe we have a waltz to attend to."

They watched the pair join the twirling couples on the ballroom floor, twinkling through the couples as Miss Bradshaw reflected every light.

"Well... That was unexpected." Mrs. Travers made the understatement of the evening. "How are you?"

She turned to her sister, who seemed to have pulled herself together. One wouldn't know that a moment before her whole world had been shaken.

"I'm fine. It's no surprise Mr. Brandon has found such a lovely girl to court. I wish them every happiness." Silas could almost believe her if he hadn't witnessed her initial reactions firsthand.

"It's okay to be upset..." Mrs. Travers trailed off as her husband whispered something in her ear. Sighing with reluctance, she let the topic rest and followed her husband to the dance floor, leaving the two of them alone.

Before he could offer his own hand for a dance, Miss Taylor excused herself, saying something about going to the powder room. After a brief moment of restraining himself, Silas gave in and followed.

CHAPTER NINE

Caraway struggled to remain calm and keep a steady pace, although she wanted to run out of the ballroom. Brandon was courting Miss Bradshaw! When he'd escorted the young woman to their group, her chest had tightened in fear. Miss Bradshaw represented a perfect English rose and the ideal candidate for Brandon to marry.

And when he mentioned their courtship... Caraway blinked away the impending tears. She thought she'd been making progress. Yes, it had been slow, but he'd seemed receptive to her gestures. Even reciprocated at least a part of her feelings. While all along he'd actually been dreaming of his London love.

Spying an empty room after exiting the ballroom, Caraway darted inside and shut the door. Hand on her heaving chest, she braced herself against the back of a leather chair. Moonlight filtered through the room, playing across a desk and bookshelves. The smell of paper comforted her, reminded her of Papa's study. Oh, how she wished her parents were still here.

Of course, all of their lives would be different if they were. And only hers would be for the better. Her sisters would still most likely be in Hampshire, unmarried and with no prospects. Except perhaps Lily.

Funny how she, the eldest, would still need her parents to live a normal life instead of being adrift in her current one. Rubbing the ache over her heart, Caraway closed her eyes, sending hot tears streaking down her cheeks. Her life wasn't supposed to be like this.

Purposeless, not belonging anywhere.

Husbandless, not belonging to anyone.

Chasing a man she'd loved for years who didn't even notice her. Her shoulders shook with more force as each pitying thought stabbed her like needles in a pincushion. God, she'd been stupid. Ridiculous. Hoping in a girlhood dream.

Suddenly, a light appeared, and the sound of the door opening and closing reached her. Caraway tried scrubbing any evidence of her distress away. She couldn't even be alone in her misery.

Warmth encased her back as the mysterious intruder stepped forward. Tilting her head slightly, she recognized the familiar scent of home. *Not home. Trees. A nameless forest.*

"Please go away." The words scraped her raw throat. She wasn't up for polite conversation—not that Riverton was known for being polite.

"He doesn't deserve your tears." His large hands circled her upper arms, stroking over the exposed skin. "You're worth a thousand Miss Bradshaws."

Caraway laughed at the ridiculous statement. His idea of comfort was sweet, but she knew the truth. "Don't lie."

Jerking away from his touch, she walked to the glass panes overlooking the driveway. Carriages lined the pavement, waiting for their guests to return. Maybe she should find Hazel and tell her she wasn't feeling well and wanted to leave. Her sister would understand, however humiliating it'd be to admit Hazel had been right.

"I don't lie," Silas growled as he spun her to face him. He was in all black again—the man mustn't own any other color. Reaching up, his rough palm cupped her cheek, smoothing away the salt tracks left by her crying. "What do you see in him?"

He spoke the words as if to himself, and Caraway refused to answer. She didn't see any reason why he'd need to know, not that he'd understand. From what she'd seen of Silas Riverton, he held very few emotions—none of them resembling love or affection. In fact, they seemed to gravitate toward annoyance or desire.

"Would you like to forget him, little Venus? At least for a bit?" His odd endearment confused her along with his entreaty. But before she could question him, he lowered his head to brush his lips against hers.

Shock froze her limbs, stopping her from making any moves. He pressed his mouth against hers again—this time more firmly, and his tongue swiped at the seam of her lips, surprising her into a gasp, which he took full advantage of.

Caraway had never been kissed before. She knew it was ridiculous and a bit pathetic that at thirty years of age, she'd never received such a token of affection from a man before. She'd imagined all sorts of scenarios, from sweet gentle pecks to passionate embraces. As varying as the kisses were, they all kept to one theme: the man who kissed Caraway loved her and she loved him. And for the past decade, that man had always been Miles Brandon.

Her imaginings didn't account for a northern factory owner fifteen years her senior.

Yet Silas's kisses caused a strange tingling to bubble through her, racing lower to the secret part of her ladies weren't supposed to know about. Incapable of retreating, Caraway melted into his tall body and grabbed the sides of his wool coat. His arms circled her hips and tugged her closer, so no space remained between them.

I was wrong.

His beard wasn't scratchy. It abraded her delicate skin, yes, but the texture served as a catalyst to awaken more of her senses. One of her hands stroked the roughness causing a gravelly sound to rumble from Silas.

In the back of her mind, she registered the scandalous picture they must make alone in a secluded room, but she'd lived her entire life by the rules. And her one fantasy was all but destroyed. What did it matter if she allowed herself this one reprieve? If she took just this small risk?

As if on cue, she heard a gasp and "I say!" burst through the pleasure-filled bubble that surrounded her. Immediately, Silas broke away and placed his body between hers and the intruders.

"What's going on here?" An outraged male voice boomed through the room.

Shame crashed into Caraway, shaking her with its force. What had she done? Scarlet crept up her chest, the heat engulfing her. She needed to get out of here. This was turning into the worst night of her life: first Brandon and now this.

"The lady and I were discussing a private matter. Nothing to concern yourself with," Silas answered in a low voice. She groaned at his response. A lady didn't discuss *any* matters—private or not—with a single gentleman alone. She peeked around his broad shoulders to see if she knew the witnessing couple, and another groan threatened to leave her as she saw Lord and Lady Gibbons, the ball's hosts.

"Now see here, we won't stand for scandalous behavior under our roof! This is a respectable family!" Lord Gibbons shouted, his rage punctuated with a wagging finger. By now, a crowd had assembled in the hallway, a dull roar of voices relaying the news of her sure ruination.

"I assure you. Nothing untoward happened here tonight." *So much for not lying*. Caraway almost snorted. Their kisses were definitely untoward.

"Lord and Lady Gibbons, if you'll excuse us, we asked Miss Taylor and Mr. Riverton to meet us here for a private discussion. Unfortunately, my wife and I were held up at the punch bowl. I apologize for any misunderstandings that have occurred due to our tardiness."

Caraway covered her mouth before a hysterical laugh escaped. The whole situation was turning into a farce with lie upon lie piling onto each other as Jonathan and Hazel pushed their way into the room.

"I don't care if you were supposed to be here to chaperone. It doesn't negate the fact that my husband and I caught these two in a most compromising position," Lady Gibbons snipped, her fan waving frantically in front of her.

Prone to fainting, Caraway waited for her to succumb to the excitement.

"Apologies again. We were just about to make our farewells. I trust this will suffice." Jonathan gathered Caraway in his arms with Hazel joining her other side. Her brother-in-law shot Silas a lethal glare before hustling them past the onlooking crowd and out to their carriage.

Once they were settled, Jonathan braced his elbows on his knees, his hair wild from his hands running through it. "What the hell were you thinking?"

Caraway jolted at the harsh words. She wasn't accustomed to someone yelling at her. Usually, she took on the role of scolding her younger sisters for any bad behavior. It didn't sit well being on the receiving end of a lecture.

Hazel placed a calming hand on her husband's knee, stopping the agitated bouncing. Covering her hand with his, Jonathan took a deep breath before continuing more calmly, "Seriously, Cara, why were you in that room with Riverton? I thought you were interested in Brandon."

Resting her temple against the cool window, she watched houses go by as they traveled home. "I am or was..." A sigh of rejection huffed out at the reminder of Brandon's courtship of Miss Bradshaw. "Silas, I mean Mr. Riverton, followed me. It's not my fault."

She refused to let them know of her own participation in tonight's activities. It was bad enough to profess affection for one man while being caught in another man's embrace.

"However it happened, it's sure to be all over town come tomorrow. I will personally see to it that Riverton does right by you."

A GENTLEMAN NEVER SURRENDERS 65

At that, Caraway's jaw tightened, her spine straightening in attention. "What do you mean 'does right by' me? Surely, you're not suggesting I marry the man!" Horror filled her tone at the notion.

Marry Silas Riverton? Not in this lifetime.

A small inkling of hope lay buried beneath her sadness at the discovery of Brandon's interest in another woman. He wasn't married yet, and courtships ended all the time with no one worse for wear. Perhaps if she tried harder to prove herself worthy of him, she could show him she'd be just as good a wife as Miss Bradshaw.

"If you don't marry soon, you'll be ruined, Cara. I don't want you to have to deal with those repercussions. It'll be bad enough the way everything stands now," Jonathan explained.

"I can deal with repercussions. I'm basically an old maid anyway. Things will blow over soon enough."

"You're not an old maid," Hazel defended. "And this is the sort of thing people remember, especially since you're the sister-in-law to an earl. You won't be invited to any events or allowed visits to the Trent Estate. People will turn their noses up at us on the street—not that I mind so much for myself but..." Hazel paused before shaking her head. "Oh, never mind all that. We've weathered our storms with Jonathan's past and Iris's father's debts. This can hardly add any more dents to our name. We'll support you whatever you choose."

Caraway squeezed her sister's outstretched hand, grateful for her support. Hazel was right, they'd survived several troublesome events. But Caraway didn't want to cause more trouble, especially when she was supposed to be the responsible sister.

She would figure this out.

She needed to get married, but it didn't necessarily have to be to Silas. *No, it could be any man.* Hope flickered in her heart as a wild idea swept through her. Maybe Brandon would offer for her after hearing of her plight. Maybe this would be the thing to force his hand and realize his true feelings for her.

Caraway knew it was a long shot, but she couldn't resist the sliver of excitement that filled her. Stories sold all the time with a heroine in distress and the dashing hero coming to save her. Life may not be a fairy tale, but perhaps this once it could be for her.

"I appreciate your concern. Both of you." She grabbed Jonathan's hand as the carriage came to a stop. "I'll do what needs to be done."

With that, they made their way inside, separating into their private chambers. *Brandon will come for me*, Caraway prayed as her maid undressed her. *He will.*

CHAPTER TEN

The next morning dawned with a rare burst of sunlight in the usual overcast Manchester. Silas decided to take that as a good omen for the day to come. He knew what was expected of him after last night's debacle—to go to the Travers's home and propose to Caraway. It was the only solution to save her from ruination.

Straightening his necktie, Silas studied his reflection. The black coat and vest looked crisp in the mirror, not a wrinkle in sight. While this may not be a love match, he could still present himself in an appealing manner, not that the bride had eyes for anyone other than Brandon, and his body stiffened at the reminder.

She'll get over him soon enough. Caraway Taylor will be my wife.

After calling for his carriage, he quickly mapped out the errands he needed to run before presenting himself to his bride-to-be. Procure a ring from Cavendish's, notify his staff he wouldn't be at the mill today, arrange for roses to be sent to Caraway ahead of his visit—he ran through the list, wondering if he missed any other important proposal details. He'd never bothered with such frivolous things before, but he wanted Caraway's proposal of marriage to be as normal as possible given the circumstances.

A quarter of an hour later, his carriage stopped in front of the jewelry store, and Silas dodged the people crowding the pavement in front of Cavendish's.

An older gentleman exited the shop as he entered. "A woman's appetite for pretty baubles never wanes, does it?"

He nodded in agreement to the stranger as metallic scents greeted him. Walking further into the store, Silas considered the man's comment. Past liaisons consisted of bedding a woman, nothing more because they knew the score—an occasional pleasurable night. No trinkets or gifts, no strings. But now he had a lady deserving of such extravagances.

Strangely, he looked forward to learning about Caraway's appetite for "pretty baubles" and satisfying it along with the rest of her needs.

"Welcome, how may I help you, sir?" A middle-aged man approached Silas, the jeweler's enormous belly leading the way.

"I need an engagement ring." Silas cut straight to the point. "Something fit for a goddess." Embarrassment caught him by surprise as soon as the words left his mouth. He didn't know where that bit of fancy had come from. Sure, he envisioned Caraway as his little Venus, but he wasn't about to share that information.

"Of course! We've plenty of divine pieces in stock for such a lady." Reaching below a glass counter, the man pulled out a tray of twinkling jewels. An array of diamonds, rubies, and more glinted back at Silas. Clasping the counter with both hands, he bent closer to examine his options.

Studying the pieces carefully, a gold ring with a large pearl perched atop the band drew his attention. Smaller sapphires surrounded the opalescent mineral, reminding him of Caraway's blue eyes.

"This will do." He handed the ring back to the jeweler. "I'll be opening a line of credit under Riverton."

"Certainly, Mr. Riverton. I'll package this for you and your lady."

Finishing the rest of his errands, Silas headed toward Ellesmere Park where the Travers resided. An up-and-coming neighborhood for the affluent, Ellesmere Park boasted tree-lined lanes with gated drives. As the poor became more prevalent in Manchester, the city's fortunate residents spread further out to create suburban areas.

The carriage stopped in front of the three-story home surrounded by precisely trimmed hedges, and Silas entered the home as a butler directed him to Travers's study. Obviously, he'd been expected. Travers waited at his desk, a glass of whisky sitting half-full next to him as he shot a withering glare in Silas's direction.

"About damn time you showed up. What the hell were you thinking last night?"

Silas sighed, unsure how to answer a question he'd been asking himself. His reasoning had nothing to do with common sense but following the undeniable attraction he had to Caraway. He doubted that would go over well with her brother-in-law. "What's done is done. I assume Miss Taylor knows why I'm here?"

Draining the last of his glass, Travers nodded. "I told Jenkins to alert her maid and have her sent down. I'll warn you. We support Caraway in whatever decision she makes."

"What do you mean? Surely, you wouldn't let her refuse my suit. She'll be ruined." Silas questioned the man's protective instincts if he'd so easily allow one of his family to weather the storm such a scandal would make. He'd come to salvage what he could of the situation—do the right thing. There was only one possible outcome in his mind: Caraway's acceptance of his proposal.

Travers's eye caught on something behind Silas, and he shook his head. "Nevertheless, we'll abide by Cara's wishes," he muttered under his breath. Raising his voice, he continued, "Dear sister, I'll take my leave now. You will not be disturbed."

As he exited, Silas turned to see Caraway keeping to the edges of the room. She wore a plain grey gown buttoned to her neck, not exactly a joyful ensemble. "Miss Taylor." He bowed. "I trust you received the roses I sent earlier."

"Yes, thank you. They're lovely." Her voice rang out clear yet distracted as she'd yet to meet his eyes, instead perusing a painting of a robin.

Moving closer, he asked, "Shall we take a seat? We have much to discuss." His hand gestured to the settee in the middle of the room, and Caraway settled at the edge of the cushion, looking ready to bolt. Her back stood ramrod straight while her gaze remained forward. He disliked this attitude of ignoring him. She answered when spoken to, but she acted as if he was an apparition, invisible for her to see.

"I know our situation isn't ideal, but I believe we can make this work. I'm willing to provide you with all the comforts you would expect as my wife: accounts at the best shops and full run of my household. You will want for nothing."

"Except love." Her cheeks turned scarlet at the naive comment as if she realized how childish it was to expect love in such an arrangement. Most marriages were built on family alliances and business transactions. Love matches were exceedingly rare and frowned upon—marrying someone you loved too gauche.

Unless you come from the Taylor family. It seems they're chock full of them.

"You will have something better than love from me. Respect. That is more than most wives receive from their husbands. I will treat you well and obey our vows. You don't have to worry about me straying from our marriage bed." No, he would not look for satisfaction outside his wife. Though trussed up more tightly than a turkey on Christmas morning, he still noticed the bountiful curves of her body. Their marriage bed would be quite pleasurable indeed.

"I see... I'll take that under advisement." She stood from her perch. "Is that all?" Finally, her eyes met his, a challenge lurking behind the blue irises, and he was beginning to understand Travers's earlier comment. The woman insisted on making this difficult.

"Well, your consent to the marriage might be appropriate." His dry tone belied the roiling storm brewing in his gut. Would she really refuse him?

"Seeing as you haven't actually asked me to marry you, I didn't realize there was a question to be answered. You seem to have worked everything out on your own without any input from me."

"Pardon the lapse, my lady. As our situation preceded any gestures of courtship, I assumed the matter was a foregone conclusion. You must marry me or else face scandal." He presented the bald facts in the face of her blatant dodging.

"Ah, yes... our situation." Her voice seethed with venom as she neared him. "The one where you followed me. Where you kissed me in full view of everyone. This is your fault. You trapped me!" Her chest heaved with the exertion of her anger, and this close he could smell her lemon soap.

"I trapped you?" He scoffed at her retelling of the events. "You were clearly distraught after that prick Brandon showed off his shiny new heiress. I was doing my duty as a friend to your family in making sure you were okay. And don't act like I forced you into anything you didn't want to do. You kissed me back."

By now, their heated breaths mingled in the short distance between them—somehow ending up only inches apart. "And you liked it," he whispered, smugness coating each word. "You want me to do it again, don't you, little Venus?"

His mouth lowered but Caraway jerked back, and Silas noticed the small trembling in her hands before she clasped them tightly in front of her.

"Thank you for your visit, Mr. Riverton. I will notify you when I've made my decision. Good day." The staccato sentences betrayed her lack of composure as she ignored the kiss that almost happened again. He'd allow her to ignore their chemistry... *for now*.

He couldn't, however, let her ignore his proposal. "You really intend to not give me an answer today? For what purpose does it serve whether you say yes now or later?" Her resistance confused him. She didn't have any other choice.

Caraway paused in her exit. "I am exploring other options."

Exploring other options. *What the hell?* "What are you talking about..." He stuttered to a halt as a sickening realization crept in. "Surely, you don't mean Brandon. You think he'll step up to save you?" The rigid set of her shoulders somehow managed to gain more steel while the rise of her chin gave truth to his inquiry.

Fury—hot and uncontrollable—surged through him until his palms slapped the door on either side of Caraway's head. A shudder ran down her spine while her grip on the parlor door handle turned white. Leaning down so his lips brushed her ear, he gritted out, "That *boy* will never come up to snuff. Are you willing to sacrifice your entire future by waiting on him?"

She didn't answer, but he could tell she didn't like his question. Her fingers pulsed with tension as she tightened and released her grasp.

"I said good day, Mr. Riverton," she reiterated, then opened the door. Silas immediately stepped back as the entryway revealed a maid dusting a vase.

After watching Caraway escape upstairs, he retrieved his belongings and escaped himself. A turmoil of emotions flooded him—anger, confusion. And deep down he thought he detected the bitterness of rejection, a vulnerable spot he hated within himself.

CHAPTER ELEVEN

Caraway held herself in check as she ascended the stairs, walked down the hallway, and closed the bedroom door behind her. She exhaled the breath she'd been holding as her head rested against the door. Not accepting Silas's proposal had been more difficult than she'd expected.

A woman learned early on that her sole purpose in life was to marry, and she never refused a man especially with her reputation at stake. But Caraway had to give Brandon a chance—as slim as it might be. Taking another bracing breath, she straightened her shoulders. She'd done the right thing. It's not like it was an outright refusal. She said she'd consider his proposition. Technically, that meant she could still accept.

But, oh how Caraway hoped she wouldn't have to, that Brandon would come riding in like a knight in shining armor. A desperate laugh bubbled up, imagining him as a medieval knight coming to her rescue.

However unlikely it seemed, though, Brandon *did* visit later that afternoon. Caraway made sure every curl was in place along with wearing a dress to show off her figure to its best advantage. A bit light-headed in anticipation of what Brandon might say, she took a sip of the cold tea leftover from earlier and went to meet him in the same parlor she'd met Silas in.

"Miss Taylor." Brandon rose from his seat by the fireplace. Resplendent in a hunter green velvet coat and striped trousers, he certainly looked the part of a valiant rescuer. "I wondered if you'd be accepting company after last night's scene, but I knew I had to risk being turned away to see how you are faring."

Caraway smiled, encouraged by his concern. "I'm as well as I can be considering the circumstances. Thank you so much for coming. You are always a welcomed visitor." She sat across from him, careful to remain serene and graceful.

He nodded his head in acknowledgment of her compliment. "It came as a surprise when I'd heard from the Gibbons' about what happened. To think of Mr. Riverton accosting you in their home! I almost feel honor bound to call him out for the pain he's caused you. Has your brother-in-law stepped in to defend your reputation?"

This conversation was going much better than Caraway had expected. He wanted to fight for her honor? A small shiver of pleasure wracked her body. Certainly a man wouldn't do such a thing for a woman he didn't care for.

"Jonathan believes matters can be solved without violence, namely through marriage." She admired the way the words fell from her lips so calmly. Now he just had to take the bait.

"Ah, yes... That makes sense." He paused in fiddling with a piece of lint on his coat to glance up at her. His grey eyes studied her face, a questioning lilt filling them. Now's the moment, she thought, almost too giddy to remain still.

He'll do it now. He's finally realizing we should be together.

Her heart pounded as she became acutely aware of every little sound in the room. Their breathing, hers fast and erratic while his remained steadfast. The fire crackling as the wood broke apart. Even the sounds of maids moving about out in the hallway.

Right as she felt ready to break with the tension of waiting, Brandon's tenor voice reached her. "You know, I thought someday you and I might marry."

Relief coursed through her, a sense of euphoria overwhelming Caraway. The beginnings of a smile tugged at the corners of her mouth.

Yes, he feels it, too.

"But I've found Miss Bradshaw, and even if that doesn't work out, you'll be married to Mr. Riverton. Life's full of surprises, I suppose." He shrugged nonchalantly, and just as quickly as her adrenaline spiked in excitement, it deserted her. Leaving a wake of exhaustion and numbness.

"Indeed," she managed, hardly recognizing her voice. Somehow they talked for another quarter of an hour before Brandon left. She couldn't recall what they discussed, only that one moment she was with him in the parlor and the next she was alone in her room.

Heartbroken, Caraway gingerly lay down on her bed. Supper would be in a few hours, but she'd plead a headache. She felt nothing, let alone hunger. Years of wishing and fantasizing had been destroyed in a few words. Her gaze traced the ceiling, replaying all the time wasted. Remembering events differently now that her rose-colored glasses had been removed. Orchestrated moments where she'd built up a touch or phrase, used it to fuel her own naive dreams.

And now she had but one choice: to marry Silas after all. Wetness on her cheeks surprised her, then all of a sudden the gates broke open, and she turned her face into her pillow to cry out the pain. What was wrong with her? Why didn't Brandon want her?

There was a knock on the door followed by a quiet, "Cara?" Hazel must have been apprised of Brandon's departure. "Are you alright?"

"Please go away," Caraway stuttered, unable to control the tidal wave of emotions crushing her.

"Oh, Cara... What can I do? Please let me..."

"Please go." No one could help her now. She wanted to be alone. Then she'd pull herself together and be the practical, eldest sister who didn't secretly pine after their childhood friend.

The pathetic spinster aunt of Hampshire's Garden Girls.

Caraway assumed Hazel left when only quiet greeted her. Closing her eyes, she hiccuped as her sobs slowed, fatigue finally dragging her into a deep sleep.

CHAPTER TWELVE

A few days passed before he received a visit from Travers at the mill. The younger man strode into Silas's office, ignoring his assistant's irate pleas to wait. Silas waved the assistant away and waited for the door to close before asking, "To what do I owe the pleasure, Travers? Our meeting is scheduled for tomorrow."

He didn't bother looking up from his work and briefly wondered if Caraway had sent her brother-in-law to give him her answer before dismissing it. He doubted Travers would agree to be her errand boy.

"I thought you might like to know Brandon stopped by the other day."

Silas's pen skittered over the ledger before continuing in smooth strokes. "And what does Brandon's social call have to do with me?"

He'd sequestered himself to work after the Gibbons party and his disastrous proposal. He couldn't care less about the goings on about town.

"Hazel believes Cara expected Brandon to propose to her."

Swallowing hard, he muttered, "And did he?" So, his guess had been true. She'd been waiting for Prince Charming to ride in and carry her off into the sunset.

"If Cara's mood lately is anything to go by, I'd say no. Which means you need to come by again."

Silas scoffed, "So, I can be her sloppy seconds?" The thought rankled despite the fact he still wanted her. It disgusted him that he was willing to take her however he could.

"Watch it," Travers growled. "You caused this mess, and you're going to fix it. Besides, don't act like this is some hardship for you. I've seen how you watch her: like a lion eyeing a gazelle."

Silas spun around in his chair to observe the workers on the ground floor. The clanking sound of machines rang loud as the looms weaved cotton together. He'd wondered if Travers knew of his fascination, now he had his answer.

"I'll visit tomorrow." Silas met Travers's gaze. "But if she refuses, I won't bring it up again."

"Understood. Cara knows she's free to choose, but I think she'll accept you now. She might have a childish fancy for Brandon, but I've seen the way she watches you as well. It might turn out to be a good match." With family matters out of the way, he moved onto business affairs. "Now about the factory layout..."

THE GRANDFATHER CLOCK chimed the noon hour as Caraway read a book in the library. Silas would arrive any minute. Yesterday Jonathan had informed her that he would be back today and to have her decision ready. She could still refuse him; her family would support her.

But her reputation and the family's would suffer the cost. And if she didn't marry now, she most likely never would. No man would approach her for any respectable union.

If Caraway wanted to have a family of her own, a husband and children, Silas Riverton was her only choice. Love wouldn't be a part of their marriage, but that was only a small part of what made a marriage work. He'd mentioned respect, and she agreed about its importance. Mutual respect would be a strong foundation for a good relationship. They could be friends, she decided, shoving any doubts away.

A rivulet of tea fell to the book in her unsteady hand. Annoyed by the betrayal of her nerves, Caraway carefully set the porcelain aside and mopped up the droplets. The pages absorbed the liquid quickly, though, causing a few of the words to bleed together.

"Blast!" The curse flew out as she set the damaged book down. Rubbing her temples, trying to head off the headache she felt coming, Caraway circled back to what kind of relationship she and Silas would have.

They'd proven they could get along with each other, even if he frustrated her with inappropriate comments or induced strange feelings when she caught him watching her. And love didn't guarantee happiness. Her failure with Brandon proved that particular point. Friends would be best. Everything would be safer that way.

"Mr. Riverton, miss," Jenkins announced at the doorway. Caraway hastened to her feet as Silas entered the room. He'd chosen a lighter scheme today, wearing dark gray instead of black. His silver-edged hair lay close to his head, not a strand out of place.

"Miss Taylor." He bowed in greeting as she curtsied in return.

"Mr. Riverton."

They stood in an awkward silence, both remembering the last time they'd seen each other. Back when she'd still had hope for a love match.

"Please take a..."

"I believe..."

They both paused as their words tumbled over each other. "You first." She waved her hand for him to continue.

Nodding his head in acceptance, he restarted, "I believe you know why I've returned. I have reason to think you're ready to accept my proposal?" He stepped forward as he pulled a small wooden box from his pocket, "And lest I am remiss again, I am officially asking. Will you consent to becoming my wife?"

He opened the box to reveal a beautiful pearl ring with sapphires. Her eyes jumped between the ring and him. Here it was: the moment her life changed forever.

"Yes, I will. I accept your proposal." Offering her hand, she trembled as Silas slid the ring onto her finger. The brief touch set off a sliver of sparks up her arm. Bringing her hand to her chest, she tried to rub the disconcerting feeling away.

What looked like relief and satisfaction mingled in Silas's dark eyes, but she couldn't be certain. Why would he be relieved at her acceptance? To be sure, society had forced him into this as much as it had her.

"We'll be married without delay. I'll obtain a special license, and we can be married within a fortnight." Silas plowed ahead with plans now that their engagement was set.

"So soon? Surely, now that we're engaged, we don't have to rush things. A June wedding..."

"Is out of the question. That's nine months away. It's best for us to marry as soon as possible so gossip can move on to more interesting stories."

Caraway sighed, knowing he was right. But she'd always imagined herself as a June bride with the summer flowers in bloom. Of course, if she couldn't have her ideal husband, why think she could have her ideal wedding at least?

"Don't worry," Silas said. "It won't be so terrible being saddled with me as a husband. We already know we suit in the physical department."

"Yes, that's what got us into this mess in the first place," she countered.

"You know, as a newly engaged couple, I believe it's tradition to seal our deal with a kiss." He stepped nearer, invading her space with his heat and woodsy scent.

"Ha, I don't think so. You just made that up," she retreated, but he followed until she backed into her chair. Stumbling into the cushion, she sat caged between his arms as his hands gripped the chair. Her breathing picked up at the powerless position, dominated by Silas's larger body hovering above hers.

Caraway's hands covered his, ostensibly to shove him away, but instead her nails dug into his skin, waiting for him to make a move. Her tongue peeked out to lick her dry lips, and his gaze followed the quick movement.

"It's *our* tradition," he decided. And without any more warning, his mouth possessed hers, the pressure forcing her head further into the leather chair.

He must have chewed a few leaves before coming because he tasted like mint. The clean, icy hot flavor energized her as she eagerly opened for him. This kiss felt different than the one before. At the ball, the specter of Brandon hovered between them with Silas intent on eradicating it. This time felt like victory, like he'd won, and he was claiming his prize: her.

Before long, Silas separated them, leaving her struggling for breath and control. "I trust you'll notify Travers of our pending wedding. I'll take care of everything else."

His words barely registered in her kiss-addled brain. Blinking rapidly to rid herself of the dazed look she must be sporting, Caraway made a low sound in her throat, unable to gather enough brainpower to speak. Taking that as her assent, his hand caressed her cheek and with an "Until next time, little Venus," he was gone.

Her shoulders sagged into the chair, her whole body devoid of anything resembling bone matter. Silas was right about one thing. They definitely suited physically.

"I DIDN'T IMMEDIATELY fall for Jonathan when I met him," Hazel stated nonchalantly. Caraway had joined her after accepting Silas's proposal, and they sat together writing their personal correspondences: hers to Iris and Lily to notify them of her impending nuptials and Hazel to acquaintances in town.

"I fail to see what that has to do with me," Caraway responded, focused on how to explain to her sisters the mess she found herself in.

"It should give you hope. Although you and Mr. Riverton aren't marrying under auspicious circumstances that doesn't mean you won't be happy. That the two of you won't form a loving bond."

Her sister had always possessed a fanciful imagination. It's what made her such a wonderful writer. But she tended to view the world a little too optimistically. Odds were against a love match forming between her and Silas. And she'd given up on romantic dreams—her abysmal failure with Brandon had seen to that.

"I wouldn't get your hopes up, Haze," Caraway cautioned. "You've mentioned before how unfeeling he seems, how everyone perceives him as a cold man. I doubt a forced marriage to me will change that."

"I know I said those things, but he's different with you."

Caraway scoffed at the cliche sentiment, but Hazel continued, "No, really. Somehow you bring whatever emotion he has to the surface. I've never seen him so engaged as he is when in your presence. I honestly believe he's enamored with you."

"While I'll concede that you *think* you see some sort of attachment from him, I doubt it'll translate to the deeper emotion of love. If anything, he's probably in lust." Caraway redirected her attention to the page in front of her, finished with the useless conversation.

"Cara, listen. I've been married for a few years now, so I have a bit more understanding of men than you do."

Caraway whipped her head up to glare at her youngest sister. Hazel raised her hands defensively. "I'm not trying to belittle your own knowledge, but you haven't exactly been acquainted with many men. Just Papa, Owen, and Brandon when we were growing up. And now Jonathan and Clarke."

Humiliation flushed her skin at the truth of Hazel's words. However, true as they may be, she didn't appreciate getting advice on men from her youngest sister. It galled her that their roles were so reversed. *She* should be the experienced woman doling out words of wisdom. Instead, she felt like the last child picked for cricket, an outcast.

"I'm well aware of my inexperience, Hazel," she snipped. "I don't need you reminding me."

The day's troubles were finally catching up to her. First, accepting Silas after coming to terms with Brandon never wanting her, and now being condescended to by her younger sibling. It was all too much.

"Cara, I'm sorry. I didn't mean—"

Caraway cut her off by abruptly pushing back from the table. "I know. I just don't want to talk about it anymore. I'm going to lie down. It's been a trying day." She gathered her unfinished letter and left Hazel sitting, subdued.

All Caraway wanted to do was take a long nap and dream up an alternate life that was very different from the one she somehow found herself in. So many things had gone wrong. Nothing looked as she'd expected it would.

All of her grand plans to arrive in Manchester and capture Brandon's affection had failed. Something she wasn't used to experiencing.

From the moment she left Hampshire, it seemed her good sense had deserted her. She'd given in to a girl's fantasy of love and fairytales knowing full well they were a piece of fiction.

I was blind. Silly.
But no longer.

CHAPTER THIRTEEN

True to his word, a fortnight later, Silas and Caraway married in an intimate ceremony at the Travers home. Thankfully, her sisters were able to take trains to arrive in time. The night before they'd enjoyed a sleepover like they hadn't had since Iris's wedding, and after assuring them of her determination to marry, they'd moved on to more pleasant topics like Iris and Lily's pregnancies.

"We're home." Silas's quiet voice filtered through her thoughts. After a brief family reception, they'd left for Ashley Mills and her new home. Caraway's belongings had been sent earlier in the day.

"I thought I might take you on a tour of the mill. However, if you'd like to rest after this morning's excitement, we can go tomorrow."

"Today's fine. I'm curious to see what you and Jonathan have been discussing." She followed him from the carriage, placing her gloved hand in his for assistance.

Once she was on solid ground, Silas kept her close to his side and led her inside the mill. Loud machinery assaulted her upon entrance while the scent of cotton mixed with oil permeated the space.

As Silas explained each part of the building, she observed the workers bending then straightening as they helped the machines create textiles. Tufts of white fluff floated in the air. Reaching up, she caught a piece in her hand to examine.

"Travers's factory will have a state-of-the-art ventilation system to decrease the number of pollutants in the air. It will greatly improve the health of his employees." Silas raised his voice to be heard as he saw her fascination.

"What about your own employees' safety?" Caraway's brows furrowed in concern. It didn't sit well with her that they'd profit from workers risking their health when there was a safer alternative.

"We'll be installing the new system here soon. We have to wait for certain parts to arrive." Mouth quirking in relief, she nodded in approval. She'd never taken Silas to be a cruel man, but it raised her esteem for him to know he cared about those under him.

As they continued their tour, numerous men approached Silas needing his advice on one thing or another. Caraway quietly observed as he put out fire after fire: giving calm, detailed instructions or firmly doling out consequences for errors. She found this authoritative side of him quite intriguing. She'd known he was a competent businessman or else Jonathan never would have trusted him with his own business plans. But seeing Silas in his element brought a different perspective.

A frisson of awareness infused her as she watched his strong hands direct another man. For someone who sat at a desk most days, he was incredibly fit—especially for someone forty-five years of age. She'd noticed his strength before, but here where he ruled, his authoritative manner paired with the muscles bunching beneath his coat created a much stronger feeling in her than before their marriage.

Sweat formed under her chemise between her breasts. Trying to surreptitiously tug at the fabric of her dress to separate it from her skin was of no use. The whale-boned corset made sure everything stayed in place, and an ache traveled down her chest to settle between her thighs.

Surely, she couldn't be feeling arousal for her husband out in public. At his place of work. Confusion and embarrassment warred within her at the notion.

"Are you alright?" Silas asked, taking note of her flushed face. "That's enough for today. I've overexerted you. You feel feverish." The back of his hand settled on her brow for a moment, serving only to heighten the heat in her body.

What was happening to her? She married, and suddenly she couldn't control the basest of urges?

"It's just overly warm here. I'll be better once we leave." The reasonable explanation seemed acceptable as Silas guided her outside. Their home was only a short walk across the street, but long enough for her to reign in her hormones. The fresh air helped clear her mind and body of the unwanted reaction.

Once they entered the brick home, Silas led her upstairs to a large suite. "This is the master bedroom. You'll be sleeping here with me from now on."

Surprise etched itself on her face. Normally married couples kept separate rooms, only joining for their marital duty. She knew her sisters didn't observe this tradition, but they were love matches.

"I won't have my own rooms?" she asked, double checking his meaning.

"You will have full run of the home. There are several parlors you can commandeer for your personal use. However, this will be your main residence. I've had your maid unpack your things, so you should have everything you need here."

He studied her as if preparing for a fight, but she had no true objection to his decree. It was her wifely duty to obey her husband, and this demand didn't seem so terrible.

"Thank you. It's a lovely room." She perused the furnishings, carefully avoiding contact with the massive bed set against the wall. Although obviously a bachelor's lodgings, the furniture looked comfortable and well-made. Spying a door, Caraway opened it to find a sumptuous bathroom suite with a large clawfoot tub set in the middle and a water closet in the corner.

"I see you've spared no expense. You've plumbed in hot water as well?" Her hands traced the lines of the tub, taking in the gold fixtures with embossed H and C.

"I prefer to take advantage of every convenience if available. What's the use of making money if I can't at least enjoy a hot bath from time to time?"

"Indeed." The reasoning shocked her. His reserved nature alluded to a man focused on saving and making his money work for him, not spending on extravagant luxuries.

She turned her attention to the collection of bottles and artifacts by a sink. Picking up a stout bottle of clear liquid, she brought it to her nose. The familiar pine scent she associated with Silas wafted in the air. Disconcerted, she

A GENTLEMAN NEVER SURRENDERS   93

set the glass bottle back down. It seemed too familiar to be touching his private accouterments, yet she was his wife. Intimacies such as these were to be expected.

"I'll leave you to settle in. Supper is at seven." Silas exited, leaving her alone, and she explored more of the room, studying the sparse walls.

While he hadn't spared any expense on creature comforts, apparently, he drew the line at home decor. Of course, she reasoned, that might be the way of most bachelors. Usually, that particular task fell to the woman of the house.

Eyeing the bed frame now that she was alone, her earlier arousal returned in full force. While her sisters had prepared her for the marriage bed, and she knew enough about her body to understand mechanics, it was difficult to imagine the actual act with Silas.

Catching a glimpse of herself in a mirror, anxiety filled her at the thought of disappointing him. He was probably used to experienced women. Beautiful women. And while he seemed attracted to her, he had yet to see her unclothed. What if he changed his mind and regretted his decision to wed her?

She shook her head in defiance. Nothing she could do about it now.

Calling for her maid, she undressed, watching as the girl put her wedding gown away—the confection of lace and ribbons a reminder of the events that morning. Disbelief still coursed through her at the fact that she was married. Only a few months ago, she'd arrived in Manchester prepared to win Brandon, and now she'd married another man.

Donning a light blue dress, Caraway ventured out into her new home. She discovered the library and several lounging rooms, but no Silas. He must have gone back to the mill.

The housekeeper, Mrs. Frost, explained the staff's routine. "If there are any changes you'd like, my lady, you've only to ask."

"You've done a marvelous job, Mrs. Frost. I'm not sure you'll need much of my help."

The older woman squirmed in reluctant acceptance of the compliment, but it was true. Caraway hadn't found a spot undusted or a painting out of place. Everything seemed to run smoothly under the housekeeper's care, which left Caraway in a quandary.

With the home needing minimal input from her, how was she supposed to spend her time?

CHAPTER FOURTEEN

Dinner came and went without preamble. Silas and Caraway kept the discussion to general topics, never verging into personal territory, and before she knew it, she found herself alone in their bedroom preparing for her wedding night.

Excusing the maid Mary for the evening since she preferred to take care of her own ablutions, Caraway finished lacing up the front of her white nightgown and took a seat at the vanity. She removed the multitude of hairpins containing her hair, letting the curling tresses fall to her shoulders in a wild sprawl. Running her fingers through the strands, she contemplated what the night had in store, trembling with nerves at the intimacies she'd share with Silas.

He'd been the only man to ever kiss or touch her, but they'd never gone past her clothing. Now she would be on full display to him, vulnerable like she'd never been before.

A click reverberated through the room as Silas entered the bed chamber, but she continued finger-combing her hair as he approached, waiting for him to say something. He wore a loose, undone shirt with trousers, and it startled her to see his feet were bare. Raising her eyes back up his body reflected in the vanity mirror, she met his hungry gaze.

"This is a pretty sight to see when I come to bed—my wife waiting for my arrival." His low voice tantalized her senses, leaving goosebumps in its wake. Silas traced a curl to the end and let it bounce back into place before gently pulling the shoulder of her nightgown aside.

His beard scraped the bared spot with a gentle kiss, eliciting a shiver in response. Trailing his lips further up her neck, he asked, "Is my little Venus afraid? There's no need to worry. I'll be gentle with my virgin wife."

His words spun a seductive spell around Caraway as her mind fogged with desire, momentarily overcoming her nerves.

"I'm not afraid. I know what to expect." She latched onto enough brainpower to answer his question.

"Do you now? I suppose your sisters explained things?" His palms skimmed down her sides, slipping over the gossamer fabric.

"They were quite informative... Should we move to the bed?" They'd mentioned how Silas should prepare her and how enjoyable it could be, but she'd assumed it would still be done under the covers.

"Not yet, love. Look in the mirror." She obeyed his command to see his large hands follow the curves of her body until they cupped her breasts. A swift inhale caused her chest to rise, pushing her further into his embrace.

Surely, he didn't mean for them to do this so exposed. Her body wasn't perfect, and she didn't want him to discover the truth this close. Not while she could see his expression.

"Are you sure this is how it's done? It doesn't seem very decent," she argued as his fingers began untying the laces holding the bodice together.

"Mmm... Yes, very indecent." In quick succession, her gown fluttered open to reveal the pink points of her nipples, and his fingers toyed with the hardened pebbles until the heat of his body seeped into her skin. Silas's eyes never left hers in the mirror as together they watched the color on her chest blossom from blush to scarlet.

Caraway clung to the vanity tabletop, her nails digging into the wood, unable to do much more than draw labored breaths into her lungs. They made a lewd sight with his towering form hunched over hers. His rough fingertips pinching and plucking at her swollen nipples.

Once he was satisfied with his ministrations, Silas urged Caraway to her feet, stabilizing her when she swayed forward. The action left her completely exposed for her husband's perusal as the nightgown shimmied to the floor in a cloud of white. Shoving the vanity stool out of his way, Silas held her tighter to his chest. "Fuck, you really are a goddess, aren't you?"

The awe in his voice unraveled some of her fear. He couldn't fake that kind of admiration. He didn't have a talent for artifice, that much she knew for sure about Silas.

Leaving one hand to continue playing with her breasts, the other drifted lower until her own hand stopped him out of reflex. "Sorry." She knew she couldn't prevent him from touching her there. After all, it was where they'd join to officially consummate their marriage, but no one had ever even seen the curls between her thighs, let alone parted them for his own pleasure.

"No need to apologize." He kissed the side of her neck as he continued his path after Caraway removed the barrier. Two fingers delved through the intimate lips of her sex to create a slick sound of their parting. Arousal made his invasion easier as he circled her opening before rubbing his thumb over her clitoris.

Reaching back to grip Silas's head, she clutched the silver strands in a daze. A pulsating sensation began under his experienced touch, emanating from her core to the tips of her fingers and toes. Their heavy breathing mixed with the sound of his fingers moving in a repeated pattern, the scent of her arousal blooming between them.

Caraway knew her body was building towards something. Something the kisses they'd shared had only hinted at. Arching her hips forward, she tried to rush toward it, eager yet nervous about what she'd discover.

"Easy... let it come to you. You don't have to strain for it. I'll make sure you come." Silas's wicked promise echoed in her mind, sifting through the blood rushing in her head. His hips pressed against her backside, guiding her body in a rhythm to match the movements of his fingers plunging inside.

"Silas..." she moaned his name, entranced by the vision they made in the mirror. The silver threaded in her husband's hair—on his head, in his beard, peppering his chest—contrasted against the brunette of her curls sticking to the skin exposed by the loose vee of his shirt. It accentuated their age difference. Painted it in taboo shades of gray.

And Caraway liked it.

Suddenly, the tension released inside her, shooting off a wave of sparks as her body shook with newfound pleasure. Silas gentled his motions, and she felt boneless, leaning heavily on him until he hoisted her into his arms and carried her to bed.

Quickly, he removed the rest of his clothing, revealing his tall, muscular body in its spectacular glory. Again, she wondered how he maintained such a virile physique while spending his days in an office. Most men his age sported paunches and bald spots but not Silas. The only true sign of his maturity was the silver in his hair and the work-weary lines around his eyes and mouth.

Then Caraway's eyes dropped to his jutting member, standing proud in arousal. While she should've felt nervous, all her satisfied body could conjure up was curiosity about what happened next. To the point where the wanton woman she apparently became in his presence drew her knees up and let them fall apart to welcome his claim.

"I'll try to go as slowly as possible, but I'm afraid this may hurt a little. But just this once. Afterward, you will feel nothing but pleasure," Silas assured her as he joined her on the bed. Nodding in assent, her eyes drifted closed while he positioned himself at her opening.

She startled at his first careful push forward, surprised by the girth and the stretch it caused her untrained muscles. Immediately, Silas reached down again to circle the sensitive bud where her pleasure centered. Relaxing into his touch,

Caraway felt him slide a little further, but this time her body opened more easily for him. The dreamy state leftover from her earlier orgasm dissolved as Silas's new movements began building the pleasurable tension again.

When he was fully seated inside her, he groaned, and Caraway opened her eyes to note his trembling body as he reared back only to push forward again, each stroke controlled by his iron will. Sweat dripped down his temples at the deliberate effort he made to ensure he didn't hurt her.

Unable to resist, she brought her hand up to the salty drops and wiped them away, letting her hand wander down his cheek, neck, and torso. The wiry curls intrigued her. They mapped a path down to his groin—a path she wanted to follow.

But Silas grabbed her hand and slammed it against the bedding by her head. "Don't do that. I'm already near my breaking point." He gritted the words out as his strokes quickened. The change of pace ratcheted up her own wildness, and she temporarily forgot her plan to explore his body as she lifted her hips to meet his more forcefully. Shifting Caraway higher, he hit a delicate spot inside that arched her back on a desperate cry for release.

"Don't stop... Please, Silas..."

Her words ignited something in him as his body slammed harder and faster into hers, burying his thick cock deep until the world paused. Everything lived in perpetual stillness before one final thrust burst the bubble, throwing them both into a maelstrom of pleasure. He jerked inside her as his release spilled down her thighs, then he briefly crushed her with his heavy body before rolling over and dragging her with him.

They lay replete, trying to catch their breath, and Caraway couldn't believe this was what she'd been missing out on for so many years. No wonder her sisters were always running off with their husbands in the middle of the day.

However, as she replayed the past hour, Caraway stopped in her stroking of Silas's chest. "We never kissed." It was odd that all of their former physical contact consisted solely of kisses, yet during the most intimate act of all, their lips never met.

"Yes, we have," he reminded her. "That's why we're here tonight—married."

"No... I mean yes, but *tonight* we didn't kiss. Not once. Yet we did... everything else." She raised her hand in a vague gesture.

"I wouldn't say *everything* else, but we covered the main parts." Silas teased as he turned his head toward hers. "But if it's a kiss my wife wants, I'm happy to oblige."

He cradled her head in his hand and closed the short distance between them. The lazy kiss eased her—this one act at least, familiar territory. His tongue stroked hers, mimicking what they'd just done, urging her closer to him as she crawled up his body for easier access.

They lost track of time, enjoying the intimate aftermath of such explosive passion, and when Silas pulled back, she sighed in satisfaction, settling in the crook of his shoulder. Sleep had almost taken her when she heard his quiet question.

"Why weren't you married before me? Was it all because of Brandon?"

Her muscles stiffened at the mention of her longtime crush. She'd managed to box those feelings away for the day. And he didn't belong in their marriage bed now, but she understood her husband's query. She didn't want him wondering what could be so wrong with her that she'd remained unwed.

"Brandon wasn't the only reason. I had a Season in London years ago while my father taught at King's College. Unfortunately, I'm fairly reserved, especially when it comes to strangers, so I had a hard time speaking with eligible gentlemen. It didn't help that I was outshone by a veritable garden of debutantes with wealth and beauty that far eclipsed my own. I didn't fit in."

How humiliating it had been to be a wallflower, ignored by all the men, while the prettier girls received all the attention. The pain and fear of never being wanted came back tenfold at the memory. That's why she'd held onto the idea of Brandon so tightly. It didn't matter if those men hadn't wanted her. She'd believed Brandon knew the real Caraway and could want her—the plump, responsible mother hen of the Taylor sisters.

Foolish girl.

Silas pushed a wayward curl behind her ear and traced the fragile shell. "Of course, you didn't. You are a divine creature. Too complex for those bastards to understand when they were too enamored of the easily caught misses who cropped up around them like daisies."

She buried a grin in his shoulder at the generous interpretation of the scene, secretly pleased by his conclusion. "I'm a mere mortal, hardly divine. Those men saw my faults and chose to deal with the less flawed women on display."

He dragged her underneath him again and nipped at her ear. "Do I need to remind you again, little Venus, goddess of desire, how much I enjoy these non-existent faults of yours?"

He didn't let her reply as his mouth crushed hers, the time for talking clearly over.

CHAPTER FIFTEEN

Silas woke up with Caraway draped over him. Memories of the night before flashed through his mind causing his cock to rally for another go, but he ignored it to ponder this new situation.

He'd never had a woman in his home, let alone his bed. Whenever he needed relief, he sought out one of the women he kept a standing arrangement with, never lingering longer than necessary.

But being able to massage a hand down Caraway's bare back was a nice change.

She shifted to a more comfortable position, exhaling a soft sigh, and an unnamed emotion ballooned in his chest at the sound. He had a wife now—someone other than himself to care for and protect.

It was at once an exhilarating and terrifying prospect.

Eventually, the rumblings of the house waking up infiltrated their quiet chamber, and he gingerly extricated himself, needing to get ready for the day. He'd suggested they take a short honeymoon after their wedding, but Caraway had refused. She'd reasoned they could go at a later time when there was more time to plan. Which meant the mill would be expecting him today.

He scrubbed away the dried sweat of last night's activities and brushed his teeth before dressing and going downstairs for breakfast. Sparing one longing look toward his wife who lay peaceful, and altogether too tempting, warm in his bed. As usual, the newspaper sat in front of his place setting in the dining room as he took a seat. He liked to peruse the articles while partaking in his coffee and eggs.

A few pages in, a motion in the doorway caught his attention. Caraway entered wearing a dressing robe over her nightgown, and his body readily leaped to attention in remembrance of undoing those ribbons lacing her top.

"Good morning."

The sentiment was returned with a sleep-filled voice as she filled a plate with bacon and toast. Once seated, she commandeered the teapot and poured a steaming cup of tea.

"How did you sleep?" he asked, intensely curious to learn her feelings, considering the trouble it took for Caraway to agree to marry him in the first place.

A fascinating blush bloomed under her skin, spreading from her chest to her cheeks. He found it amusing and encouraging that she could be embarrassed after their lovemaking.

"Quite well, thank you. You?"

"Quite well," he repeated, pleased.

"Will you go to the mill today?"

"Yes, work doesn't stop just because a man's married, unfortunately. And I have a meeting with Travers later. You're welcome to join me, so you can visit your sister." He figured they'd want to talk after last night. It seemed like the things women, especially, sisters would do.

"Thank you, I'll be ready when you are." She paused before adding, "May I see the society pages when you're done? I'd like to see what they wrote down for our marriage."

He pulled the pages she wanted out and handed them over. "They're all yours. I never bother with that fluff."

A hearty chuckle followed the insult. "I agree most of it is nonsense, but I'd like to save any mention of us for a memory book," she explained as her eyes scanned the sheets. Speculation passed through him at her statement. If she wanted to create a memory book for them, that had to be a good sign. Surely, she wouldn't bother if she didn't care.

They settled into a comfortable silence with him reading the finance section while Caraway searched for a mention of their marriage. Picking up his cup and realizing it was empty, he reached for the coffee carafe before pulling back. The memory of how she'd filled Brandon's teacup before the man had even finished it taunted Silas.

Now that *he* was her husband, she would be performing such caring tasks for him. Surreptitiously, he set his cup down a little closer to Caraway, hoping to catch her attention. The crinkle of turning pages sounded as she continued her reading.

Placing his arms on the table while holding the paper slightly lowered, he cleared his throat and gently bumped the cup. Still nothing from her. Wondering how else he could get her attention, he kept his gaze on her.

She must've felt it because she finally glanced up in confusion. "Did you need something?" Her brows furrowed in question.

Sudden anger swept through him at her obliviousness. Brandon hadn't had to stoop to ridiculous measures for her to tend to him, and he'd be damned if he continued. Jealousy, or any other emotion, had never ruled his life or actions. They wouldn't start now.

"No," he barked, tossing the paper down and shoving his chair back to leave. "I'll be back to pick you up around three o'clock." With that, he left, annoyance buzzing in his veins.

BEWILDERMENT SUFFUSED Caraway after Silas stalked out of the dining room. She didn't understand the flare of animosity. Everything had seemed fine, then she caught him watching her as if waiting for her to make a move. But what he expected her to do, she wasn't sure. Studying the tableau in front of her, nothing stood out as out of the ordinary.

Giving up, Caraway shrugged her shoulders and chalked it up to one of those things she'd eventually learn about her husband. Returning to the words in front of her, she read through pieces about a ball and theater sightings until she found what she wanted—their marriage announcement.

"Mr. Silas Riverton wed Miss Caraway Taylor on the eighteenth of October, the year of our Queen Victoria. The small gathering attended by family alone came together rather quickly in this journalist's opinion. Some may remember a certain tete-a-tete at the Gibbons party some weeks ago."

While she didn't appreciate the snide remark about why they married so soon, she still tore the paragraph out for posterity's sake. One of these days, their family may like to look back through their history, and the article would be wanted.

Blame her parents for the need to document their lives as if they were the plants Mama and Papa studied so devoutly.

CHAPTER SIXTEEN

A month passed, early autumn barreling toward winter, and life remained the same despite Caraway's changed marital status—nights filled with Silas's lovemaking, notwithstanding. She helped Mrs. Frost with menus and household tasks, a marked contrast from doing everything herself in her Hampshire cottage, and visited Hazel a few times a week.

Wasn't marriage supposed to be when your life officially began?

That's the story society told, yet restlessness plagued Caraway. For years, she'd been responsible for her sisters, for keeping the family together after their parents died. Been the authority figure, the maid, the cook—by default, a woman whose role as the eldest meant she carried the burden of everyone else's well-being on her shoulders. Except now, Caraway was on her own. Free to do as she pleased since servants maintained the home and Silas was far from requiring tending after living so long as a self-sufficient bachelor.

"This is ridiculous." Caraway snapped the book she was attempting to read shut. The same page had stared back at her for nearly an hour as her attention kept drifting out the window where everyone else in the world seemed to actually be accomplishing tasks. Not lounging about in the middle of the day.

Perhaps Silas could use some help at the mill like notetaking or filing papers—anything to get her out of the house. She'd never approached him at work, not wanting to be a bother, but sitting at home twiddling her thumbs was not in Caraway's nature.

Decision made, she gathered her cloak and hat and walked across the street to Ashley Mills. The factory formed a U-shape around a spacious area left clear for the loading and unloading of goods. Or for employees to gather during breaks based on Caraway's observation.

Groups of two or three loitered about the edges of the square while eating their lunch when a bread roll bumped into her boot. A young woman hurried over to retrieve the errant pastry, inedible now with dirt clinging to its surface.

"Beggin' yer pardon, m'lady. 'Tis difficult to balance meals out here."

Caraway noticed her hands held a precariously balanced napkin filled with a piece of meat and cheese. "Don't concern yourself. The issue's obvious... There's nowhere else for employees to take their repast?"

"No, ma'am. Most days we eat out by the barrels of cotton. 'Tis dreadful on a rainy or wintry day." Then as if realizing she might get in trouble, the girl backpedaled, "But I'm not complainin' none. I'm grateful for the job. Mr. Riverton is a right fine master."

Nodding in agreement, Caraway offered a commiserating smile. "Yes, I know. I'm Mr. Riverton's wife, though you may call me Caraway. Please don't worry about speaking your mind. It's good to voice any concerns you have. Have you mentioned this to Mr. Riverton? I'm sure he'd rectify the situation."

The girl tightened her grip on the napkin. "Oh, no, Mrs. Riverton! It's not my place to be causin' trouble."

"It's no trouble. I'll say something to him today." Perhaps she'd found the perfect job to occupy her time—ensuring the mill workers' contentment while Silas focused on the business side of things. "May I ask your name? I'll keep your confidence, but I'd like to know what I may call you since we're sure to meet again."

Hesitation stiffened the girl's features before she reluctantly answered. "It's Joan, m'lady. Joan McCormack."

"Nice to meet you. Thank you for sharing your concerns."

Joan dipped into an abbreviated curtsy before racing back to the two women she'd been dining with, and Caraway wondered what else she might learn about the mill. Silas wasn't above improving his workers' conditions. His hearty support of Jonathan's plans with the modernized mill proved that, so maybe she could help him here at Ashley Mills.

It may be exactly what she needed to snap out of her boredom.

The mill offices bustled with activity as clerks moved back and forth between file cabinets and desks. Navigating through the chaos with aplomb, she quickly found herself in front of Silas's assistant, Mr. Lyman's, desk.

"Good afternoon. Is my husband free?"

The thin man jumped to his feet and bowed. "Mrs. Riverton, we weren't expecting you today. Mr. Riverton is going over a few accounts at the moment, but I'm sure he'll see you. Right this way." He motioned for her to precede him before knocking and opening the office door for her.

"Mr. Riverton, your wife is here."

Silas looked up from the sheet of paper he'd been scribbling on, a pleased smile peeking through his beard. Standing, he offered one of the chairs in front of his desk. "Hello, little Venus, to what do I owe this pleasure?"

"I thought it might be nice to visit. I haven't interrupted something important, have I?" Accepting his invitation to sit, she settled into the stuffed leather chair, testing the plushness of its arms with her fingers.

He made a dismissive sound as he returned to his previous position and folded his hands in front of him. "Nothing's more important than you. You're always welcome here."

Abashed, heat colored her cheeks at the sincerity in his tone. Their conversations, while congenial, remained mostly surface level. They avoided discussing anything approaching emotions, except for times when Silas would surprise her like now. Dropping some comment that implied his pleasure at being in her company.

"Thank you..." Forging ahead, Caraway got straight to the point. "I spoke with one of your employees outside. She mentioned the mill doesn't have a common area for people to take their lunch?"

Sunlight filtered through the windows behind him, glinting off the silver haloing his head. "No, it doesn't. Why were you speaking with my employees?" Thankfully, curiosity rather than censure filled his tone.

"It was by accident that we happened upon each other, and once we began talking I learned of the deficit. Is there a reason they're not provided a proper place to rest?"

"I didn't realize there was any need. They've been fine taking meals outside for years now." He shrugged, sitting back in his chair. An authoritative air emanated from him like a king on his throne, and Caraway found it distractingly arousing.

Now's not the time.

"Well, if you're not opposed, I'd like for us to arrange some kind of shelter for them. It would be a lovely diversion from needlework." Or napping the day away. Or reading the same page repeatedly. Or any combination of tasks she'd attempted to use to occupy her time this past month.

A pause bloomed between them. Would he deny her request?

"If it's what you wish, then it'll be done. I think we have an empty storage area we can convert into a gathering hall."

"Wonderful!" She clapped her hands together in excitement. "I'll arrange for seating to be delivered soon. And maybe we could add a kitchen space and provide..." Her mind raced with possibilities, and Caraway wished she had pencil and paper handy to make a list of tasks needing to be completed.

"You want the mill to start serving their meals?" Silas's voice cut through the points she was checking off in her head.

"Would that not be possible? Can we afford the extra expense? I'm sure it would be appreciated if they didn't have to take from their own food store and haul it into work."

It was unusual for a place of employment to provide such things, but Caraway figured the kind gesture was worth it to show their appreciation for the workers. It's not as if they'd be destitute from adding this employee perk. At least, she didn't think they would be. Goodness, was Hazel's impulsive nature rubbing off on her?

"It's not a matter of money, although it would be an unexpected expense. We'd also have to hire a cook and purchase ingredients..." The explanation trailed off as his gaze studied her fallen expression. "But I suppose that's easy enough. The mill is doing well financially. If this is something you care about, we'll make it work."

"You're sure? I know I'm overstepping, but—"

"You're not overstepping. What's mine is yours, remember? It's smart to keep our employees happy."

A smile brightened her face as she hurried around his desk. "Oh, thank you, Silas! You won't regret this!" Her hands squeezed his shoulders as she pressed a kiss to his cheek, ignoring the urge to linger and perhaps press a kiss lower to the enticing promise of his mouth. Flustered, Caraway scrambled backward and practically ran for the door. "I must visit Hazel. She should be able to help me commission what we need. I'll see you at home later tonight."

Then, like a whirlwind, she was gone, eager to start her new project and forget the entirely inappropriate thought of seducing her husband in broad daylight. In his office, no less!

Meanwhile, the man in question sat in a stupor as warm satisfaction weaved around his heart. Silas enjoyed making his wife happy. And if she showed her gratitude through kisses, then God help him, because he'd never be able to refuse her anything.

CHAPTER SEVENTEEN

The Travers invited Caraway and Silas over for dinner a week later, and she was excited to inform her sister of the progress made at Ashley Mill's soon-to-be dining hall. Long wooden tables and benches had been delivered that afternoon while the finishing touches for an added kitchen were done in remarkable time.

Jonathan had been most helpful when it came time to find craftsmen for the woodwork, having contracted men for additional aid at the school and boarding house in Devil's Haven. Amidst the flurry of construction, Joan had approached Caraway with wonder, and she took advantage of the girl's willingness to chat by learning about the issues some employees faced, particularly the women with young children. Word spread like wildfire through the factory of the upcoming changes, and everyone looked forward to using the new facility.

It satisfied Caraway as nothing had in a long time, if ever. She'd chosen to complete this project. It hadn't been foisted upon her because she happened to be the firstborn Taylor girl. Or because being responsible and always overanalyzing potential pitfalls of decisions made her an anomaly in her family.

No, she'd chosen to become the liaison and champion for Ashley Mills' employees, and remarkably, Silas supported her endeavor.

Giles guided them to a parlor occupied by Hazel and Jonathan as they discussed her upcoming book release before noticing the arrival of their guests. "Cara, Silas, welcome! I was just telling Jonathan about a meeting with my publisher."

They joined them at a table where several sheets of drawings were laid out, and Hazel explained the book's plot while indicating corresponding scenes. "Willoughby thinks this might be my highest-selling book yet." While the money didn't concern her, she loved the idea of encouraging thousands of children to read.

"That's wonderful!"

Hazel's imagination and drawing skills had always led to fantastical stories, and Caraway was glad that people could finally appreciate them.

"Yes, my wife is quite talented. It's not surprising her books practically leap off the shelves," Jonathan concurred, the gaze he sent his wife full of love and admiration, as Hazel took his hand in hers, a proud smile gracing her face.

She felt uncomfortable witnessing their affection for each other, so at odds with her own marriage. While Caraway and Silas got along well enough, he certainly didn't harbor any secret feelings of adoration for her. And she couldn't envision herself feeling so entitled to his body outside the marriage bed.

Silas shifted closer to her, and the tablecloth swayed with the bouncing of his knee. Glancing up from a picture of a fairy and rabbit drawn in pastels, she caught him studying her with a calculated light in his eye before his hand brushed hers. Dismissing the accidental contact, she returned her attention to Hazel until Silas leaned closer, his warm breath tickling her ear as he whispered, "Take my hand."

"Pardon?"

"Take my hand, wife," he demanded again.

Annoyance buzzed through her at the odd dictate. She didn't understand his urgency, and it bothered her that he wanted to force a physical embrace, however innocent.

He can do whatever he wants. He's your husband.

But Caraway didn't care. She bristled at being told what to do.

Growing up as the eldest child, she'd grown used to being in charge. And while she accepted advice from elders, that didn't extend to edicts made by her husband. Especially irrational ones.

Reluctantly complying so as not to make a scene, she slipped her hand under the table and into his rough palm but kept her hand loosely clasped around his, sticking to the bare minimum of what could be considered hand-holding.

As if to make sure she didn't pull away, his hand immediately took a firmer hold.

"Caraway, how's your project at Ashley Mills going?" Hazel asked.

Silas brought their joined hands to rest on his knee which stopped bouncing at the contact, and she redirected her attention to the question, endeavoring to ignore whatever mood plagued her husband.

"It's going well. We received the dining furniture today, and the kitchen's completed."

"That's excellent news! Aren't you glad you married such an enterprising woman, Silas? Cara will make Ashley Mills the envy of every factory in Manchester."

"Until our mill is built, sunshine," Jonathan added teasingly.

"Yes, I'm fortunate to have Caraway." The low tone sent a shiver down her spine. His words implied an ownership beyond the usual of man and wife. It at once irritated and intrigued her—the idea of him *owning* her appealing to a previously hidden wicked streak connected straight to her core.

Didn't you just cite your displeasure with being told what to do?

"I'm sure she's already the envy of every factory owner."

The outrageous compliment brought a scarlet blush to her skin. She doubted the veracity of his statement very much. She'd never inspired jealousy in her life.

"I'm sure you're right," Hazel agreed smugly, her youngest sister retaining hope that their marriage would turn into a love match.

"Pardon the intrusion, but dinner is served."

Caraway pulled her hand from Silas's as they headed to the dining room and wiped the sweaty palm on her dress as her husband eyed the action with dismay.

Well, what did he expect from holding her hand for so long?

SILAS BERATED HIMSELF for being a damned idiot. He didn't know why he'd commanded Caraway's touch. He just knew that seeing Hazel grab her husband's hand caused a stirring in him for his wife to do the same.

After all, they were married, dammit.

She'd been overly affectionate with Brandon every time she'd been near the man, and there had never even been a *promise* of something more than friendship. Yet she kept him at bay. Since their marriage, Silas's focus had been on winning Caraway for himself and ignoring her past with Brandon.

But when she distanced herself from him to the point of scrubbing his touch away, Silas couldn't help but be reminded of the man.

Her eagerness to be free of him was palpable compared to what he'd witnessed between his wife and that bastard.

Silas didn't understand her. She willingly accepted his attention when it came to their marital bed, actively participating in a way that surprised yet pleased him. It was an unexpected reaction considering his idea of virgin spinsters.

But when they were outside the bedroom, a separation appeared. She remained pleasant and proper. In fact, he supposed she acted like any other English wife except for her sister. Or really any of her sisters. He recalled their wedding reception where all three of her siblings and their husbands had so obviously been enamored with each other. Sharing secret touches, playful teasing, and adoring looks.

The clear love that filled the room had made him uncomfortable yet envious. Why couldn't he inspire such passion in his own wife?

CHAPTER EIGHTEEN

"My father's coming to visit." Silas continued to read the letter he'd received notifying him of his father's impending arrival as Caraway glanced up from her book. A fire roared in the fireplace, creating a warm and cozy atmosphere, while they savored a quiet afternoon at home after attending church that morning.

"When will he be in town? I'm happy to finally meet him. I was disappointed when he couldn't attend the wedding of his only child."

Silas didn't comment on his father's absence from his nuptials. He'd informed Elias of his upcoming vows and promptly received a note back stating his father had business meetings that couldn't be rescheduled just because his son had gotten himself in trouble. It came as no surprise to Silas that his father would find business more important than his family. It was the story of his life.

"He'll be here in a week."

"A week? Mrs. Frost and I must hurry to make sure everything is arranged for his arrival." She set the book aside and moved to the writing desk to scribble down a list of tasks. "We'll need to air out the guest room, clean the sheets, tidy up some of the lesser used rooms... Does your father have a favorite meal or any allergies we should know about?"

Her pen paused over the sheet of paper as she waited for his answer.

Silas lowered the letter and moved to stand behind her. Placing a comforting hand on her shoulder, he soothed, "No allergies. He'll eat anything. Don't work yourself into a fit over his visit. The house is fine as it is."

Caraway shook her head in denial. "I want everything to be perfect. I'm his daughter-in-law now, and first impressions are everything."

Silas squeezed her shoulder, unsure of what to say. Deciding to relay the truth, he explained, "Sweetheart, I don't want you to get your hopes too high. My father is a strict man. He only cares about making money and building companies. I'm afraid if you were hoping for a father figure, he's not it."

"Surely, he can't be that bad! He's your own father!" Her voice dropped a little as if realizing that may not have been the best defense. He knew he embodied more of his father's characteristics than he'd like to admit.

"Exactly and look how I turned out. Cold, never letting emotions get in the way of what I want."

"That's not entirely true..."

"Don't lie, Caraway. It doesn't suit you." He returned to the seat behind his desk, organizing the rest of his correspondence.

Caraway contemplated his words. "I know most people would agree with your view of yourself. And maybe I did, too, in the beginning. But I've gotten to know you, and even before we married, I knew they were wrong. Why, anytime we were around each other, anger fairly poured off of you."

"That wasn't anger. That was frustration at not being able to claim you the way I wanted, which can be chalked up to physical attraction rather than emotions."

Caraway laughed at his explanation. "Whatever you say, but I stand by my opinion." Her humor faded as she studied the list of preparations for a guest. "However, I'll try to temper my expectations when it comes to your father. I trust you know him best."

With that, she left to find Mrs. Frost and begin checking off items on her list while Silas stewed over her last comment. He wouldn't say he knew his father best. Yes, he knew Elias's tendencies and character, but his father refused to let anyone into the inner workings of his mind or heart.

He was locked tight like a vault—the same way Silas was.

THE DAY DAWNED CLEAR and blue-skied, a rare occurrence in Manchester. For once, Caraway rose before Silas, intent on ensuring everything was perfect for his father's arrival. Nerves skittered through her veins at meeting her father-in-law, and Silas's warnings heightened her anxiety.

So, she quietly grabbed her clothing and escaped to the washroom to prepare for the momentous occasion. Finishing with her dress, Caraway twisted her mass of curls into a simple chignon and twisted to view her handiwork from all sides before giving a curt nod of approval.

People bustled below stairs as Caraway entered the kitchen searching for the housekeeper. Heat wafted from the oven where pastries were being removed from breakfast.

"Mrs. Riverton, what are you doing in here?" Mrs. Frost shooed her back out to the dining room.

"I wanted to go over our preparations for the senior Mr. Riverton's arrival today."

"Everything's settled. You've done a wonderful job getting the house ready, my lady. There's nothing more to be done." The robust housekeeper guided her to a seat at the dining table. "Why don't you take a seat, and I'll have some breakfast sent out to you."

"But..." Caraway trailed off as Mrs. Frost disappeared back into the kitchen. She supposed she should be glad things were organized already, but the urge to double-check the preparation made her fingers twitch.

Sighing, she tried to even her breathing and calm her racing heart. A maid brought in trays of meat and bread along with a pot of tea. Laying a place setting before Caraway, the girl left with the empty carrying trays.

A small grin tipped her lips as she realized she should have stayed abed with Silas. It would've been a much more enjoyable morning waking up to her husband's attention rather than worrying over nothing. Then, as if her thoughts had conjured him, Silas entered the dining room and sat next to her rather than at the head of the table.

"You got up early this morning," he commented as he stole a piece of bacon off her plate. His arm wrapped around the back of her chair and massaged the tense muscles at the back of her neck.

"I thought I'd make sure things were ready for your father with Mrs. Frost, but it appears I wasn't needed, after all. Everything's well-handled." She pushed her plate a little closer to him, so they could share. Picking up a slice of apple, she bit into the tart fruit, offering the other half to Silas.

He gently took the offering, kissing her fingertips before retreating. "You've been working non-stop for a week preparing the household for him, along with keeping the mill's dining hall on schedule. Ever since you learned of his visit, you haven't taken a break. Is it any wonder there's nothing left to do?"

"I know." She turned to rest her head on his arm. "I'm just nervous." His 'don't get your hopes up' spiel was, no doubt, forthcoming, but she raised a hand to stop him. "I know, I know. You can spare me the warning. But that doesn't mean I don't want to at least try and start out on the right foot with him."

"Caraway, I guarantee whatever foot you start with won't matter."

Silas had told her how his father only cared about business and that people didn't matter to him unless they served a monetary purpose. For the past seven days, it was all she'd heard about. But she couldn't reconcile that description. His father was human. Surely, a part of him loved his son and wanted to see him in a happy marriage. Wanted to know his daughter-in-law. It seemed only natural.

Silas fed her a torn piece of buttered biscuit, affectionately swiping at a few crumbs clinging to the corner of her lips. Chewing thoughtfully, she swallowed and then asked, "What time do you think he'll get here? Has he sent a message ahead to let you know?"

"You know as much as I do. But if I were to hazard a guess, I'd say, he'll arrive on the afternoon train from London, so around noon." *Only a few hours away.*

"Why don't we strive to rid you of your nerves?" His low voice warned her of the different track their conversation was heading down.

"Silas, we don't have time for that." She sat up straight in her chair, grabbed the teapot, and poured him a cup of tea. "Here, drink this. Maybe it will calm you down."

He chuckled at her attempt to distract him, "I'm perfectly calm. It's you, dear wife, who needs a little help." His lips lowered to her ear and nipped the tender lobe. "Come now, we have hours before he'll arrive—plenty of time for me to help you relax." Nuzzling into her neck, his free hand rested on the curve of her waist.

"I don't think so. Besides, I'm already dressed."

"That's never stopped us before. I'm pretty sure I recall how to divest you of your clothing fairly well." The teasing lilt of his voice sent a rush of pink to her cheeks. Yes, he certainly knew how to do that.

"You are incorrigible," she relented, eyeing his state of undress. The heavy robe he wore gaped open to reveal a sliver of his hair-covered chest. Unconsciously, her hand came to rest on the exposed skin, warm to the touch, and his heart beat a rapid tattoo beneath her palm.

"And you're irresistible," he countered as he dragged her closer to meet his kiss.

Caraway sighed, melting into him. She couldn't deny he had a gift when it came to soothing her.

All her life it had been her responsibility to mediate between stubborn sisters or remind her parents of practical matters. Peacekeeping had fallen to her as the eldest daughter which, for the most part, had never bothered her. However, it was a relief to have someone else step in and tend to her, instead.

A throat clearing in the background forced its way into their bubble, and Caraway broke off the kiss, burying her embarrassed face into Silas's shoulder.

"Yes, Giles? Did you need something?" Silas's gruff voice betrayed his annoyance at being interrupted.

"Apologies, sir, my lady. A telegram arrived announcing the senior Mr. Riverton's detainment. He'll arrive later tonight on the seven o'clock train."

"Thank you. If there's nothing else?" Giles shook his head and swiftly exited.

"It would seem time is no longer an issue." Pushing back from the table, Silas grabbed her hand before tossing her over his shoulder.

"Silas, put me down! You'll injure yourself!"

A firm swat landed on her bottom as he continued the journey toward their bedchamber. "Don't let age fool you. I'm still strong enough to whisk my luscious wife to bed for a thorough debauching."

"OUCH!" A GROAN OF PAIN vibrated from Caraway just as he was settling into the role of caveman but had he gone too far? Immediately placing her feet back on the ground, Silas ran his hands over her body, searching for a sore spot.

"Fuck, did I hurt you? I'm sorry. I—"

Caraway rose from her bent position and winked. "Tricked you. Seems all my years in Hazel's plays have perfected my acting skills."

"Why, you little..." He leaped forward but she danced out of his grasp.

"Uh-uh..." She wagged her finger at him like a naughty schoolboy being scolded by his teacher. "You forced me to fake an injury before you were felled by a real one. I'm not waifish or willowy. I'm—"

"Curvy and gorgeous. Plump and delicious."

Caraway darted down the hall and into the library with Silas quickly on her heels, then he slammed the door shut for privacy. "I'm also not a feathered turkey! If you insist on calling me anything, such as your 'little Venus,' I suppose it's only fair I call you by the name of one of her lovers," she teased as he stalked her around the library. "Do you prefer Vulcan or Mars?"

"You shall call me by my name, wife. No other man's," he warned, his body tightening in response to her jest.

"Now that wouldn't be fair," she continued, tapping a finger on her cheek. "Of course, it's not fair to compare me to Venus when I haven't had as many lovers as she... Perhaps I should broaden my—"

Her words ended in a delighted gasp as Silas pounced and pinned her to the library bookshelves. "You will do no such thing, goddess of mine." His teeth nipped at her bottom lip in aggression. "You're mine alone."

His hips pressed harder into hers, urging his hardened manhood into the vee of her thighs, and a desperate moan trembled from her throat at the contact. She wanted to push him past his breaking point, force him to lose control of the reserve he held so tightly.

Caraway never imagined she'd act this way: be brave enough to seduce her husband in broad daylight. She'd grown up thinking the marriage act belonged in bed at night under the covers. Of course, she'd never imagined enjoying the act quite as much either, and clearly that was a misguided belief.

"Am I? As a goddess, I'm practically required to entertain the attention of multiple men, especially as the goddess of love, beauty, and sex." The last word dripped from her mouth like honey. It felt unbearably delicious speaking so explicitly.

"Poor wife." He leaned more heavily into her, caging her against the shelves. The smell of books and Silas's woodsy musk combined into a strangely erotic mix of comfort and desire.

Heat emanated from him, causing her dress to become unbearably hot and constricting. She yearned to be free to absorb his warmth, their skin gliding against each other in passion. "Have you been suffering from lack of attention? I see you require more satisfaction than initially thought."

His beard abraded her skin as his lips drifted lower to where he roughly tugged at her bodice. Hearing a tear, Caraway glanced down to see his hands pulling the fabric past its limit to settle beneath her breasts. Without her corset, the stretched neckline pushed her breasts to an unseemly height—her nipples, eager for attention, barely concealed by the thin muslin chemise she wore.

"Shall I satisfy you, sweet Caraway?" He didn't seem to need an answer as he suckled one of her breasts, the wet fabric outlining the hardened nub when he pulled back as if to examine his handiwork.

Though the ability to speak was rapidly deserting her, she managed to challenge, "You think you can? One man compared to many?" She knew immediately she'd made an error and pushed too far.

Spinning her around, Silas roughly raised her hands to clasp the shelf above her. "Don't let go."

The guttural words were barely discernible as he ruffled around the bottom of her skirts. Wondering what he was up to, everything became clear when a rip sounded and cool air washed up her rapidly exposed legs.

He'd torn her skirt up the back!

Wetness coated her thighs at the barbaric action. Feeling like a needy wanton, Caraway slid a little further down the bookcase until she was bent forward, providing easier access for his entrance, her breathing deepening in anticipation.

Finding her suitably situated, he covered her body with his own as his hand searched through her slit to assure himself of her readiness. With her cheek pressed to *A Tale of Two Cities*, she closed her eyes in relieved pleasure as his rough fingers stroked her.

"You'll want for no other man." A harsh thrust of his hips accompanied the promise, surprising her with the sudden invasion of his cock. Silas usually entered her in measured degrees. Careful of her body's acceptance. This was nothing like that, but she discovered it suited her nonetheless.

He kept a steady pace of hard strokes that jostled her body into the unforgiving wood. Her nipples swayed back and forth over the leather tomes in a tantalizing rhythm while slick sucking sounds followed every time her body reluctantly released Silas's cock.

The erotic symphony added to the onslaught of her senses. Touch, smell... *I'm missing taste*, her fogged brain realized.

She tried lowering one of her hands to reach for Silas, but his larger palm stopped the movement.

"Don't. Let. Go." He repeated, punctuating each word by burying himself deeper inside her each time.

"Silas," she moaned. "Kiss me, please... I need your—"

His mouth tilted to the side and crushed her mouth in a clashing of teeth. Greedily, she accepted the punishing kiss, needing him to dominate every part of her.

A brief frisson of fear shot through Caraway at the odd thought then quickly faded as she succumbed to pleasure. Sparks radiated from their intimate connection, but Silas didn't slow his movements. Her orgasm only served as encouragement to power even deeper, harder.

Dropping his hand from a bruising grip on her hip, he slipped through the tear in her skirt to renew his efforts on her clitoris.

This new fervor scared her as she tried to escape the heightened sensations. "Please..." she protested, tearing her mouth from his. It was all too much.

"What's the matter, little Venus?" he taunted in her ear, his hot breath tickling her. "This is what you wanted. Do you think your lovers would stop fucking you after one peak?"

She spasmed around his cock at the expletive. "No, sweet girl. They'd make sure you were pleasured until your body lay soft and replete. And that's what I'm going to do because you're not done yet, are you? You're slick with the need for more."

His incendiary words ignited her blood. Impossibly, her sensitivity ebbed and flowed with his strokes, bursting into bright color then bringing her back down only to relive the cycle.

She lost track of time as her body experienced peak after pleasurable peak until finally Silas shuddered behind her, and his warm seed seeped out between them. Slowly, they crumbled to a heap on the floor, sweat darkening their still-clothed bodies.

Caraway felt dizzy as her head buzzed with satisfaction. Unable to move her exhausted limbs, she haltingly commented, "You're definitely Mars, god of war."

Silas chuckled behind her as his body curved around hers. Nuzzling the curls stuck to her cooling skin, he murmured, "I suppose I can accept that."

"Although I much prefer Ares. I can't call you a planet," she mused dreamily, relishing the lingering kisses he placed on her neck.

"But that would be the wrong mythology, love," he reminded her.

They lay in a warm patch of sunlight shining through the window, and she'd never felt as safe and relaxed as she did lying on the library floor, staring at a bottom shelf filled with historical tomes, the accumulated dust attesting to their disuse.

Rolling to her back with a groan, she studied Silas, noting the lines around his eyes and the silver dominating the black in his hair. "For a man of forty-five, I wouldn't expect such stamina. You're uncommonly fit for your age."

His lips twitched at the observation. "You act like I'm a decrepit old man. But I'll admit the majority of my peers seem content to waste away with gluttony for spirits, food, or women."

Caraway lifted her hand with great effort to trace his hairline. "Hmm, you have a point. I wouldn't say you have a problem with overindulgence."

"Really?" An amused eyebrow quirked in question. "I thought it was obvious I love overindulging in one very specific pastime." To punctuate his meaning, he claimed her mouth again, his tongue mimicking their earlier actions. The kiss wasn't meant to incite passion, though. Instead the slow movements kept them safely wrapped in a hazy afterglow.

She felt like a prize won by some Viking or berserker of old. Taken, used, dominated. Maybe her earlier comparison of Silas to a barbarian hadn't been too far off, and she realized she didn't mind this side of him. Besides, Caraway doubted any marauding villain of the past kissed so sweetly after the conquest.

CHAPTER NINETEEN

Silas finished adjusting his necktie, then turned to help Caraway button the front of her dress. The flushed color of her chest tempted him to toss her back on the bed, while her clumsy attempts to tame her mussed hair amused him.

"I take it you're feeling better," he asked smugly.

Caraway ruefully shook her head. "You know the answer to that."

They'd spent the entire day in bed after dragging themselves from the library to their personal chambers—something he'd never done before with a woman, just talking and making love—until the time came to get ready for Elias Riverton's arrival.

A knock sounded on the oak door before a maidservant scurried into the room with her head down and murmured, "A carriage has arrived," before making a hasty retreat.

"Well, she's a nervous one, isn't she?" Silas commented before moving to leave himself. "I will greet my father as you finish dressing. Take your time. No need to rush on his account." He grinned, reveling in the enticing picture she made with her hair and dress askew.

Silas sauntered down the staircase in time to see his father walk in. He remained as imposing as ever despite his sixty-five years. His tall form wasn't bent with age and his eyes sharply examined his surroundings. The only real concession to his age was the white hair strictly styled on his head.

"Father." Silas offered his hand, and his father shook it firmly, returning the one-word greeting, "Silas."

"How was your trip?"

"As expected. We were eleven minutes behind schedule due to a farmer's cart stuck on the tracks in Helton." Elias's eyes narrowed on the embroidered throw pillow gracing the settee—a clear mark of his son's newfound marriage. "And where is this daughter-in-law of mine?"

"She'll be down momentarily. She's finishing getting ready," Silas explained. Going to the sidebar, he poured both of them a tumbler of brandy.

"She's already had seven extra hours to get ready. What's taking the chit so bloody long?" Elias gulped down the rich liquor as Silas gritted his teeth, forcing a semblance of calm in the face of his father's derogatory tone.

Before he could respond, Caraway floated into the room, her serene presence instantly bringing him peace. An afterglow clung to her body, causing her pale skin to appear luminescent.

"Mr. Riverton, we're delighted to have your company. I've felt woefully behind as Silas has already met my entire family, and I've yet to meet his."

"That could've been avoided easily enough had you not trapped my son in this farce of a marriage," his father accused. Caraway gasped at the outright attack, a trembling hand smoothing down her front.

Silas growled, "She didn't trap me into anything, Father. I was and am her willing servant." He moved to his wife's side and wrapped an arm protectively around her middle to urge her closer.

"Pretty words coming from you," Elias snorted. "I thought I'd taught you better than to be such easy prey. If you wanted to marry, there were dozens of girls I could've arranged a contract with. Women who would've brought connections, business mergers."

Of course, that's what mattered to his father. It always came back to the best business decision. And a few months ago, Silas might have agreed. But that was before meeting Caraway. She'd changed everything for him.

"If I'd been interested in that sort of arrangement, I would have married years ago." Silas argued, "However, I am quite content with my current circumstances."

"And I assure you, sir, though I don't have many connections, my brother-in-law Jonathan Travers does quite well and works with your son on a new state-of-the-art factory. And the Earl of Trent is also my brother-in-law," Caraway cited, squeezing the hand he had on her waist.

"You don't have to defend yourself to him, little Venus," Silas whispered in her ear.

Elias scoffed, "Oh, yes. I've heard about this venture you're entangled in Silas. It's reached my desk in London. My good friend, Lord Brooks, informed me of the ludicrous scheme."

Silas bristled at the description of months of hard work he and Travers had spent making this mill a reality, and he pocketed the information that Lord Brooks was spying on him. He should have known his father would have someone keeping tabs on him after all these years, but this was the first time he'd actually had confirmation.

"It's a good thing I've come to save you from yourself. Left to your own devices you've fallen in with a former criminal and mercenary spinster."

Silas was reaching his breaking point with his father, and the man had only been there for less than an hour. How was he going to tolerate a whole week's visit?

Thankfully, Giles announced dinner, and they adjourned to the dining room, where Silas sat at the head of the table with Caraway on his left and his father on the right.

Mulligatawny soup arrived first, the shredded chicken and vegetable broth smelling delightful as everyone began eating, and Caraway managed to direct the conversation to safe topics concerning the unusually clear weather and how the theater was producing a version of *A Midsummer Night's Dream*. Elias, caring nothing for such frivolities, remained blessedly silent, focusing instead on inhaling the hearty meal.

After dinner, the three of them moved to the parlor before his father stopped Caraway. "It's customary for the men to enjoy a drink before the ladies join, is it not?"

"We're not so formal when there's only one lady to speak of, Father, and she's the lady of the house," Silas informed him.

"Nonetheless, I have business matters to discuss with you that feminine ears don't need to concern themselves with." Condescension dripped from his tone.

"It's alright," Caraway soothed. "I'll join you in an hour. Catch up with your father." She placed a gentle hand on his arm before leaving them alone to sit in two leather chairs facing the fireplace.

Staring at the flames, Silas considered how best to deflect his father's meddling. He assumed the man wanted to discourage him from continuing his partnership with Travers.

"Tell me what I must do for you to abandon this venture with that rookery rogue." His father wasted no time getting to the point. Unsurprised, Silas explained the benefits of updating the way current mills ran, detailing increased productivity and profits.

A part of him was disappointed his father held little interest in learning how his son was doing as a married man. Then frustration at himself followed the useless emotion. He should know better than to entertain such juvenile thoughts, wishing his father would finally start acting like one over four decades after Silas's birth.

The church may believe in miracles, but Silas sure as hell didn't.

"... and Jonathan Travers hasn't been a rookery rogue for years. He's a responsible businessman now. I'd think you'd admire him for the strength and smarts it took for him to rise above his previous station in life."

"Admire the man? Nonsense. He's reeled my only son into his scheme—hook, line, and sinker. He likes causing trouble, riling the Mill Owners Board like he has, and he's dragged you into the muddy pit, too." Elias tugged at his collar, irritation stamping his stiff movements. "Which by association means *my* name is sullied."

"Because, of course, this is about you." His father may tout the benefits of leaving emotions out of business, but this reeked of petty pride.

"You're damn right it's about me! It's my legacy you're dismantling brick by brick."

"Careful, Father. Those pesky emotions are showing." Silas emptied his glass tumbler and rose to refill it—to the brim. "I'm not dismantling anything. Frankly, I didn't give you a thought when I joined Travers, and why would I? You've made it abundantly clear you want no part of my life or business dealings, whether they succeed or fail."

"It's a harsh world, boy. I taught you how to survive, though, it seems all it took to make you forget the lesson was a tight cunt and her rabblerousing family."

Glass shattered against the wall. "What did you just say?"

Elias had the gall to laugh. "Now, who's lost control of their emotions?" Rising from his seat, he sauntered toward the door. "It's obvious there's no reasoning with you tonight. Perhaps in the morning, you'll be able to think with something more than your cock."

His footsteps faded down the hall as Silas collapsed against the wall at his back. Clenching his fists, the bloodthirst coursing through him heightened every sense, and he wanted to go upstairs to fuck Caraway into oblivion. To erase this conversation with his father.

But he knew he couldn't visit his wife yet. He'd be too rough. Too rabid. No, a visit to The Warehouse was in order. At least there he was free to loosen the reins on his control, could drown in the fury boiling in his gut, unleashing it on someone prepared to handle it.

Unlike his little Venus.

CHAPTER TWENTY

Tension permeated the home over the next few days as it became clear Elias was unwilling to accept Silas's wife or his business dealings. So it was fortunate when a previous engagement, the Calhoun family's annual masquerade ball, provided a much-needed respite.

Caraway eagerly opened the box containing her finished costume from Madame Fleur. Gossamer layers of white chiffon floated beautifully through the air as she unfolded the dress, but the sheerness of the fabric concerned her. Madame Fleur hadn't mentioned how transparent the costume would be.

Perhaps it's a trick of the light.

A knock on the door interrupted her doubts about the gown, and Caraway promptly called for the visitor to enter, setting the dress aside for now.

"I won't keep you from getting ready, but I wanted to drop off this gift for tonight." Silas strode into the room and presented a velvet box hiding behind his back. Intrigued by the gift, Caraway opened the casing to reveal a long strand of pearls overlapped to fit the rectangular space. "Those should match your outfit tonight. Madame Fleur said you'd be iridescent."

Caraway recalled the shimmery white material and couldn't fault the woman's description. It was touching that he'd gone through the trouble of discovering details of her dress and gifting her with matching jewelry.

"They're beautiful." She stroked the small orbs glowing in the light. "But you didn't have to—"

"You're my wife. Not to mention the goddess Venus tonight, and as such you deserve whatever kind of bauble I wish to adorn you with."

Pressing a swift kiss of gratitude to his bearded cheek, Caraway accepted his generous offering and laid it with the rest of her accouterments for the evening on the vanity.

"Speaking of Venus, are you ready to embody Mars, my god of war?" They thought it would be fitting to wear matching costumes to emulate their own secret nicknames.

"I'm pretty sure I've already embodied him... or do you need a reminder?" He arched his eyebrows in mock seriousness.

Laughing, she shoved him away. "Not at the moment. We need to get dressed. Is your father sure he doesn't want to join us?"

Elias had turned his nose up at her initial invitation, stating his lack of interest in such ridiculous soirees. "A waste of time," he'd stated, and she'd released her breath in relief at his refusal. However, it was only polite to double check.

"Don't worry. He hasn't changed his mind. He's holed up in my study working as usual." The bitterness in his voice rang loud and clear. Silas's childhood hadn't been warm and rosy, but now after meeting his father, she felt even more sympathy for the young boy he'd been. And for the man who still couldn't bring himself to stop caring, no matter how much he'd deny that fact.

"Maybe another time." She rubbed his arm comfortingly before changing the subject and pushing him into the adjoining chamber where his costume awaited him. "For now, I expect my Mars to be properly outfitted in an hour."

"The same goes for you, wife." Silas shot a mischievous grin over his shoulder, one that punched her in the gut with its carefree nature. The layer of ice that used to surround her husband seemed to have melted completely, and its disappearance allowed a playful and passionate man to emerge.

Something she must have seen over the past few months of their marriage but hadn't consciously realized until that moment.

"Are you ready, my lady?" Mary lifted the Venus costume from the bed once Silas left, allowing Caraway to avoid the implications of such a drastic change in her husband.

"Yes, of course."

They proceeded to remove layers of her day dress until Mary reached to remove Caraways' chemise as well.

"Wait, this stays on." She pushed the fabric back down.

"Beggin' your pardon, ma'am, but there's a note in the box. It says, 'To be worn alone for full effect.'"

Caraway grabbed the note and read the short instruction with Madame Fleur's signature underneath. "Alone? But surely she didn't mean without undergarments... that doesn't sound right. Maybe there was a mistake." Without undergarments shielding her, the costume would surely be too revealing.

"I don't think so." Mary's head shook in denial. "When I worked for Mrs. Field, she attended the Calhoun ball as Eve from the garden and went without underthings, too." The maid's wide eyes betrayed her thoughts at such scandalous behavior. "I believe it's what's expected at these types of parties. They're less formal, ma'am."

Biting her lip in consternation, Caraway warily considered the costume. Never in her life had she wanted to expose herself so openly to a crowd, yet here she was contemplating such a thing. Glancing down at her overly abundant body, she feared what the gown would reveal, and her excitement for the night dimmed.

Was it too late to beg off? Her thoughts raced as she imagined entering the masquerade ball—a pale imitation of a real goddess next to her sure-to-be arresting husband. They'd probably laugh her off the ballroom floor.

Mind made up, Caraway prepared to tell Mary to put away the gown and notify Silas of their changed plans when the girl asked, "Why don't you try it on? Just to see if it's really that bad?"

She had a point. Even though Caraway would forgo her usual undergarments, it didn't necessarily mean the fabric wouldn't cover her properly. Nodding, Caraway pulled the chemise over her head and stood still as Mary draped the light chiffon on her body.

The featherlight gown drifted down, eliciting goosebumps in their wake. Soft layers created a dreamy, air-like sensation against her bare skin. Moving to the mirror, Caraway studied her reflection. Although not as transparent as she'd originally feared, if she turned a certain way, she could almost detect a darkening where her nipples stood out and the curls between her thighs lay.

Facing Mary, she asked, "Well? What do you think? It's too indecent, right?"

Mary shook her head in awe. "Oh, no, my lady. You must wear it! You'll be the grandest lady of them all!"

Caraway doubted the declaration, but she couldn't resist the curiosity burgeoning to see everyone's reactions at her audacity, to see if Mary could be right. Or, a titillating idea floated into her mind, at least observe Silas's reaction to such a state of undress.

Steeling her courage, Caraway decided to let some of Venus's confidence infuse her. A goddess wouldn't care what mere mortals thought of her body. She was a goddess, for crying out loud. Meant to be worshiped.

An impish smile formed on her face, and desire heightened her color. Yes, she would like to be worshiped—by one man in particular.

The evening held all sorts of possibilities.

"Thank you, Mary. I'll wear it. Now let's finish my hair. And I was thinking some face paint might add a nice ethereal look. Oh, and let's put these on." Caraway settled on the vanity bench and reached for the pearl necklace, which Mary looped a few times around her neck, letting one strand hang low to draw attention to the low cut of the neckline. With that completed, she moved on to attempting a Roman-inspired hairstyle with Caraway's curls pulled back into a loose chignon, curls draping down the back underneath and around her neck. A silver crown adorned the top of her head coming to a point that rested over her forehead.

Mary dabbed a bit of face paint around Caraway's eyes to catch more light, then sprinkled a shimmery substance to create a sparkling countenance.

Studying herself in the mirror, Caraway hardly recognized the woman staring back at her. She felt like Cinderella with such a magical transformation.

After thanking the maid for her help, Caraway headed downstairs to meet Silas, who stood at the bottom of the staircase unaware of her descent. Examining his Roman costume, he seemed like a man out of time. His muscular build matched the warrior's uniform while a breastplate met on one of his shoulders, leaving his other broad shoulder exposed. The toga he wore underneath reached just below his knees, the dark hair on his strong calves standing in stark relief. It wasn't difficult to imagine him as a Roman god.

Caraway hoped she lived up to his goddess counterpart.

On her last step, Silas finally noticed her, his eyes traveling from her sandal-covered feet then higher, pausing briefly on her thighs and chest.

"Giles, go see that our carriage is ready," he ordered, never taking his attention from her. The butler bowed before discreetly disappearing. Once alone, Silas approached her like a cat about to pounce. "You're not leaving the house in this." His hand trailed down the bold neckline, brushing over the curve of her breast.

"I know it's a bit risqué, but most of the women will probably be wearing worse."

"I don't care about other women. I don't want every man in attendance to have such a free view of my wife. I can see the shadows of your nipples," he groused.

"That's just a trick of the lighting. And no one will be staring at me. You forget I'm not a young debutante. I'm a thirty year old wallflower."

"You're not a damned wallflower now," he gritted out.

She shouldn't be pleased with his edict to change, but she couldn't help feeling a rush of pleasure at his clear desire for her. And his irrational jealousy of other men.

"No matter, it's too late for another outfit. I have nothing else to wear, and our carriage is waiting outside." She headed toward the door and hurried outside before Silas managed to keep her home. Glancing back, she caught him scowling as he followed her, and once they were in the carriage, she couldn't resist adding, "You know, I could ask you to change. You're exposing too much skin for my liking too. The ladies will be swooning."

It was primarily meant to tease but a frisson of jealousy flamed to life, as well. Silas wasn't traditionally attractive with his somber demeanor, but his strong physique and exposed muscles would be sure to draw attention.

"Let them fall," he replied darkly, shaking his head in reprisal. "I should've known better than to go along with your idea of costumes."

"You mean *your* idea. You started the whole goddess thing. I was just continuing in our tradition." She smiled, trying to charm him into a better mood.

A quarter of an hour later as they approached the Calhoun home, an innumerable amount of carriages lined the drive. "Looks like it'll be a crush tonight. All of Manchester is apparently here."

And it occurred to her that Brandon might be one of the guests. She'd managed to avoid him since her marriage. It helped that she wasn't staying at the Travers home anymore, where she assumed he still met with Jonathan and Silas for business meetings. Wayward thoughts of her former feelings were swiftly tamped down whenever they appeared, but it might prove difficult tonight if she was actually in his presence.

Her relationship with Silas wasn't an unhappy one, and she did care for him—after all, Caraway wasn't a heartless corpse. But did she love her husband? A jumble of emotions knotted in her stomach at the question.

Why had tonight already been a roller coaster of emotions and they hadn't even entered the ball yet?

Stopping in front of the Calhoun mansion, they disembarked and joined the flow of guests inside. Silas kept a protective arm around her waist as he guided her through the masses, but when they approached a line of servants relieving guests of their outerwear, nerves drenched Caraway in a cold sweat. Was she really prepared to advertise such a revealing costume?

Scrutinizing the other female guests, she found Marie Antoinette, a cat, and an Eve, just like Mary had mentioned earlier. The costumes varied in coverage, but she had to admit the Eve look alike had much less covered than Caraway. Buoyed by the sight, she unveiled her costume before ambling into the ballroom with Silas.

A myriad of characters meandered through the glittering room. Laughter rose from friends as they judged the cleverness of their costumes, and Caraway's fascination grew with each new outfit that came into view.

"Oh, what a good idea!" She pointed to a man with a small periscope and the woman emulating a star next to him.

Silas followed her direction and agreed, "And much more covered up."

"Riverton! Happy to see you out and about, old chap. Seems marital bliss suits you." The stranger ushered them into his group with a wide grin, and Silas introduced her to the circle of men before they launched into a discussion on cotton prices.

It wasn't the most invigorating of conversations, and thankfully, her presence wasn't required for long when she noticed Hazel and Jonathan enter the ballroom dressed as two of her sister's book characters.

"I'm going to say hello to my family, if you'll excuse me." Caraway eased away from the men as Silas nodded in understanding. Interestingly enough, she could've sworn she felt his penetrating gaze tracking her retreat rather than paying attention to his business associates, and the sensation shot a bolt of awareness straight to her core.

Inhaling a heavy breath to dispel the untimely spike of arousal, she considered her earlier musings. She may not know if she loved Silas, but one thing was certain—love or not, her body responded to him at the drop of a hat.

An unsettling experience for a woman who'd spent decades carefully in control.

CHAPTER TWENTY-ONE

Silas watched as Caraway weaved through the crowd to her sister and brother-in-law, making sure she reached them safely. The room overflowed with all sorts of characters, and he didn't want anyone—any *man*—accosting her. When she'd descended the staircase enveloped in gossamer white, the need to hide her away for himself alone had nearly knocked him over in its intensity.

And now they were at a masquerade ball—the Bacchanalian atmosphere teeming with lack of inhibitions. Anything could happen when people felt so free behind their costumes, but he would ensure no one thought to steal his Venus away.

"How are things at Ashley Mills? I've heard rumors of potential trouble."

The group's gaze shifted to Silas in speculation. *It's the first time I'm hearing of it.* His jaw tightened as he tried to keep a neutral expression on his face.

"Everything is fine. I'm not sure what you've heard or from whom," he said, his eyes boring into Brooks. "But business is moving as usual."

Brooks held his hands up in defense. "Don't shoot the messenger, friend. I'm just making conversation."

Silas dipped his head in acknowledgment, waited another ten minutes to seem unbothered by Brooks's comment, then excused himself. He'd had enough of pretending friendship with these men. They were noblemen who'd never had to work a day in their lives. They were hardly qualified to comment on the state of his own company. Besides, the only *friend* Lord Brooks had even remotely familiar with the business was Silas's father, and he already knew that man's derogatory thoughts.

Searching the crowd, his eyes sought Caraway and found her alone on the side of the ballroom watching dancers twirl in the middle of the room. But as he got closer, he noticed her gaze following a particular couple as they swept across the polished floor—Brandon and Miss Bradshaw.

Silas hadn't seen Brandon since that fateful night he and Caraway were caught alone, ending the dandy's attendance at the meetings with Travers and himself. According to word about town, the man had spent some time wooing the heiress in London for a spell before returning to Manchester to complete her father's business dealings.

Silas hadn't realized Brandon was back yet, and neither had Caraway based on her fascination with his movements.

Jealousy—insidious and murky—rolled through him. She shouldn't still have feelings for Brandon, not when he'd spent the past two months impressing upon her the benefits of being his wife. Not when she responded so enthusiastically to him in their bed each night.

Creeping up behind Caraway, he slipped a finger beneath the pearls around her neck and tautened the strand by slowly pulling it down her back.

"What..." She jerked at the action before turning her head to see him. "Oh, Silas, it's just you." Relaxing, her attention refocused on the dance floor, causing his eyes to narrow at the clear dismissal.

"Something, or should I say *someone*, catch your interest?" He tugged the pearls back further until they reached their limit and gently pushed into Caraway's neck, eliciting a stuttering breath at the slight pressure.

"Nothing in particular," she denied unsteadily.

Knowing otherwise, he growled, "Let me remind you, wife, that you're married to me not Miles Brandon." She shuddered in front of him as his hand reflexively squeezed the delicate necklace in his hand, urging her deeper into his body.

Caraway tilted her head up in defiance. "I know exactly who I'm married to. It would seem you've gotten a little *too* into your role of god of war, husband."

A hard swallow caused her restricted throat to undulate against the pearls,

"Perhaps you're right," he murmured, breathing in the scent of lavender in the crook of her neck. All evening his body had pulsed with desire for her, and her focus on Brandon taunted him to assert his claim on her.

"Come with me. I think it's time Mars showed Venus exactly who she should be paying attention to." Silas released the necklace and reached for her hand. She tried to object to being dragged away from the crowd, but he ignored her protests. He needed relief, and she needed a reminder of who owned her.

"Silas, we absolutely cannot do this again. Last time we were alone at a party we ended up married to avoid scandal."

"Which means we're allowed to do whatever the hell we want," Silas countered.

A brief snicker burst from her. "Hardly. It means we can't create any more scenes."

Ignoring her comment, he navigated the Calhoun halls nodding at guests and servants, searching for privacy. "You realize if the last time culminated in our marriage, perhaps this time will be in your pregnancy. It's the next logical step."

The idea of her pregnant with his child appeased some possessive part of him.

Finally finding an empty room, Silas pulled her behind him then shut the door. A couple of chaises occupied the space along with a writing desk against the back wall.

Perfect.

He strode toward the shadowed desk with Caraway in tow before propping her bottom on the desktop.

"Silas, I really don't think—" she paused as he began removing the necklace around her neck. "What are you doing?"

"These beads can serve more than one purpose." His cryptic words confused her as her nose scrunched in question. After wrapping the strands around his fingers, he leaned forward, forcing her head back to accept his kiss.

Silas loved her taste, and no matter how often they kissed, she always started shy and timid before passion pushed to the forefront. On cue, desire trumped reservations and her nails dug into his shoulders, urging him closer.

While she was distracted, Silas ran his pearl-covered knuckles down her neckline, the thin fabric giving way to his nudge until her breast was exposed. Releasing her mouth, he whispered, "Watch," and tilted her chin down to see him graze her nipple with the pearls. Her chest rose with a deep inhale at the touch.

"You shouldn't..." The words faded as he captured the hardened nipple with his mouth while his hand drifted to trace the pearls over her other breast.

Switching sides, he devoted himself to the sweet bounty before him, nipping and sucking the darkening nipples as he continued the pearls' journey south. The slit of Caraway's dress drifted open, exposing one pale leg, and he loosened his grip to let the necklace brush against the inside of her thigh. Lifting higher, he sifted through damp curls to tease her wet center.

Raising his head, he kissed her again before saying, "If you don't like this, let me know, and we'll stop. Okay?"

Caraway studied his intent expression and nodded. "Okay."

His gaze remained on her as he gently eased the pearls inside her clenching channel. He noted the widening of her eyes at the new sensation, but she didn't deny him entrance, instead her thighs contracted around him, her body adjusting to the foreign intrusion. Once satisfied with the placement, Silas removed his hand, leaving the necklace behind.

"How does that feel?"

A contemplative expression crossed her features as Caraway shifted on the desktop. "Strange... but not unpleasant," she conceded. "But are you going to... you know..." She gestured to his obvious erection, and he understood her concern.

"No, there's a party we must return to." Straightening her clothing, he carefully lowered her feet to the floor.

"What? No! I can't—"

"Yes, you can. If anything becomes painful, I'll remove them, but they're not coming out just because you're nervous," he explained. While they'd been intimate, this was the closest he'd pushed her toward his usual kind of bed sport.

She debated her choices before sighing. "Fine. I guess they can stay. What difference does it make anyway?"

He hid a grin as they walked back to the ballroom. *A big difference, little Venus.* But he'd wait and let her discover that for herself.

The first chords of a waltz rose in the ballroom upon their entry, and couples gathered in the center of the room, preparing for another round of dancing. Silas offered his hand in invitation which Caraway immediately accepted, his larger hand covering hers as the other settled on her waist.

He'd caught Brandon staring at them and wanted to impress on the man that Caraway belonged to him alone. Drawing his wife closer than was strictly proper, they spun around the room, bright light from the chandeliers causing Caraway's skin to glow. Her skin flushed from the dance, and no doubt, the pearls readjusting inside her with each movement.

When the dance came to an end, she requested a drink, so he escorted her to the punch bowl, pouring her a glass and spying the slight tremble in her hand as she brought it to her mouth.

"Silas." She looked around to see who was near before stepping closer. A slight sheen of sweat dotted her forehead. "How long must I endure this... predicament?"

"Is it such a terrible task to endure?"

"Not exactly. But I fear I might... That is I don't want to..." She stumbled over her words before clasping his hand and pulling him behind a potted plant further away from listening ears. Her heavy breathing could be heard in the quieter atmosphere. "I don't wish to experience... *in public*." Caraway's hands flustered about in the air as she was unable to intelligibly voice the problem.

Understanding, Silas held back a chuckle at her quandary. Of course, his proper wife wouldn't want to orgasm in front of a hundred people even if they had no idea what was happening. Thinking to tease her a bit more, he enacted a disappointed expression.

"Can't you wait a little longer? It's only been one dance, surely your tolerance is higher than that."

"Silas!" She fairly growled his name in desperation, and his jaw latched shut in an effort to appear neutral rather than amused. Rubbing the small of her back to soothe her ire, he finally took pity on her.

"Don't worry, goddess of mine, I'll take care of you."

CHAPTER TWENTY-TWO

Thankfully, their earlier escape remained unoccupied as the couple reentered the room moments later. However, this time Silas guided her to a chaise sitting in the moonlight, the beams casting a dreamy haze over the spot.

"Lay down, little Venus."

Caraway didn't hesitate before lowering onto the plush cushions and reclining until her body lay flat before him.

"What an enticing picture you make, wife." His knuckles ran down her cheek, over her breasts, then further down her round belly, and the mewling sounds Caraway made in response set his blood aflame. "The very image of sex and hedonistic pleasure with your lush curves on display for your husband."

Kneeling on the floor, Silas braced his hands on either side of her hips. The costume skirt gathered next to his fists, leaving his wife's pussy obscenely open to his hungry gaze. Glossy arousal coated the loop of pearls he'd allowed to hang outside her walls to draw the orbs inside down in a slick, sensitizing journey.

Looping the strand through his fingers, he gently tugged on the beads as his lips circled her clitoris, laving the tender bud with his tongue. Caraway arched at the dual attack, a throaty moan reverberating through the air.

"Silas... Please..."

Once the last pearl slid out, Silas tossed the necklace aside and devoured the gleaming gush of arousal with a long lick. "Shh... little Venus. I'll satisfy this sweet pussy. Haven't I promised to never leave you wanting?"

And Silas never broke a promise.

Lifting his toga skirt, he buried himself inside his wife's hot channel—he knew foregoing underclothing would be useful. Caraway's body stilled at the thick intrusion before her silken walls bore down on him, drawing him deeper with each pulsing clasp.

This wouldn't be a slow and gentle affair. No, this would be a quick and dirty fucking, he decided as his body slammed into hers, forcing Caraway forward until her head butted against the chaise arm. She braced her hands above her head to prevent it from hitting the firm structure, and the move caused her chest to rise higher, tempting Silas with the shadowy points of her nipples.

Suckling one turgid nipple his strokes became harder. Her breathy pleas spurred him on. He wanted to please her, and his need to mark her as his heightened. Scratching his bearded cheek against her neck, Silas bit down and sucked on the salty skin before licking the small bruise left behind.

Finally, he felt her pussy tighten around his cock, and as Caraway's pleasure peaked, Silas let go with a roar, following her into oblivion.

Moments later, a rumble of satisfaction coursed through Silas's chest, vibrating against her cheek. "I doubt your precious Brandon could have made you feel that way." The pride in his voice was obvious, and Caraway stiffened before pushing him away and scrambling to her feet.

"What did you say?" she asked in disbelief, her arms crossing over her chest.

"You heard me. Tell me Brandon could've brought you that kind of pleasure. Did he ever even kiss you?"

"That's none of your business, and it's disrespectful to even think of mentioning Brandon at a time like this." Venom dripped from her words. "So, you're skilled when it comes to lovemaking, no doubt due to a string of women before me. It means nothing. At least with Brandon, there would have been love." Caraway's chin tilted defiantly as she hit her mark, and Silas's eyes narrowed as he slowly stood to face her.

"Oh, yes, precious unrequited *love*," he mocked, marching a step closer. "What a life you would've lived—seeing to every single one of Brandon's needs while he saw to none of yours."

"There's more to a marriage than physical satisfaction, but I wouldn't expect you to understand. You think you can force me into affection by demanding it."

"I shouldn't have to demand it, dammit. You're my fucking wife! *Mine.* You should want to care for me." Anger and confusion laced his tone. He didn't understand why she didn't care for him. What was it about him that failed to inspire even a modicum of affection? First his father, and now his own wife.

"You trapped me in an unwanted marriage by following me that night. You forced me to abandon the love I'd held for Brandon for years. And you wonder why it's so difficult?"

She turned away and stalked to the windows overlooking the gardens. "I've been trying, Silas, truly I have." Her shoulders slumped as she sighed. "We've only been married for nine weeks. You can't expect me to just switch love on and off, from him to you. I know now that he didn't view me as I did him, although I'll always wonder if I had more time, if that would've made a difference..."

Caraway shook her head as if to physically shake off that way of thinking. Turning to face him, she explained, "I'm angry at you. More so than I think I even realized before now. I've been trying to push it down and ignore it by putting on this facade. And I've been torn because I *do* like you. You're a good man. But you took my choice away, and you can't demand feelings from me that just aren't there yet."

He studied her sad eyes pleading with him to understand. A blanket of numbness iced over him. Clearly, any headway he thought he'd made was all a lie. She felt nothing for him, still longed for another man.

Schooling his expression, he said, "I understand. I'll endeavor not to demand anything more of you. If you're ready, I believe it's time we took our leave. Suddenly, the party seems to have lost its allure."

She didn't respond for a moment then nodded in agreement. "Yes, I think that would be best. We're both in no mood to socialize anymore tonight."

The drive home was silent as they sat on opposite sides of the carriage, and once inside their home, they went their separate ways. Calling for his valet, Silas requested a change of clothes be sent to one of the guest rooms.

Since his wife had been transparent about her feelings, or lack thereof, he saw no reason to force his presence on her. He'd sleep in a different room for the foreseeable future, ensuring her privacy.

Discarding his Mars costume, Silas marveled at how far the night had fallen. Things had started so well with his goddess earlier that evening. He'd thought her teasing—calling him her 'god of war'—had meant progress. So much so that he'd agreed to wear this ridiculous costume just to earn her affection.

He tossed the offending fabric to the floor.

He'd been a bloody fool.

A headache formed at his temples as he replayed her words from tonight. He supposed he should be thankful she'd finally been honest with him, but he couldn't muster any sort of emotion. Rubbing the ache over his heart, Silas walked to the door and answered the quiet knocking. His valet stood with a stack of clothing.

"Here you are, sir."

Silas thanked him then shut the door. Once dressed, he went downstairs to his study. It seemed he'd be returning to his old routine—working late into the night. Sitting behind his desk, he pulled out a ledger, determined to put the night's events out of his mind.

CHAPTER TWENTY-THREE

Caraway lay awake waiting for Silas to come in. After getting home from the ball, she'd immediately changed out of her costume into a white nightgown and scrubbed the make up from her face before climbing into bed. She hadn't bothered summoning Mary to help her, wanting to be alone with her thoughts.

They'd had their first fight, and it had been terrible. She groaned as she remembered the horrible things she'd said to Silas. She'd meant every word although they may have come out a little too adamant at some parts. While she was angry with Silas, some of that anger was also directed towards herself, at how easily she'd been able to accept him. Despite her denial, it hadn't been very difficult at all to begin caring for Silas.

Closing her eyes, she pictured his face when she'd said she didn't feel anything for him. It was like a shutter had fallen, blacking out any sort of emotion from him. *But he hadn't been blameless*, she tried defending her actions.

Silas had no right to insinuate such a horrid thing about Brandon. He would have made a lovely husband, and if the stories she heard from Lily were true, he certainly had a way with women—apparently leaving a string of broken hearts across the Continent during his tour with Owen.

Turning her head, Caraway strained to read the clock—after midnight. Where was he? He usually came to bed much earlier. Granted they'd only returned an hour ago, but still. Surely, he'd want to get out of costume.

Nerves filled her in anticipation of the awkwardness that would occur when he joined her, but they'd have to get through it. It's not like they could avoid each other as husband and wife. They needed to work through their disagreements.

Yawning, she flipped over, shifting closer to Silas's side of the bed. The maids must have changed the sheets because she couldn't detect his familiar scent on the pillow, and its absence made her uneasy.

RAYS OF SUNLIGHT WOKE Caraway the next morning as she stretched her hand for Silas but came up empty. Confused, she patted the bed searching for him, as if his large body could so easily be hidden. But the lack of indent on his pillow and tucked in covers told a disheartening truth—he hadn't come to bed last night.

Insecure thoughts that he'd sought attention elsewhere last night flitted through her mind before she squashed them. Silas would never betray her that way, no matter what transpired between them. He was a man of his word.

Perhaps he wanted to avoid more harsh words being exchanged and decided a night apart would be best. A frown wrinkled her forehead as she hugged his pillow to her chest. *That must be it*, she decided. And now that they both had cooled down, a calm discussion could ensue—except his father remained in residence.

She contemplated how little privacy they would have with their house guest. A house guest who had already made his dislike of her known. If Elias found out about their fight, he'd just make things worse, taking it as confirmation of his bad opinion of her.

Maybe she could sneak over to Ashley Mills and speak with Silas in his office. While not exactly private, at least she could be sure no one would eavesdrop on their conversation in the loud mill.

Yes, that's a good plan. Snuggling deeper into his pillow, Caraway fell back asleep now that she had a course of action for the day, a weight lifting off her chest.

A FEW DAYS PASSED WITH Caraway only seeing Silas at breakfast and dinner. Whenever she thought she could take a break to visit him, something happened to distract her like Mrs. Frost requiring assistance or the dining hall at Ashley Mills needed attention.

So it happened that on Elias's last night with them they still hadn't spoken since the ball. Silas hadn't returned to her bed, and she had no idea where he was sleeping. She'd surreptitiously looked through all the guest rooms and failed to find ruffled linens evidencing his whereabouts.

Doubt began to creep up, making her question if maybe she was wrong and he really would seek solace in another woman's arms. The sharp pain that pierced her heart at the idea surprised her with its depth. Perhaps more of what she said had been a lie than she'd realized.

"I've heard Travers's venture has reached a snag—some building permits were never filed. No surprise a man like him tried to cut corners." Elias informed them as he took a bite of the roast duck in front of him. Caraway cast a worried glance at Silas, who glared at his father with an annoyed expression.

"They were filed but conveniently lost."

"Hmm... likely story," Elias muttered. "Doesn't change the fact that you should back out while you still can."

"Even if I could, I wouldn't. Travers's mill is the future. Innovation needs to happen for our businesses to sustain an ever changing market," Silas explained for the umpteenth time. His father refused to trust his son's wisdom, no matter how often Silas explained the benefits, and she didn't understand the blatant distrust. Silas was one of the most respected businessmen in Manchester.

Elias scoffed. "There's innovation then there's a naive pup sticking his nose where it doesn't belong. What experience does Travers have when it comes to the textile business?"

"Mine. He has my experience. And I believe this is the right direction." His son countered testily as he stabbed a Brussel sprout. Caraway took a sip of her wine, worried he was reaching the brink of his tolerance—afraid of what might happen if his father kept pushing the subject.

"And what do you know about new ventilation systems or hydraulic machines? You sit behind a desk all day." Elias's insult fell like a brick in the suddenly quiet room.

Unable to take anymore, Caraway stepped in. "To be fair, sir, your son does much more than sit behind a desk."

"Oh, really? And tell me, what would you know about it? Don't you spend your days in this home my son's providing for you, throwing his money away on useless baubles?"

Ignoring the sting of his estimation of her, she said, "I've been through Ashley Mills with Silas. He knows everything that goes on there, understands the workings of the mill. And he's been in communication with factory owners in America who have already adopted this updated system."

Silas was much more than his father gave him credit for.

Elias turned to his son. "Is this why you have a wife? Dazzle her with a little business knowledge to make her feel useful and to fight your battles?" Caraway flinched at the man's icy tone. "Why don't you focus on maintaining this drafty old place? Dust covered the mantel in my room and this duck is cold. It's intolerable, especially when your cunt can't be that good."

The insults to her wifely duties irked when she'd done her best to ensure his stay was as comfortable as possible. But the reference to her sex... Never in her life had she been subjected to such treatment.

The scrape of Silas's chair resounded in the dining room. "Maybe it wouldn't be cold, if you'd bother to stop insulting my wife. I've tolerated enough of your crude and malicious criticisms in my own house. Caraway's been nothing but gracious to you while you've been an absolute bastard."

Caraway gasped at the harsh name. "Silas..." she tried to temper his ire, but he ignored her.

"You'll apologize to my wife then you'll finish this meal in silence or else get the hell out of our home."

Elias sputtered before shoving away from the table. "I wouldn't stay here any longer anyway. If this is how you're going to treat your father now that you're married, then good riddance. What a waste of time you've been ever since you were born." The terrible words hung in the air as shouts could be heard as he called for his valet to pack his things and ordered a carriage to be brought around.

Reaching for Silas's hand, she tried to comfort him, but he pulled his hand back. "I'm sure he didn't mean..."

"And I'm sure he did. I apologize for his bad behavior and thank you for trying to defend me. Although, as you saw, it's quite pointless with him." With that, he left, leaving her alone in the dining room with a table full of uneaten food.

Deflating in her chair, Caraway rested her head on the back of her chair in resignation. What a horrible night. *Scratch that, a horrible week.*

CHAPTER TWENTY-FOUR

Silas entered Travers's office the following day, the newspaper held tightly in his grasp. Striding up to the large desk Travers sat behind, he slammed the paper down.

"Can you believe this tripe?"

Travers reached for the piece in question and quickly scanned an article detailing the imminent bankruptcy of Ashley Mills. "Who is this reliable authority they keep referring to?" he asked, laying the sheets down.

"Hell if I know." Silas paced back and forth like a caged circus animal. His hand ran through his hair, disheveling the dark strands. "But clearly it's someone who holds a vendetta against me. I lost five men today who defected to other factories. They feared for their job security with me." A harsh expletive burst from Silas as his strides became more erratic.

Travers moved to a side table and poured him a drink. "Here, drink this. You need to calm down. I've never seen you so distraught."

"I'm not distraught. I'm fucking pissed." Silas tossed the drink back and returned the empty glass. "I need to go to The Warehouse, at least there I'll have somebody to beat to a bloody pulp."

"Or you can go home. Release some of this energy on your wife," Travers suggested. Silas shot him a horrified stare.

"Good god, man, not like that!" Travers objected, interpreting his shock. "I mean you can either fight or fuck, and personally I'm always partial to the latter. Go home and let your wife soothe you."

"I'm not going home... Who do you think wants me gone?" he asked, changing the subject back to his original purpose for visiting.

"Hard to say." Travers shrugged. "You've been racking up enemies left and right since you started working with me on the new factory."

Silas nodded his head, finally settling in a leather chair. Steepling his fingers in front of him, he leaned forward to rest his elbows on his knees. "Good point. People haven't been hesitant to voice their opposition. My father in London has even been informed of my business dealings."

They sat in silence, each going through a mental list of who could be the culprit behind spreading lies about Ashley Mills. The person would need serious clout to bribe someone at the newspaper into printing false information.

Considering his options, Silas said, "I'll have someone visit the newspaper offices to see if they can find out who spoke to the reporter. Maybe we can get a name."

"Surely, the perpetrator wouldn't be so dumb as to leave such an easy trail."

"Maybe not, but it's still worth pursuing."

Anger roiled like lava in his veins. He didn't want this article to snowball into more employees leaving the mill for his competition. It was imperative he speak with the mill leaders to get them to calm their people down. A thought toward asking Caraway to talk with her friends at the mill flitted through his brain, but he dismissed it. Silas didn't want her worrying about anything until he had more concrete answers. Besides the mill was his responsibility. It was his duty to make things right.

"I'll put some feelers out to see if I can dig up any information as well. Someone knows something and is bound to talk with the right incentive," Travers said. He had an extensive underground network still despite being out of the seedy underworld of Manchester for a few years. Travers maintained his contacts for times such as these.

"Thanks, I'll take my leave now." Silas stood and shook Travers's hand before hurrying out the door.

"What's it to be? Fight or…" He trailed off, having enough decency to not shout an obscenity sure to be heard throughout the house.

Silas didn't even hesitate before gritting out a stiff, "Fight."

LATER IN THE AFTERNOON, Giles brought Hazel to the small room Caraway had commandeered as her own personal space. She'd filled it with her favorite books along with a pretty writing desk for her correspondence. The cozy space reminded her of their family cottage in Hampshire.

It was only since her sisters started marrying that she had regular access to large, luxurious homes. Their cottage in the country had barely fit the four sisters and their parents, and while cramped, sometimes Caraway missed the close feeling. Silas's home, or rather their home, wasn't as spacious as Lily and Owen's estate, but it still showcased how well he'd done for himself.

Caraway rushed forward to hug her youngest sister who looked like a ray of sunshine in a yellow linen dress. "Hazel, what an unexpected surprise!" She embraced her sister tightly, glad to see someone who loved her. Something she needed more than she could say.

"I should have sent word ahead, but I didn't think you'd mind an unannounced visit." Hazel removed her hat, tossing it on the desk.

"And you're exactly right. I feel like it's been ages since we've talked." Caraway motioned for her to take a seat in front of the biscuits and tea laid out. Hazel had chosen the perfect time to stop by—the tea had just been delivered as if it knew it would be needed.

"We spoke at the Calhoun ball, although you and Silas left rather abruptly. Did something happen?" Hazel asked innocently as she selected a raspberry tart and accepted the hot tea offered her. She wrinkled her nose at the taste of chamomile. It wasn't her favorite, but Caraway had needed the calming tincture.

Blushing, Caraway recalled that indeed a lot happened that night—like the illicit sexual game they'd played before everything exploded with their fight.

Unsure of how much she should share, she settled on, "Silas and I had a disagreement. After that, we weren't really in the mood to stay."

"I see." Hazel nodded knowingly. "That's happened to Jonathan and me before. Marriage can be full of ups and downs, but you get through them. How are you both doing now?" She set her tea down and relaxed more into her seat, preparing for a long chat.

Caraway mirrored her actions and sighed. "We're slightly better. It's helped a lot that his father left." Just the thought of Elias Riverton raised her ire. "While it wasn't a pleasant visit, I learned more of how Silas was raised, and it's helped me understand certain actions from him. It's amazing he's not more like his father."

"Was he really so bad?" Hazel asked. Since Travers's parents died years ago, she'd never faced the trials of in-laws. At the moment, Caraway envied her that particular fortune.

"Yes," she stated unequivocally. "He belittled everything Silas has worked so hard for, disapproved of me because I didn't advance his son's career in any way. Overall, he seems like a very unhappy man who's determined to make everyone around him unhappy. If you don't earn him money or power, then you're of no use to him." And what a poor way to grow up for her husband.

She imagined him as a little boy with ruffled hair and serious dark eyes forced to learn his father's business instead of running outside and playing. A lonely boy with no mother, only an uncaring father who refused to show any sort of love or affection at all. A pitying shudder ran through her.

His childhood differed so much from hers. She knew her parents had loved their children even if most of the time they were caught up in whatever fascinating plant species they were researching. And siblings dashed the possibility of secluding herself—she'd never been alone.

"How terrible! Poor Silas. At least now he has you."

What was meant as encouragement only served to embarrass Caraway. He *didn't* have her, or at least that's what he thought after the horrible things she'd said.

I've been childish.

And she resolved to do better by him, to become a better wife.

Caraway nodded then changed the subject. They spoke about her improvements at the mill, and it was refreshing to have something of her own to contribute to the conversation. Usually, she sat quietly as one of her sisters enumerated on their various projects, but now she had one of her own.

It felt good.

CHAPTER TWENTY-FIVE

Elias had been gone a few days, yet the atmosphere at home remained chilly. Silas still took his breakfast and dinner with her, but their conversations never strayed too far from the weather, her family, or the progress with the mill's mess hall. Even then his answers stayed within short, polite sentences.

His distance was wearing on Caraway, and she could tell he wasn't faring any better. Dark purplish circles surrounded his eyes while a rigidity tensed his muscles.

She wanted to declare a truce but found it a difficult topic to broach. It shamed her to remember what she'd said to him, while pride made her wonder why *she* had to be the first to apologize when they'd both committed errors.

The only positive outcome of their separation was her ability to finally deal with her frustration over their forced marriage. Silas had set into motion the events of that fateful night, but it's not like he planned for the Gibbons' to discover them. Besides, she shouldn't have run off like a child in a temper tantrum after seeing Brandon with Miss Bradshaw.

The past couldn't be changed. So, it was of no use holding it against Silas. She needed to forgive him and move on, which she'd done. But how to tell him of the latest development in her feelings?

Deciding enough was enough, Caraway read the clock—midnight. She wasn't about to spend another night alone in their bed. Hopping out from under the covers, she grabbed her dressing robe and tightened the belt around her waist firmly. She was going to find her husband and bring him back to their bed if she had to drag him through the hallways kicking and screaming.

Systematically, Caraway searched each room on the floor until she determined he wasn't upstairs before tiptoeing down below where light slipped under the study door. Her lungs released a breath of relief at finding him home. A small, fearful part of her had wondered if he'd gone out.

The door eased open to reveal Silas slouched over his desk. Piles of paper surrounded him while the only light came from a dying fire. No wonder exhaustion weighed on him if this was how he spent his nights.

Crossing the Aubusson carpet to stand beside him, Caraway placed a hand on his shoulder causing him to jerk awake. "It's alright. It's me. You need to come to bed."

He shook his head and rubbed his eyes. "No, I still need to finish looking over these measurements for the new system going in at the mill. You go on. I won't bother you." One of his hands gently pushed her away.

Frowning, she tried again. "Nothing needs to be done at this minute. It can wait until morning. You've clearly been working yourself into a stupor and need rest. Come on, I'm not taking no for an answer." The stern authoritative tone she used on her sisters when they wanted to disregard her wisdom brooked no argument. Wrapping her hands around his arm, she tugged. He resisted for a moment then relented.

Helping him from his seat, she hugged his waist and guided him up the stairs to their room. Once she closed the door behind them, she proceeded to remove his rumpled clothing.

"I can do it." He tried batting her hands away but his unsteadiness couldn't compete with her determination.

"So can I. Just relax."

When he was down to his drawers, she urged him to his side of the bed before climbing in to cuddle up behind him—going so far as to throw a leg over his to ensure he couldn't escape while she rubbed circles on his back.

Slowly, his muscles released their tension, softening under her touch, and when she heard his even breathing, Caraway tucked herself closer to him, hugging him tighter.

Closing her eyes, she contemplated the feelings of peacefulness in his presence. She hadn't realized how much she'd come to depend on having his strong body next to hers in bed. They'd only been married a short time while she'd slept alone for years once her sisters began moving out to build their own lives.

Yet, she knew it'd be impossible to go back to that again.

Somehow, Silas had become essential to her in this minute way, making her question how else he'd managed to ingratiate himself in her life.

SILAS SIGHED AS HE floated in the odd sphere between wakefulness and sleep. Fatigue had plagued him day and night since he'd taken to falling asleep slumped over his desk. The bad habit was beginning to intrude on work, too. Focus was hard to come by at the mill, which could be dangerous on the machine floor. Something obviously needed to change, but he couldn't bring himself to talk to Caraway yet. To be honest, he feared hearing more about how disappointed she was in their marriage.

So, he stayed in his office each night.

Except he didn't remember the office being this comfortable. Softness cushioned his back, a giving presence unlike the wood of his desk. Blinking his eyes open, Caraway's familiar form greeted him, and delighted confusion rocked through his gut.

He barely recalled Caraway entreating him to come to bed in her dressing robe. But his mind had decided it must be a dream like every other night—imagining her coming to him, wanting him. Apparently, his imagination had been wrong.

"Good morning." His wife's sleep-softened gaze punched a hole in his heart. He'd missed waking up to her every morning, falling asleep next to her every night.

"Morning... How did I end up here?"

"You don't remember? I found you in the study and hauled you back to bed. We've been apart for too long." Scarlet bloomed on her skin as she bit her lip. "I'm sorry for what I said. It was neither fair nor kind, and you didn't deserve the lashing."

Another morning surprise! Silas hadn't expected Caraway to apologize first, but he gratefully accepted it. "I apologize as well. You were right to be upset when I brought up Brandon. He doesn't belong in our relationship. I'm a proud man, and it... bothers me that you've harbored affection for him so long. It's hard to compete against."

Admitting his weakness felt like torture. Like being beaten to a bloody pulp in the ring.

Caraway shifted to rest a hand on his chest, hovering over his body, her curls cascading into a curtain around them. "There's no competition. Brandon is my past. You are my future. We both need to remember that going forward. It may not happen overnight, but it's not supposed to. Relationships take time to grow. If you'll recall, we skipped the entire courting process where all of this probably would've been worked out prior to our ever marrying."

"You're right... I'll endeavor to avoid letting jealousy control my actions."

"That's all I ask." Caraway dropped a kiss over his heart. "All's well between us?"

Silas tenderly traced her brow and offered a half-smile. "All is well."

CHAPTER TWENTY-SIX

A hive of activity surrounded the mill as Caraway walked to the mess hall. It was finally finished, and she was excited to see it in use. She'd sent a message to Joan to meet her there on her break and saw the young woman waiting for her outside the front door.

"Joan! I'm so glad to see you. Have you been inside yet?"

The girl shook her head as she bounced on the balls of her feet. "No, ma'am, but I 'eard from a couple of girls that it was mighty fancy."

Caraway laughed. "Well, that's encouraging news. Let's go in and see for ourselves, shall we?" She took Joan's arm in hers as they strolled inside. The girl tensed at the gesture before relaxing as they took in the freshly built hall. The smell of pine and lunch permeated the air, a welcome change from the smoke of outside. Gleaming wooden benches and tables lined the walls as workers filled the seats with trays of food.

"It's like a shiny new half-penny, isn't it?" Satisfaction settled in Caraway at having helped accomplish such an undertaking, and some of her fears of being a useless wife to Silas ebbed away.

"Yes, my lady." The awe in Joan's tone echoed Caraway's.

She wondered if Silas had visited the new addition to his factory yet. He wasn't above associating with his employees, but perhaps visiting during their lunchtime would seem too personal.

"Do you know if Mr. Riverton has been down yet?"

"I haven't seen him, but I only just arrived a few minutes before you," Joan explained. They stood in line at the back of the room to receive bowls of stew, a bread roll, and a cup of water. The server hesitated a moment at seeing a refined lady in such a place before placing the food items on her tray. Thanking the woman, she and Joan found empty seats before digging into the simple fare.

Caraway watched Joan for a reaction as she spooned a bit of broth into her mouth. "Well, how is it? Worth forgoing your own cooking?"

"Oh, yes. 'Tis proper good stew." The girl eagerly ate more, and Caraway decided to try it for herself. Indeed, the meat was tender and flavorful while the roll offered an airy bite.

"You must call me Cara. We're friends, and as such, I believe we can dispense with formalities."

"But, my l—" She stopped at Caraway's stern look. Sighing, Joan relented, "Alright... Cara."

They ate in silence for a few minutes, taking in the conversations floating around the room. It seemed everyone enjoyed the opportunity of a free hot meal and a dry, clean place to eat it. Studying the open expressions on the workers around her, it occurred to Caraway there might be more that could be done to improve their work lives.

Turning back to Joan, she asked, "Are there any other problems needing to be addressed? Or hassles we can remedy?"

Joan paused with a piece of bread half-raised. Setting it down, she leaned forward. "Do you truly want to know, my... I mean, Cara?" she stumbled over the familiarity.

"Yes, I want to help if I can."

That's when Joan launched into a list of grievances—some small and others so big it was out of any kind of control Caraway could muster—but there were quite a few she could mention to Silas about fixing.

"What if the mill provided childcare?" Caraway interrupted a diatribe about the trouble of tending to sick children at home and being required to work or else possibly lose the job. The question stopped Joan in her tracks, her eyes widening in surprise.

"I don't know. Who would look after the children?"

"We could hire nannies or... teachers," she suggested as the thought took root. Her own sister served on a school board. Surely, she could help them. "The children could be taught while their parents worked. New educational reform bills are being discussed in Parliament. We could be early adopters with the dual purpose of aiding the people who work here."

Joan contemplated the idea. "I'm not sure... Most people don't believe in schooling since the children will just be growing up to take their place in the mill when they're old enough."

"But that's the point. They wouldn't need to follow the family tradition if they didn't want to. They'd have a choice with an education." A million possibilities raced through Caraway's head as she imagined all the children they could help.

Joan shrugged her shoulders, not entirely convinced, but Caraway was sold on the plan. She just required Silas's approval first—which hopefully proved to be successful.

They were cordial with each other, past their argument in theory, but they hadn't begun talking freely with each other again. Maybe this would break the ice. Guide them back to deeper topics beyond the weather or her family.

Seeing Joan nervously eyeing the door, Caraway surmised it was time for her lunch break to end. "Thank you for letting me know about everyone's concerns. I'll talk to Mr. Riverton about them. In fact, I'm going to head his way now, and let you get back to work."

The girl offered a relieved smile before darting off, and Caraway followed at a much slower pace. She walked across the factory floor before ascending the stairs leading up to the offices. The sound of machines from below mixed with the ping of typewriters as assistants typed up receipts and inventory lists.

"Mrs. Riverton," Mr. Lyman the assistant bowed. "Mr. Riverton didn't mention you'd be by today."

"I visited the mess hall and decided to drop by and surprise him. Is he available?" She noticed his door was closed, but sometimes he did that to close off the loud noise of the mill.

"He's in a meeting currently, but I can interrupt—"

"Oh, no, it's fine. I can wait." She took a seat along the wall while Mr. Lyman wrung his hands anxiously.

"But I don't think…"

"It's alright. I don't mind waiting. I can observe the goings-on here and see more of how the mill runs." She smiled, trying to soothe his nervousness. Silas was a busy man, and she didn't want to become some needy wife who insisted he cater to her every whim—like stopping by unexpectedly while he worked.

Her gaze swept over the room, taking in smaller details she'd missed before. Only men worked up here, she realized, and wondered why there weren't any women assistants. They were on the floor downstairs yet none graced the upper echelons of the mill. A frown marred her face at the blatant hole in diversity. Plenty of women were just as educated as some of the men here, and she wagered a good handful were probably smarter.

The discrepancy was added to her mental list of things to address with Silas, but first the childcare business needed to be settled. Once she had his okay, she'd see Hazel about the proper steps for setting up a school. The new education laws would outlaw children under twelve from labor and require school attendance. A school at a mill would be out of place, but part of the point was to keep the children near to their parents for peace of mind.

The office door opened, and Silas followed a white haired gentleman out. He spied her immediately but finished his meeting first with a handshake and promised to contact the man later.

"What are you doing here? Is something wrong?" Silas glared at Mr. Lyman. "And why didn't you notify me of my wife's presence? Instead of having her wait out here like no one of consequence."

She quickly placed a hand on Silas's arm. "It's not Mr. Lyman's fault. I told him not to disturb you. Let's go inside and chat." Gesturing to his office, she gently guided him in that direction.

"I ate at the mess hall this afternoon. Have you visited yet?"

Silas leaned back in his chair as his gaze traveled from her face to her chest then back up. The obvious appreciation in his eyes distracted her for a moment, kindling a slow heat. They hadn't been intimate since the costume ball, and she wondered when the ban would be lifted.

You could break it yourself.

"I stopped by before it opened for employees to ensure everything was in working order. You did a good job down there. Everything looked perfect, and from what I've heard, it's a success." A blush colored her cheeks at the praise. It was nice that he saw her as more than just a feminine body to warm his bed.

"Thank you. I spoke with Joan again—the girl I met who inspired the mess hall idea. She let me know about a few other things that could use changing around here. Like adding childcare for the workers."

Wrinkles formed on his forehead as he contemplated the idea. "Childcare? For what purpose? Surely, someone's already been looking after the children, and with no trouble for years."

Caraway understood his reluctance, and he had a point. But just because it was the way things were done, didn't mean they were right or couldn't be improved upon. "Yes, that's true," she conceded. "But most of the time, it's children watching children or an elderly relative or neighbor trying to corral ten or more young ones. If anything were to happen, parents risk losing their livelihoods to leave work in the middle of a shift to care for a sick or injured child."

"No one would lose their job here if they needed to deal with a sick child," Silas asserted. And while Caraway believed him, she wasn't so sure his employees did. The factory owners were tough taskmasters, brooking no tardiness or missed days. Unfortunately, he was lumped into that group by default.

"I know, but think of how much more efficient workers may be if they weren't worrying about their kids at home, if they knew for certain they were being looked after. I thought we could build a school for the ones old enough to learn along with nannies to watch the babies. I'm sure Hazel has connections that could help." She hoped her passion for the project and Silas's good sense would sway him to her side.

His head tilted to study the work being done outside his window as if it held the answers he needed while Caraway fidgeted in her seat, trying to remain calm but determined in her stance. After a couple of achingly slow minutes, he refocused on her. "This is something you really want to do?"

"Yes, I think it's important to do as much as we can for those employed here."

Sighing, he ran a hand over his beard and acquiesced. "Alright. I'll have Lyman see about dedicating a spot for a school. We may have to convert more storage space."

"Thank you, Silas! You won't regret this. I'm sure this will work out favorably for the mill." Her effusive gratitude brought a rueful smile to his face.

"Is there anything else you'd like me to address? I know you mentioned a list of items, although I warn you I won't be so lenient on every request." His tone tried to remain stern but the look in his eyes belied any true refusal.

"I think that's all for now. Best to address one thing at a time."

A low guffaw erupted from Silas. "Now you have me worried about these other items... What do you have planned for the rest of the day, now that you've succeeded here? Will you have a celebratory shopping trip?" he teased, resting his elbows on the desk.

"No, a visit to Hazel is in store. I'm sure she'll have opinions on a new school. In fact, I should probably get going before it's too late to call. I'll see you at dinner?" Lately, he'd been returning home past dinner time. She wasn't sure if it was still in response to their argument or this was just an extra busy time at the mill.

"Yes, I'll be home by then. I hope your chat with Hazel proves fruitful." He stood and walked her out. "Did you bring the carriage?"

"No, I walked. It's such a nice day, and we're just across the street. Nothing a country girl like me can't handle."

Thirty minutes later, the butler showed her to the front parlor room as she waited for Hazel to arrive. Rapid footsteps rang through the hall before she spotted Callum bounding through the door. "Cawa!" The little boy shouted as he launched into her arms—clearly, still on the way to mastering the 'r' sound.

"Hello, sweet boy." She snuggled into his neck, inhaling his sweet toddler scent. Caraway lowered onto a chaise with Callum in her lap, his squishy arms wrapped around her neck.

"Good afternoon!" Hazel swept into the room with a bright smile. "What brings you by?"

"We're going to build a school and provide childcare for the employees of Ashley Mill," Caraway stated proudly. The whole carriage ride to her sister's home, she'd mapped out the possibilities and was excited to get Hazel on board.

Hazel cocked her head to the side as if wondering if she'd heard correctly. "Really? Does Silas know?"

"He's already approved of it." Smugness filled her tone. Of course she'd get Silas's opinion before moving forward with such a large undertaking that would affect his business.

"Wow... How very progressive of him," Hazel said approvingly. "However did you think of such a radical idea?" A maid entered with a tray of pastries and a pot of tea, so they waited for her to set everything out before continuing their conversation—full plates in front of both of them. Callum grabbed a biscuit and began creating a crumbly mess.

"I spoke with Joan, the young woman who gave me the idea for the mess hall. She has a list of grievances we can address to improve the mill. Maybe it's something Jonathan and Silas can incorporate in the new factory before they even become problems." It hadn't occurred to her before, but it made sense. Now that they knew about certain issues, they could circumvent them before they snowballed into trouble.

"You'll need to share the list, so I can show Jonathan. I'm sure he'd be interested. You know he's all about workers' safety and health." Yes, her brother-in-law was a huge proponent of progressive reform for the lower class. He would definitely want to know how he can help more.

"I'll send it to you soon. In the meantime, I'm hoping you can help me organize the school since you have connections to the new school board."

"Of course! I'll speak with them at the next meeting. We'll have to figure out what type of regulations and permits we'll need, if any." Plans for the future filled the rest of the afternoon, and by the time Caraway left, she was full of determination and a sense of rightness.

This was a good thing they were doing. Not only did it give her purpose, but she'd be helping those who couldn't help themselves. A happy feeling ballooned inside her causing a wide smile to grace her face. The carriage driver probably thought she looked like a loon, but Caraway didn't care.

Because purpose energized her spirits again.

SILAS WALKED THE BUSTLING building with Travers as they studied the progress being made on the factory. So far, everything was on schedule for the new ventilation system's installation, and he wished the other parts of his life would run so smoothly.

While he shared a bed with Caraway again, they hadn't progressed enough to allow physical intimacy yet. Every night she cuddled into him and fell asleep. It tortured him not to take things further, but he'd learned from his mistakes. He wouldn't pressure her into shows of affection anymore. He'd accept whatever she gave him even if it did feel like he'd die from his restraint.

"This is where our mess hall will go. Caraway inspired me with the plans she made for your mill. It's a good idea to provide healthy meals to boost morale and efficiency."

Yes, it was a good move.

When she'd first voiced her concern to him, he'd agreed in an attempt to earn her favor. But now, he believed it to be the best course of action regardless.

"She's talking about creating a childcare wing next," he mentioned casually. The subject came up that morning at breakfast, and the cautious way she'd spoken raised his protective instincts—he wanted to relieve any fear she had about speaking to him, especially since it was the first time they'd ventured outside the usual, safe topics.

The idea of offering a place for workers to bring their children while they worked had never occurred to him before. He just assumed family members or neighbors cared for the children if they weren't old enough to be put to work. According to Caraway, it was the perfect way to ensure the children's safety while giving parents peace of mind, therefore allowing them to focus on their work.

Travers paused a step before continuing their walk. "Childcare... I don't know why I haven't already thought of that. It would keep the children off the street and aid the parents' efficiency on the job."

It shouldn't have surprised him that Travers understood so quickly. He'd been raised on the streets and had met his wife while she'd read to the very same children they'd be tasked with caring for if the childcare wing moved forward. They'd started a school for the older children already and fostered orphans when possible—like Callum.

"I like it. I'll have our architect draw up the plans for an addition. Maybe we should start paying Cara on a contractual basis if she's going to consult on such matters." Travers joked, although knowing the man, perhaps he was serious. But Silas agreed that Caraway was improving their businesses which would result in more profits.

"I'm sure she'd like that."

They walked a few minutes more before Travers said, "You know I was worried at first about the two of you marrying, considering how everything happened, but you two are good for each other. I approve."

Silas laughed. "I'm glad we have your blessing months after the fact." The wry observation didn't faze Travers.

Running his hand over a newly erected wall, he nodded in approval of the workmanship. "I'm serious. Before you met Cara, you were as cold as a witch's tit. While you weren't exactly harsh, you never would have considered adding amenities for your employees' benefits. And Cara... well, she needed purpose. With her sisters taken care of, she had no one left to wrangle."

"She seemed fine enough to me. Besides, she had Brandon. Wouldn't you have preferred that match over her and me, considering her feelings on the matter?" Silas questioned, a ball of nerves rolling around his stomach.

"Hell no! What she felt for Brandon was a mix of childhood fantasies and nostalgia for a life long gone. He was familiar to her. Now she's a grown woman. She needs more than what that dandy would have provided."

"Yet you still invited him to join our company," Silas pointed out.

"I figured we should use his money instead of investing more of our own, just to be safe after last year's downturn in the stock exchange. Also, Owen asked me to help out. Apparently, Brandon was causing some trouble carousing in the village." Travers relayed the information with a shrug of his shoulders. Doing his brother-in-law a favor took precedence over his own feelings for the philanderer.

"I see. I didn't realize he led such a prolific life back in Hampshire. Caraway doesn't seem to know." He didn't think she'd approve of such behavior.

Her family must have kept her in a bubble for her to avoid even idle gossip about Brandon's unsavory activities—actively allowing her daydreams to go unchecked, her feelings developing without reprisal.

"It's not exactly an appropriate conversation, though Lily's dropped fairly pointed hints about his character. Thankfully, we don't have to worry about him anymore. I much prefer you to Brandon as a brother-in-law even if you can be the occasional cold bastard." Travers patted him on the back as Silas grinned, taking the insult with good humor. He knew what he was, what his father had made him.

"Now enough about Brandon. I almost forgot to tell you I know who started the bankruptcy rumor and placed it in the paper."

The news reignited the fire in Silas's blood. His own investigation had failed to yield any useful information, since the paper's editor refused to name their source, citing freedom of the press.

"Who was it?" Silas growled, his teeth grinding together.

"Cannon. Apparently, he paid a boy to deliver the message. I learned through the grapevine that his secretary took the dictation, so it's definitely him."

"Why would Cannon spread such a lie? We're not close, but I don't consider him an enemy." Silas mulled over this new information. Cannon resembled Elias, and honestly, it wouldn't surprise him if they knew each other. Maybe he'd been the mole informing Elias of his business deals.

"I'm not entirely sure. But from what I've gathered he's against what we're doing here. He doesn't like the upending of the old ways, and wants things to stay the same. I'm guessing he's afraid his own company will suffer with defecting workers if they can find safer accommodations that pay more." Travers leaned against a doorway leading outside. The smell of fresh cut timber drifted in as teams of men worked around them.

"Hmm... Still seems like a large risk. Slandering me and the company. I can sue him for such lies."

"I doubt it. Who's going to step forward and risk their own livelihood just because there's some beef between you and Cannon? I only found out this information because of the guarantee of anonymity." Silas kicked a loose wood chip out of frustration.

"I suppose you're right. But it's frustrating because people are still moving to other mills because of the rumor."

"You haven't settled that yet?" Travers asked, concern in his voice.

"I've tried, but with every step forward, something happens to set me back two more. There's more than the article going on. I think someone is personally riling everyone up. Maybe Cannon's hired an agitator."

He'd tried the best he could to calm his workers' fears, and he thought he got through until a few more men showed up at his office to quit. So far, he'd managed to hire quick replacements, but eventually his luck might run out. And if there was a mass exodus, production would come to a standstill. He couldn't risk that.

"Want me to get someone on it?" Travers asked. Complete with their inspection, they proceeded outside to separate carriages.

"I'd appreciate it, thanks. I know you have a way with these sorts of things."

"You mean underhanded sneaking around?" Travers chuckled. "You've got the right man for the job. I'll contact the man who discovered Cannon was behind the news article—see what else he can find. In the meantime, I'm heading home to my wife. It's been too long since I've seen her."

"We've only been gone for a few hours," Silas argued as his footman opened the carriage door.

"Like I said, much too long. My wife needs a good... well, never mind. Suffice it to say, a husband's duty never ends." The smile he shot Silas belied any sort of resentment, and his obvious eagerness to perform such duties couldn't be ignored. Silas only wished his own wife wanted such attention from him.

He knew Caraway enjoyed their marital relations to a point. She'd made it clear that it didn't mean anything, though. And while he'd participated in countless meaningless sexual encounters, it bothered him, reducing their own physical intimacies to such a base state. Which was rather humorous in a sad way—Silas wanted an emotional connection with his wife while they made love.

Perhaps his father was right about avoiding emotions...

CHAPTER TWENTY-SEVEN

Silas rubbed his sore jaw—tonight's opponent had been more than he'd bargained for at The Warehouse. Entering the bedroom, he shrugged out of his jacket as Caraway brushed her hair at the vanity.

"What happened?" She caught his reflection in the mirror, concern clouding her features over the marks on his face. A second later her fingers lightly traced the discoloration of the nasty bruise.

"I moved too slow tonight." He'd lost focus for a moment, which left him open to his opponent's left hook. Usually problems outside the ring disappeared once a fight began, but the stress of learning about Cannon had managed to follow him. Along with his struggle to figure out the tangle of emotions he harbored for Caraway.

"How did this happen? Were you in a fight?" Her voice was muffled as she poured water from the washroom into a bowl and returned to hold a wet rag to his face. He reveled in her attention, unused to someone caring for him after his bouts at the club. It was almost enough to make him believe he meant more to her than he knew he did.

"Just a boxing match."

"So, you did this to yourself on purpose? Why haven't I noticed any bruises before if this is your idea of entertainment?" Frustration infused her tone.

"Because I'm very good," he stated with pride. "Normally, my opponents don't have a chance of causing damage before I've beaten them." Not to mention that while Silas and Caraway shared a bed, they hadn't resumed sexual relations. She didn't have the opportunity to view any injuries even if there were any.

"I don't understand. How is this considered fun?" She gestured toward the darkening on his cheek.

Boxing offered a physical release. It reduced men to their primal natures, needing to fight to survive, but Silas wasn't sure she'd understand his explanation.

"Perhaps I can show you," he suggested, unsure where the thought came from. Women weren't allowed at The Warehouse, but a part of him perked up at the image of Caraway seeing him defeat an opponent, proving his strength. Which was ridiculous. As an educated man such an instinct seemed anathema, yet the truth remained.

Her eyebrows raised as she considered the proposal. "You'd bring me along the next time you went to the club?"

He nodded, dislodging the cloth she held to his face. "We'd have to disguise you, of course. Women aren't allowed inside."

"No surprise... Alright, I'll come with you next time. At the very least, I'll learn what's inside a men's club, why it's so special."

"Keep in mind, this isn't your usual men's club. It's a place Travers showed me."

"Oh? Now I'm really intrigued." She dunked the cloth in water again and applied the coolness to his inflamed skin. They stood there for a moment—staring into each other's eyes, and the desire to kiss his wife rode him hard. But he ignored it. Because Caraway needed to make the first move about this.

Hopefully, before he expired from restrained lust.

"ARE YOU FREE LATER this afternoon," Silas asked at the breakfast table three days later, setting the paper he'd been reading aside as he waited for her answer.

"Yes, why?" Caraway sipped her tea.

"I'm going to the club and figured today would be as good a time as any for you to accompany me."

"Oh! Of course. Shall I borrow some of your clothes to blend in?" Excitement filled her voice at the prospect, and he couldn't help but chuckle at her enthusiasm. It was adorable as hell.

"I'll have Thomas set something out for you. It'll be simple—trousers, a shirt, and jacket."

Energy rolled off of her in waves as she clapped her hands in glee. "How exciting! It will be just like one of those penny novels—sneaking around in disguise."

"I doubt it'll be that exciting." Amusement coated his words. He doubted anyone would take notice of a companion of his, especially when she'd resemble a short, young man—hardly the type to stand out in such a rough crowd. He'd need to keep a close eye on her, though, just in case.

"Do you have a fight planned? Or multiple fights? How does it work?" A barrage of questions ensued as they finished breakfast. Answering one inquiry led to two more, her curiosity endearing. Too soon, the clock struck nine o'clock, reminding Silas of the time.

"Oh, I've kept you long enough." Caraway recognized the significance of the tolling bells as well. "I've made you late for work."

"No matter. I don't have any meetings set this morning. Besides, I own the mill. I can show up whenever I please. Some owners don't even bother going into the office, preferring to delegate such tasks to a manager." Indeed, most of the men he knew conducted their business that way. It's as if they figured once they'd done the work of starting their company, they didn't need to keep overseeing it. Preferring to enjoy their profits safe and comfortable at home.

"Would you ever do that?"

"Perhaps... If my presence was ever necessary elsewhere." The thought of her pregnant with their child came to mind. While he'd never planned on having a family before Caraway, now that he was married, children were a given. And he was determined to never treat a child the way his father had treated him, even if it meant taking a step back from the everyday tasks at the mill.

"I see," she murmured, dropping his gaze, an interesting note coloring the statement. He didn't have time to analyze it though, before she returned to her normal tone. "Well, I won't keep you any longer. I need to speak with Mrs. Frost, and you have work to do. Just don't forget about picking me up this afternoon, I'll be ready."

Time flew by at the office in his anticipation of taking Caraway to the ring. He knew a husband probably shouldn't subject his genteel wife to such an atmosphere but she was willing and he didn't want to keep this part of him hidden from her anymore. Hopefully, Travers wasn't in attendance today. His brother-in-law would not view her visit favorably, he feared.

Choosing to walk home, Silas headed straight to the bedroom and found Caraway finishing her disguise by covering her hair with a cap.

"Where did you find that?" He knew he didn't possess such an article of clothing.

"Mary managed to scrounge it up from a stable boy. What do you think? Do I pass muster?" She twirled in a circle, giving him a full view of the outfit. And immediately he questioned his judgment. What man could see her curves and believe her to be a man? Although she'd bound her breasts into a semblance of flatness, her curvy hips were obvious under a tucked in shirt.

"I'm not sure this is a good idea..."

"Don't back out now! Not after I've done all this work to appear as a man." Her hands settled on said hips in a belligerent huff.

Skepticism filled Silas, but he relented, figuring he could protect her if need be. A promise was a promise, after all. "Come on, let's get this over with then. Remember to stay close to me, and don't speak. Your voice would be a dead giveaway as to your true identity."

The carriage ride seemed shorter than usual as they came to a stop and disembarked. "This is where your club is?

There's not even a sign, and it looks like it'll blow over from the slightest breeze."

He couldn't fault her assessment, but the outward appearance kept the constables away—since they assumed it was uninhabited.

"It's very exclusive." The brief statement was all he had time for before leading her inside. He made a conscious effort not to be overly courteous by opening doors for her or placing a guiding, protective hand on the small of her back. Such a thing would never happen if she really were a young man.

They trudged through the crowds gathered around multiple rings to an empty room meant for changing. Benches littered the area along while stacked crates provided rudimentary shelves. Stripping off his coat and shirt, he stuffed his folded clothing into one of the crates. Usually Silas didn't bother leaving items behind, preferring to keep them close at the edge of the ring, but he figured they might return to this room after the fight.

"Ready?" he asked before leading her back into the main arena to find an opponent. Caraway nodded, her eyes wide as she took in the surroundings.

Weaving through the mass of men, he chose a ring in the back corner with a smaller crowd, who watched as one of the men pummeled another until he finally fell. Cheers rose as money was exchanged, and when the victor looked around for another match, Silas pulled himself into the ring since these types of fights weren't organized in any particular way. Just a first come first served basis against the winners until they decided to stop.

Silas motioned for Caraway to move closer for a better view, and so he could keep an eye on her. His focus needed to remain on his opponent—knowing she was safe within reach would help with his concentration.

The first round began with the ringing of a bell. Shouts of bets echoed around the room, but Silas ignored them. He ducked and dodged a few swings before landing a hard right hook to the man's cheek. The crowd cheered as the man stumbled back but stayed upright.

Shooting a quick glance toward Caraway to make sure she wasn't getting too jostled, his lack of attention ended with a quick blow to his side. Bowling over, he clutched his ribs briefly, before shrinking into a more protective stance. A couple of rounds passed with each man getting in a few good hits, until Silas landed a knockout punch, abruptly ending the match.

He exited the ring to pats on the back from lucky winners who'd bet on him. Shaking off their praises, Silas searched for his wife in the sea of men before spotting her in the back, separated from the posse formed around him.

Usually, Silas would stay for another match, but with Caraway nearby and a win under his belt, adrenaline filled his blood—all of it heading south after his win. Leading her back to the room they previously occupied, he shut the door, effectively locking them inside with only the murmurs of the crowd outside filtering in.

Wrapping a large hand behind her neck, Silas tugged her close and kissed her hard. The tidal wave of feeling coursing through him was overwhelming. Possession. Desire. They wound around his body like twine—squeezing,

squeezing—until the threat of bursting became a very real possibility.

But he didn't want to frighten Caraway with the strength of his need. Reluctantly, forced himself to release her, shuffling away so she wasn't caged against the door like a helpless animal.

"Sorry." His hands dragged through his sweat-dampened hair, "I'm always full of sap after a bout in the ring."

"Don't be sorry," she said breathlessly as she followed him, bringing her lips back to his, teeth clashing together, until they ended up against the opposite wall, a bench digging into the back of his calves. Caraway as a sexual aggressor heightened his own sex drive. Sinking down to the wooden bench, he kept a hold on her hips as she stood in front of him.

"Now I understand why you're in such good shape." She ran a hand down his sweaty chest, tracing the gleaming drops until they disappeared under his waistband. Moving closer, she straddled his lap, their mutual attraction palpable in the room. "You're a good fighter," she mused as her hips grinded against his hardened cock. "You dodged a lot of hits."

Caraway bent to lick the salt from his chest while her fingers traced a forming bruise. "And I appreciate that you didn't let your face get bloodied... Does this bruise on your rib hurt?"

"Not with you here," he breathed out, intensely focused on her movements. The rocking of her hips was quickly becoming too much. They hadn't made love since their argument at the Calhoun ball, and his body was eager to remedy the issue.

"What a charmer you've become." She chuckled, meeting his hot gaze with a teasing sparkle.

"Must be because I won. I'm feeling magnanimous."

"My hero, my champion."

His grin at her description faded as he noticed a budding purplish mark forming on her neck where he'd gripped her earlier. Contemplating the small bruise, he murmured, "I like having my mark on you—knowing you belong to me." Gently, he ran a fingertip over the spot.

"Want to know a secret?" Her arms loop around his neck as her mouth hovered near his ear. "I like having your marks, knowing I belong to you, too."

The whispered confession shocked him. Did she *want* to belong to him? On a hairbreadth's edge, he warned, "You can't say things like that. Not while I'm barely holding onto my control."

"Maybe I want to break it."

"Then perhaps I should start living up to my Greek god counterpart and claim what I want... Remove your trousers." he growled, instructing her to stand. A brief instance of hesitancy paused her actions—her practical mind trying to override her body's needs. "I'll know if anyone tries to come in. I won't let anyone get a glimpse of what's mine."

That was all the assurance Caraway needed before bending over and following his command. The collar of her linen shirt had somehow already come untied, so it hung off one shoulder to expose a creamy shoulder.

His little Venus was undone, her feminine form emerging beneath the weak disguise, and Silas unbuttoned his trousers to stroke his aching cock at the beautiful sight.

Motioning her forward, he reached underneath her top to find the end of the cloth used to bind her chest. The bandage unraveled easily as he released her breasts from their confinement, the heavy globes striped red from the cloth.

"You're never coming here again because your body doesn't deserve this kind of treatment." Silas gently kissed the irritated skin before helping her settle over him and sink down onto his cock. Groans of satisfaction echoed between them at the slick glide of flesh, and a steady rhythm began as Caraway rode him, her curves swaying and jiggling upon every move, beckoning his roving hands to explore his wife's softness.

Soon, however, he realized they both needed more than this position offered.

"Hold on, sweetheart," he ordered as he turned to pin her to the wooden bench, giving him more leverage to burrow deep in her pussy with powerful strokes. The firm surface held her steady as he pumped his cock in earnest, rumbles of pleasure accompanying each cry or gasp from Caraway. Fascinated by the bobbing of her breasts and the passionate expression twisting her features, an odd thought occurred to him.

"You're my reward."

Confusion wrinkled her brow. "For winning the match?"

"For winning the match, for surviving my childhood, for working all these years nonstop, for all of it." He poured out his feelings—an involuntary action he couldn't resist. Embarrassment distracted him from their lovemaking until he noticed a change in her eyes as her release washed over her.

"Silas!"

With her neck arched so her head tilted back, exposing her throat, he felt a rush of tenderness for her and knelt down to brush the lightest of kisses on the center of the delicate column. Almost reverently, he whispered, "My Caraway," as he came. He'd never said her name that way before, preferring to use an endearment like "little Venus" during sex.

Such vulnerability shot a frisson of fear through Silas. He'd been so high from winning the fight—a true man's man—yet here he was exposing himself to her, confessing how dissatisfying his life had been before her. Wisps of incomplete thoughts flitted through his mind, evaporating before he could analyze them. Thoughts of how he needed her. That she had become his life.

Silas didn't think he could live without Caraway, although he wasn't ready to admit that to himself or her.

CHAPTER TWENTY-EIGHT

Caraway woke to curtains being drawn later that evening. After they'd returned from The Warehouse, she and Silas had washed off the grime and sweat dried on their skin before retiring to their room for a restorative nap. The bed covers tumbled down as she sat up to view Silas taking a seat at a table filled with pastries and sweetmeats.

"How long have I been asleep? You should've woken me." Caraway slipped her feet over the side of the bed, the plush carpet sinking between her toes as she shuffled towards him.

"You looked too peaceful to wake, and you needed rest."

When she was near, Silas pulled her into his lap, arranging her sideways so her cheek rested on his shoulder. Sinking into his warmth, Caraway huffed at the endearing yet frustrating explanation. She wouldn't fall apart from an interrupted nap and told him so.

"Nevertheless, dear wife, it's my duty to tend to your well-being. Now, would you prefer a strawberry or peach?" He motioned to the dishes in front of them.

"Peach, please." She reached forward to grab a slice, but Silas stopped her with a hand to her arm.

"Allow me."

Finding a peach slice among the fruit trays, he brought it to her lips, where she awkwardly opened for him. *This is new.* It felt far too intimate, despite the sexual escapade of earlier. After she bit through half of the peach slice, Silas brought the remainder to his own mouth.

Too intimate, indeed.

They continued eating in such a way until both were satisfied. No words exchanged aside from the occasional "yea" or "nay" to a particular delicacy. To Caraway's surprise, it wasn't an uncomfortable silence—more, a companionable one. Something she hadn't felt with anyone before. Most people tried to fill the quiet spaces, but not Silas. He tended to live there.

"What brought that on earlier? I know we haven't been intimate since... Well, in a while, but I didn't expect to be jumped by my wife in public," he teased, his arms wrapped loosely around her as she settled into him.

She didn't know how to answer him. How do you tell your husband you've decided to make your marriage work instead of pining for a former flame? Laughter threatened to burst forth at the question. Did other wives face this type of predicament?

"We weren't exactly in public... But your fight was quite invigorating, and it was the perfect opportunity for me to surprise you as you are always surprising me—with scandalous forays in inappropriate locations."

Silas had a penchant for such liaisons. From their first night together to the euphoric experience in the library to his game with the pearls.

"You certainly succeeded. My blossoming little Venus, full of delightful surprises." She turned her face more fully into him, breathing in the scent of earth that clung to him. A small smile curled her lips. It felt good knowing she'd pleased her husband.

"On a separate topic, we didn't discuss it this morning, but how was your meeting with the Mill Owners Board today? Did they agree to stop hiring your men and refute the rumors going around?"

She'd known this sudden attack against his business had taken its toll on him, but it frustrated her that she'd had to learn about the trouble through Joan rather than her own husband. When she'd questioned him, Silas only shared how he didn't want to concern her, that he had it under control.

"Not in so many words. They defended themselves by saying they couldn't help it if my employees preferred working in their mills over mine. More or less what I figured they'd say."

"But they know the real reason men are leaving has nothing to do with you or the truth, but that nasty bankruptcy rumor!"

Hazel, who'd been confided in by Jonathan, told her that the board was filled with old men who refused to enter this progressive age, choosing instead to stick with outdated modes of operation. The injustice of their treatment toward Silas riled her sense of fairness.

"True, but it doesn't change their stance. And why would it when it means their competition may go under?"

"Is it really that bad, Silas?" She raised herself higher to study his expression. Dark shadows crossed his eyes while faint purple lay beneath them. Caraway didn't know how she hadn't noticed the signs of his sleep deprivation—again. Every night he came to bed and woke up beside her, so she'd assumed he'd been sleeping, but apparently she'd been wrong.

"Don't worry. We won't be destitute. I wouldn't leave my wife unprotected due to financial troubles. I have several investments outside of the textile industry as a sort of safety net. Diversified portfolio and all that."

Caraway wasn't worried about money. She'd lived on a modest income all her life. Plus, she now had the accounts Owen had created for her—flush with funds. No, she was more concerned about Silas losing the company he'd built from the ground up. Proof he hadn't needed his father's help.

Cupping his bearded face, Caraway said, "I'm not worried about my lifestyle. I'm worried about you."

A shiver traveled down his body at the words, and a vulnerability came over him, his gaze searching hers. "Pretty words when I know you don't feel that way for me."

She supposed that was fair. A considerable amount of time had been spent reminding him of her attachment to Brandon. "Believe me or not, but I *do* care for you, Silas," she paused, trying to articulate what she herself barely understood yet. "I know things haven't been perfect between us, and I've been mostly to blame. But you're my husband, it's only natural for me to express concern over your well-being."

Silas considered the statement slowly, as if examining each word for hidden meaning. "Very well, wife. I think it's time you concern yourself to other parts of my 'well-being', then." With that, he stood with Caraway in his arms and carried her to bed.

The time for talking ended.

Relief coursed through Caraway. They'd diverged onto a road she didn't care to continue exploring at the moment—didn't want to think at all, and especially not about Brandon.

Thankfully, Silas was of the same mind, making love to her deep into the night without another question of her feelings toward him or the other man.

CHAPTER TWENTY-NINE

"My lady, Mr. Brandon is here to see you. Shall I show him in?" Giles interrupted her reading in the library. Caraway hadn't seen Brandon except in passing since her marriage. She'd hoped to speak to him at the costume ball after his return from London, but the night had quickly devolved, she remembered grimly

Thank goodness, we've overcome that hurdle.

To be honest, she hadn't given much thought to Brandon lately—not since attending Silas's boxing match. Caraway's nose wrinkled in distaste at the memory of blood and unwashed bodies. Just as quickly, though, memories of a different sort invaded, bringing with it heat and a little embarrassment at what they'd done.

No, she hadn't given Brandon much thought at all after that.

However, it didn't negate the excitement Caraway felt at seeing her longtime friend, so she told Giles to bring Brandon along with a cart of treats for their guest. Placing a ribbon between the pages, she set the book aside and straightened her skirts, wondering if she'd look any different to Brandon as a married woman. An absurd notion but so much had passed in so little time, Caraway felt there must be *some* outward sign of her changed circumstances.

A knock sounded on the door before Brandon strode in with shiny boots and a lemon yellow jacket draping his shoulders. "Cara, my dear, how I've missed you," he gushed as he bestowed a kiss on her offered hand. His familiarity confounded her—rarely did he call her by her Christian name or show such affection.

Which should've been a sign of his lack of feelings ages ago.

"Mr. Brandon." She curtsied, reverting to his surname. For a moment, she considered how appropriate it was for a married woman to be alone with an unmarried man but dismissed the thought. He'd been a friend of Owen's and by extension her family for years. No one could possibly criticize their socializing.

Brandon placed a hand over his heart as if wounded. "Cara, must we be so formal? I know you're an old married woman now, but we're close friends. Surely, you can call me Miles," he cajoled with a charming smile. The dimples in his cheeks stood in stark relief reminding Caraway of one of her favorite features of his. Oh, how often she'd dreamed of those dimples and smiles lovingly directed towards her.

"I know, but it's not proper. Besides, I don't think my husband would appreciate my being so familiar with a man other than him, no matter how innocent." In fact, Silas would probably be upset at Brandon's visiting without his presence—especially in light of her past feelings for the younger man.

"Your husband's a tough taskmaster," he said darkly. It was an odd statement coming from him considering he'd entered into business with Silas.

"He's actually fairly flexible, but when it comes to other men, naturally, he's a bit possessive," she defended with a rush of heat. His possessiveness had quickly become one of her favorite traits of her husband.

Brandon rolled his eyes, scoffing at the idea. "Are you happy, Cara? Do you enjoy being the wife of such a cold man?"

The inappropriate question raised her hackles. Straightening in her seat, Caraway raised her chin and replied haughtily, "Yes, I've been able to discover more about myself and help others in need."

"I notice you mention nothing of love." He moved to sit next to her on the settee, and she leaned slightly away as his arm went around the back of the furniture, his thigh touching hers.

"I don't believe it's any business of yours, Mr. Brandon." Her breathing stuttered at his close contact—a faint unease unfurled within her at his proximity.

"It is when I know the man you truly love is me." The smug declaration shot an arrow straight through her pride. She'd assumed he never noticed her feelings since he'd never acknowledged them before. To know now he'd been fully aware of her crush sent humiliation reeling through her again at how foolish she'd been.

"While it may have been true in the past," she admitted with a parched tongue. "I'm a married woman now. Nothing can change that."

As if he'd been waiting for her to come to that conclusion, he shook his head and shifted closer to her. "You can ask for an annulment."

She hopped up from her seat and paced away at the incredible suggestion. Wringing her hands in agitation, she said, "You must be joking. What good would that do me?"

Brandon tracked her around the room, "You'll be free to marry someone else... me, for example."

Caraway didn't think she could be anymore shocked than by his outrageous claim. Why was he talking like this? "Why now? You could have offered for me before, but you didn't. And what about Miss Bradshaw?"

Like a freight train, the memory of the elegant heiress slammed into her. She was the one Brandon planned to marry.

"Miss Bradshaw and I don't suit. I realized it while we were in London, when it gutted me to realize what a grievous mistake I made. I want you, Cara. It's always been you. I've been too blind to see it, but I've changed. If your marriage is annulled, then we can be together." His passionate admission stunned her. A shameful piece of her enjoyed his groveling, but she found it was the only emotion involved.

Not love or desire.

Caraway turned away from him to settle her gaze out the window overlooking the busy street. Searching her heart and mind, it was a relief to discover she no longer harbored such intimate feelings for Brandon. Not anymore.

Of course, she still cared for him, but as he was—a childhood friend. Somehow, without her knowledge, her affections had shifted towards a reserved man who struggled with expressing himself—to her husband, Silas.

A man who understood her needs and accepted her for who she was. Honestly, he was the first man to ever truly see her, even before they were wed. He challenged her and allowed her to find her way, offering to help if she asked. She doubted such a life would await her with Brandon.

He was a young man who enjoyed life to the fullest through parties and other social engagements. Their lives would be spent seeking the next pleasure. Although it seemed like he'd been turning over a new leaf—becoming more industrious by working with Jonathan and Silas—Hazel had informed her that he hardly bothered to show up to business meetings. And if he did, he reeked of liquor and smoke from a night spent carousing. In fact, the more she'd learned about who the true Miles Brandon was, the more thankful she became that Silas had come along, even if he did force her hand.

A shaky hand came up to settle on the wall in front of her, to steady the sudden weakness she felt at the realization. If only she were alone to contemplate such a seismic shift in her world. Or Silas was there to help her make sense of it. Instead, she stood in a room with her old crush receiving an offer she'd dreamed about for years, literally getting the one thing she'd always wanted. Only to find she didn't want it after all.

Before she could rebuff Brandon's advance, a low voice came from the doorway. "Indeed, it would be a perfect fairytale ending, wife."

Caraway whipped around to see Silas glaring at Brandon with his fists clenching at his sides. How long had he been eavesdropping on their conversation?

"It would be best for Cara, Riverton. Why don't you be a gentleman and let her marry the man she loves instead of chaining her to yourself," Brandon goaded, a taunting smile crossing his face.

"I'm afraid I'm not much of a gentleman," Silas growled as he stalked towards Brandon. He hadn't met her gaze yet, instead focusing on the younger man the entire time. "And I'll be damned before I give up my wife, especially to the likes of you." He punctuated his words with a punch to Brandon's gut, who doubled over in pain, clutching his stomach. Wheezing, he tried to say something before Silas hit him again—this time in the jaw, snapping Brandon's head up and causing him to stumble to the floor.

Terrified of what more her husband would do to the prone man, Caraway hurried to place herself between the two men. Holding her hands in front of her, she pleaded, "Stop! That's enough. You've made your point."

"Have I, little Venus?" The nickname should've been comforting, but the way he said the endearment chilled her. With his attention on her, Caraway suddenly felt the full weight of his fury. His eyes blazed as the irises completely took over, turning his gaze black.

Trembling, she nodded. "Yes, now please let Miles go."

She knew her mistake the second she let his name slip. *Of all the times to err, you choose now?*

"Miles, is it? Tell me... When were you planning to tell me you wanted out of our marriage? When you and Brandon were halfway to the fucking highlands?" Reference to the popular shotgun marriage destination of Gretna Green galled, and annoyance built inside her at the insinuation. While she may have wanted Brandon in the past, Silas should have known better than to suggest she'd ever break their vows. Should trust her enough to at least treat Brandon respectfully.

The man in question groaned, reminding her that they didn't have time to argue while he was bleeding behind her. "Think whatever you want. I need to tend to Brandon's injuries, thanks to you."

Harsh laughter barked out of him. "Of course you do. You'll never change will you? It will always be *him*." Agitated hands ruffled his hair in frustration before he looked down at her kneeling next to Brandon. Ignoring his accusation, she helped him to a sitting position and assessed his rapidly bruising jaw. When Caraway glanced up again, Silas was gone.

As quickly as he'd blown in, he'd disappeared without a word.

CHAPTER THIRTY

Dinner that evening was a silent affair.

Caraway couldn't bring herself to say anything to Silas after his actions in the afternoon. The scene hadn't been entirely appropriate, but it didn't give him permission to hit Brandon. Violence wasn't the answer. Though, even more than the punching, it angered her that he trusted her so little. Did he really think she could betray him that way?

She'd apologized for what she'd said about Brandon before, and he should know no matter her feelings, Caraway would never compromise herself or him by running off with another man.

Renewed irritation heated her blood as she stabbed a piece of chicken, wishing it was him she speared. He deserved to be taught a lesson, she thought viciously. Her own violent nature—formerly unbeknownst to her—shocked her with its force, but she supposed one could only accept so much before they finally broke.

The hypocrisy when it came to Silas's own actions versus her thoughts wasn't lost on Caraway, but she ignored it. *He* was in the wrong—not her. Finally, they retired to separate spaces. In the bedroom, she paced back and forth before spying a stray necktie of his thrown haphazardly on her vanity. Snatching it off the wooden top, she promptly shoved it back in the wardrobe.

If she didn't want to see his person, then she definitely didn't want to be reminded of it with his belongings strewn about.

Stripping down to her chemise, Caraway forwent changing into a nightgown and retrieved the book she'd been reading earlier, settling into bed while hoping Jane Austen would calm her.

However, the closer Elizabeth and Darcy got the less interested she became. Life was nothing like these romantic novels. Slamming the pages shut, she tossed it back on the nightstand beside her and flopped onto her back. The canopy above glowed with shadows from the fireplace, showcasing the fiery red-colored velvet.

One hundred. Ninety-nine. Ninety-eight.

Counting backwards from one hundred should slow her thinking, right? Should stop the thoughts of Silas running wild through her mind? He was like a disease infecting her, and there was no cure.

Turning onto her side, Caraway punched the pillow into a more comfortable position, then out of childish spite, she punched his pillow for good measure. It made her feel marginally better.

Forcing her eyes to close even though she wasn't tired yet, Caraway imagined being back in Hampshire with her parents and sisters, before the accident that killed Mama and Papa and almost Hazel.

They'd be gathered around the dinner table. Her father would regale them with the latest herb he was studying while

Hazel would jump in with a story about a rabbit intent on creating his own herb garden. A soft smile formed at the scene, and eventually, sleep won the battle in her mind.

SILAS SAT IN HIS OFFICE the next afternoon, trying to focus on work. Ever since he'd walked in on Brandon and Caraway, the scene kept playing in his mind. What if he hadn't decided to go home for lunch? Would he have arrived home later that evening to find her gone?

His grip tightened on the pen in his hand, causing the tip to break and splatter ink. Releasing a quiet expletive, he quickly tried to blot the mess with sheets of paper when a knock pounded on the door, swinging open to reveal an angry Travers.

"What the hell did you do?" He skipped the niceties as he stomped forward, slamming his fists on Silas's desk.

Focused on cleaning up the rapidly spreading black ink, Silas asked, "What are you talking about?"

"You're going to pretend ignorance? I'm talking about Miles Brandon. Rumors are flying around that you assaulted him, and now he's pulled out of the deal. And if that isn't bad enough, one of my contacts spied him visiting Horace Cannon. Now, why do you think he'd go straight to our most vocal enemy?" Travers hit the desk again to emphasize his question.

Trashing the ruined sheets of paper, finished with cleaning the spill, Silas leaned back in his chair with a sigh. It seemed like everything lately was against him, and at the core of it was Miles Brandon.

"I don't know why he'd see Cannon, but I'd wager a guess he's sharing information about our work that he thinks Cannon can use against us," Silas theorized. "As for assaulting him, I caught him alone with Caraway trying to persuade her to get an annulment and run off with him. In my own damn home he dared to suggest such a thing."

Fury boiled inside him again, and he wished he'd been able to get in a few more hits before Caraway had stepped in. Her protection of the dandy galled him.

"Are you serious?" Travers asked, shock clear on his face. "I hope you taught him better than to try to steal your wife away."

"As much as I could before Caraway stopped me." He rubbed his healing knuckles in remembrance. If he could've gotten the younger man in the ring, there would have been no contest—and no one would have halted his fists from hitting their mark.

"Good... I'll make sure to keep my guy on Cannon and Brandon. He never paid much attention to the few meetings he attended anyway, so I doubt he has very valuable information." Travers took a seat, his anger ebbing away, replaced by calm as he tried to figure out Brandon's plan.

"No, and we've done everything by the book. He has nothing," Silas confirmed.

Brandon hardly contributed to their discussions, preferring to drink the fine liquor offered and sit indolently by a fire—*when* he deigned to bless them with his presence. It seemed he considered his time better spent courting Miss Bradshaw upon their return to Manchester.

Travers and he had ignored Brandon's behavior, though, since they only really required his money.

Both of them contemplated their next move before Travers switched back to their previous topic. "So, how's Caraway? What happened after Brandon left?"

"I don't know. We haven't spoken since." Silas met his gaze, challenging him to push for more information. Last evening's dinner had been as icy as the northern tundra. Breakfast that morning had been taken separately—he in the dining room while Caraway remained abed in her separate chamber.

Travers raised his eyebrows then shook his head. "Trust me, you don't want to keep up the silent treatment for too long. Talk about what happened then move on. Otherwise your entire marriage will consist of silence as often as you're bound to have disagreements."

"This is a little more than a disagreement," Silas pointed out. His wife had thought of leaving him. It would require more than a quick apology to move past.

"They all seem like that at the time. Granted, this isn't great, but she's married to you, and I don't see that changing—no matter what Brandon tried to do. Don't let him have any more power in your life than you've already allowed him." Travers stood and straightened his coat. "All this talk about possibly disappearing wives has me needing to see my own to assure myself of her complete fidelity." He winked before taking his leave.

Travers made a good point—Silas didn't like the idea of Brandon hanging over their heads for the rest of their lives. But he wasn't sure how to exorcize the man. And to be honest, it was up to Caraway.

She was the one who'd loved him for decades.

CHAPTER THIRTY-ONE

It was only a day later when they received their answer.

"I guess we know why Brandon went to Cannon." Silas tossed the morning paper onto Travers's desk. The business sections showcased in large print that Ashley Mill and Mr. Jonathan Travers were struggling financially, lying about the progress of their new venture, and sure to fail without the backing of their former noble business partner, Mr. Miles Brandon. "He obviously sold lies and Cannon rushed them to the paper."

Travers quickly scanned the article, commenting randomly at a particularly egregious lie. "Obviously, they don't fear us suing them for libel."

"No, though, at this point, it would only drag things out and create more problems." Silas crossed his arms over his chest, annoyed with their dilemma. "The best thing we can do is be as transparent as possible and share our actual financial standing."

"Are you out of your mind? No one needs to know such confidential information, let alone all of Manchester," Travers countered, incredulity etched on his rough-hewn features. It wasn't Silas's first choice either, but something needed to be done to shut down vicious rumors.

"We can publish a sample of our statements after letting a few reputable reporters view items in more detail. And I'll see about drumming up support from other owners on the local board. Cannon isn't as powerful as he used to be. Hopefully, there'll be some members willing to vouch for me." With as much as he did to help his fellow factory owners, he sure as hell hoped that was true. He'd weathered storms before, but this one seemed particularly destructive when conjoined with his problems at home with Caraway.

Travers rubbed his eyes roughly, clear exhaustion with their predicament written on his face. "Fine, let's do it. I'm sick of having to waste our time on this shite." He crumpled the paper into a ball then strode to the fire and tossed it in. "When we're done, everything will be worth it, but for goodness's sake, it's been one thing after another since we've started."

"No one said progress is easy."

But he agreed with Travers's sentiment. He, too, was fed up with this wave of trouble. He wanted to return to normal work life and an easier relationship with Caraway, although he wasn't sure how to accomplish the latter.

Last night, they didn't speak to each other, and for some reason, things seemed worse than their previous fight about Brandon. And how he hated that all of their arguments centered around the bastard. Gritting his teeth, Silas imagined how much easier his life would be if the man was out of the picture.

Unfortunately, it didn't seem likely, instead, anger aimed at Caraway and himself seethed through him. She distracted him from his work whether by her arousing presence or her infuriating affections for Brandon. Maybe if he didn't have to worry about her, he could have foreseen how to deal with these problems earlier. Maybe things wouldn't have escalated so far.

A part of Silas knew he wouldn't change how things happened, though. Despite their fights, he still wanted Caraway, and at times, he'd been the happiest he'd ever been when he was with her.

The highest of highs and the lowest of lows—the shifting tides of his life since Caraway. All because his foolish heart and head couldn't get on the same page.

Damn emotions.

CHAPTER THIRTY-TWO

Footmen secured several heavy trunks on top of the carriage in preparation for the Riverton couple's departure to the train station. The starting point for their holiday journey to the Trent estate in Hampshire.

Silas had never partaken in such a large family gathering as this promised to be since he usually spent the holidays by himself. His father didn't hold any sort of sentiment for such days, preferring to work through them.

Like Ebenezer Scrooge.

The unfamiliar territory plagued him with anxiety. While he knew the Travers', he'd only met the rest of the family at their abrupt wedding reception, and with Caraway still not speaking to him, he feared being the outcast. Attempting to shrug off the melancholy settling over him, Silas reminded himself that such a moniker wouldn't be new. Honestly, he should be used to it by now.

A flutter of skirts notified him of Caraway's arrival as she descended the steps cloaked in a warm woolen cape and absentmindedly pulling on kid gloves. Suddenly, her bootheel caught on the hem of her dress, and she pitched forward, a frightened yelp piercing the foyer before Silas jumped in to catch her. The impact of Caraway slamming into his chest left them both out of breath.

"Are you alright?" His arms tightened around her. He hadn't held her this close in quite some time. He'd missed it.

"I think so... Thank goodness you were here." The words trembled from her shaking figure. Running a soothing hand over her back, he tried to calm her.

"Next time, maybe put your gloves on after you've completed the stairs," he suggested, his own adrenaline creating a buzz in his body.

"You may be right." Caraway extricated herself from his embrace, visibly shored up her composure. "This trip is certainly off to an exciting start. Hopefully, we won't run into any more mishaps."

He silently agreed, but wondered what the chances of that were considering their past. Guiding her outside, they climbed into the carriage and made it to the train station a quarter hour early to board the train.

A porter showed them to their private car, which boasted luxurious leather seating surrounded by red brocade on the walls. The window looked out on the bustling platform with passengers preparing to board. Thanking the young attendant, Silas sat across from Caraway as they waited to depart.

Silence fell over them as chatter from outside filtered through the car. An awkwardness lay between them, an improvement, he supposed, over the angry tension that had followed them the past week.

Finally, a high-pitched whistle signaled their departure as the landscape began to move. Silas prepared for a long, quiet ride until Caraway cleared her throat. Shooting her a questioning gaze, he waited for whatever she had to say.

"Since we're visiting my family for the holidays, maybe in the spirit of the season, we can declare a truce? I realize how damning the situation must have looked to you, and Mi—Brandon—crossed a line. I admit I may have given you cause in the past to believe such a request from him might be favorably looked upon." Sitting forward, she continued, "But I assure you: I would never do such a thing as he suggested. I take our vows very seriously."

Her round eyes beseeched him to forgive her and put this behind them before visiting her family for the next fortnight.

"I'm sorry for how I reacted, too. The troubles at the mill have been wearing on me and seeing Brandon pushed me over the edge." Silas didn't comment on her stated loyalty to their vows, though. He wanted to believe her, and normally he'd trust she'd never entertain such ideas. However, one of these days her feelings for Brandon may overcome any loyalty she felt towards him.

"I understand. I hadn't considered the pressure you must be feeling at the mill. How are things going now?" she asked, satisfied with his apology.

He released a wry laugh, thinking about the state of affairs. "Not much better, honestly. Every time I put out one fire, another takes its place. A fellow member of the board, Cannon is intent on seeing me fail, for some reason."

"Why now? It seems like odd timing," she said with a slight frown marring her face. He'd also considered the timing, but he supposed with the new factory being in progress, the older man thought to derail it by bankrupting

Silas first. He relayed his speculations to Caraway as she removed the hat covering her curls.

Removing the pins, she mentioned, "I don't understand why a modern mill is such a problem. He should want to see progress in the industry." The words sounded garbled as she tried speaking around the pins she held between her teeth.

"Apparently, if it's not coming from him, it's not good. Though, I doubt he would ever upgrade his own building. He's of an older generation that believes if strategies are still working, why change them?" Leaning forward, he gently picked the pins from her mouth before she accidentally stuck herself. "Here, let me take them while you finish."

Shooting him a grateful look, she filled his hand with pins until her braid fell over her shoulder. "I know this isn't entirely appropriate, but the combination of all those pins holding my hair together and the motion of the train would be sure to make me ill."

Silas didn't care if it was proper or not; he enjoyed viewing her loosened hair. The chestnut curls stayed barely contained in the long braid, at any moment about to spring free. "I didn't know you suffered from motion sickness. We can probably stretch our travel time out, if you'd like to disembark at a location halfway through. It will give you a small break." Concern laced his tone. They'd avoided any bruises or broken bones earlier, no need to risk a stomachache, too.

"I should be fine, but thank you. This helps." She tugged lightly on the end of her braid. "And tea when the refreshment cart comes by." He conceded to her knowledge of her own body and settled back into the leather bench.

"Would you like to play a game to pass the time?" Caraway broke the lull in conversation.

"Sure, what game?"

She proceeded to explain something called Grandmother's Trunk where she'd say an item in the trunk then it would be his turn, but they couldn't laugh or smile during the list or lose.

"So, if I start, I'd say something like 'My grandmother keeps an aardvark in her trunk'. On your turn, you'd say, 'My grandmother keeps an aardvark and a bludgeon in her trunk'. Then I'd repeat the list adding the next letter in the alphabet and so on until one of us laughs or smiles."

"It sounds like this grandmother may have violent tendencies if she's keeping bludgeons around," he teased, but Caraway rolled her eyes good-naturedly.

"You know what I mean. Now, you start."

He thought about it for a moment and said, "My grandmother keeps anchors in her trunk."

Caraway nodded approvingly. "Very heavy this trunk..." Tapping her chin, she paused before adding, "My grandmother keeps anchors and brains in her trunk." He laughed at the gory image and continued the game. They made it to G when Caraway listed 'germander' as an answer. A quick chuckle escaped him before he could stop it.

"Ha! I win!" She smiled triumphantly.

"That's not fair. Is 'germander' even a real word?"

She raised her chin, defying him to refute her claim to victory. "Of course it is. They are a type of plant, having a botanist as a father had its perks, you know."

"Beyond the plethora of knowledge to choose names from you mean?" The former Taylor girls held interesting floral monikers.

"Do you have a problem with that? I thought I might continue the tradition with our own children someday." The quiet statement surprised him. They hadn't discussed children very much despite it being the obvious consequence of their marital activities. Although those hadn't taken place since the Brandon incident.

Damn him.

"I wouldn't mind. Caraway is a beautiful name, just like its owner." A red blush rose to her cheeks at the compliment. "We could have a Willow or Rose."

"But those are girl names. Don't you want a boy first?"

"A boy first would be good to look after his sister, but it doesn't matter to me. I'll be happy with a healthy child." It went against the times not preferring a male heir first, but his child would have every opportunity: male or female. If a daughter of his wanted to learn the business, he'd teach her. She wouldn't need to rely on a husband to survive. A rueful smile erupted as he considered how Travers's progressive ideas must have rubbed off on him in all of their interactions.

"I'm surprised you feel that way. It's not the popular way of thinking. I know my father loved us, but even he wanted a boy. The only reason they stopped having children after Hazel was because of the risk to our mother." A sadness entered her eyes at the mention of her parents. She'd told him how they'd died in an accident a few years ago, but this was the first news he'd heard of her mother's pregnancy troubles.

"Would it be safe for you to carry a child?" he asked the question at the top of his mind. No child was worth the risk to her life.

"I think so. Lily endured the birth of Benjamin with flying colors." During their visit for the Christmas season, they would also be celebrating Lily and Iris's birth announcements along with Caraway's birthday.

A porter knocked before opening the door. "Good morning, Mr. and Mrs. Riverton, would you care for some refreshments?" They each chose a variety of biscuits while tea was poured, and the man pulled a shelf down from the side of the cart to serve as a makeshift table for them.

After the porter left, they moved onto safer topics while playing more games as the day wore on. When the train finally reached Hampshire, the sun had long since set on the winter day. While a chill pervaded, it wasn't quite as bitter as the weather in the north. Bundling inside the waiting carriage that would convey them to Owen's estate, they huddled together under a blanket, sharing body heat.

The Trent home could be seen long before they reached its entrance with bright candles lighting every window along the front of the mansion like a beacon in the night. Upon closer inspection, green boughs graced each sill creating a cheerful holiday appearance.

"Lily's done a lovely job decorating!" Caraway exclaimed as she pressed closer to the window to view the ever increasing home. A sound of agreement rumbled out of Silas as he calculated what an extravagant expense it must be to maintain such light.

His father had never allowed such wasteful use of resources. The Riverton Manor remained untouched during holiday seasons, emitting a cold, monolithic feeling instead of the warmth the earl's home presented.

Lily and Owen waited for them in the grand entry hall as they began removing their outer garments. "Oh, I'm so glad you both made it! Everyone else is already in the parlor listening to Iris play the piano. How was the trip? How did you feel, Cara?" Lily asked as she took Caraway's gloves and handed them to a maid.

"Everything went as expected, and I feel fine. No signs of illness from the ride, thank goodness. And how are you?" Finally free of her heavy winter garments, she held her arms out for a hug as she gently patted Lily's burgeoning stomach. The women locked arms as they turned to join the rest of the party, excited chatter flying between them.

Meanwhile, Silas stood behind with the Earl of Trent. Owen Lennox exuded authority as he carefully studied Silas. They'd met only once before, briefly exchanging pleasantries at the wedding. The man eyed him suspiciously then, and now Silas felt that same suspicion weighing on him.

"Thank you for having my wife and I for the holiday, my lord." He bowed slightly.

"Of course, Cara is always welcome." The implication that he was not included in that invitation rang loud and clear. Obviously, Silas still needed to prove himself when it came to this brother-in-law. He wondered if the same could be said for Clarke Calloway, as well, since he didn't know this silent partner in Travers's factory venture very well. His earlier anxiety returned in droves at the possibility.

Upon entering the parlor where everyone gathered, Silas saw Caraway surrounded by a gaggle of women. The Taylor sisters lived up to their names—a veritable garden of femininity, each with their own unique beauty. Lily sat on the floor in front of the fire playing with two cats and a ball of yarn while two toddlers giggled at the felines' antics. Observing the domestic tableau from a small settee were his wife and Iris, who must have given up playing music in favor of visiting with her sister. The younger woman placed Caraway's hand at various places on her round belly, clearly trying to show her something. Travers and Calloway stood to the side chatting.

"Riverton, you finally made it—took you long enough." Travers patted him on the back. Urgent business at the mill had stopped them from traveling with the Travers family. Caraway refused to leave without him when he'd suggested she go on ahead, so they'd been delayed a few days.

"Hopefully, we haven't missed too much." He forced a brief grin, trying to push away the nerves buzzing through him which were ridiculous. He knew Travers. He should feel comfortable being in the man's presence even if he was in a sea of practical strangers. Two, possibly, who disliked him or at the very least, distrusted him.

"Hardly," Calloway interjected. "We've mostly spent the time settling in, but tomorrow an outing to the pond is planned. It's frozen over, so skating is on the agenda."

Surprise bubbled up at such a possibly dangerous activity. "Is that wise with the condition of Lady Trent and Mrs. Calloway?"

A scowl formed on Calloway's face, one identical to Trent's. "Lily wouldn't hear of not going. She reasoned that she's not confined yet, so it wasn't a risk," the earl explained, clearly not happy with the decision.

Silas wondered why the man didn't just forbid his wife from taking such risks, yet he had some experience with a Taylor woman and understood the stubbornness he must face.

CHAPTER THIRTY-THREE

The next day dawned with a clear blue sky and freshly fallen snow.

"Perfect weather for an outing," Lily declared at breakfast. Footmen had cleared the pond early in the morning so it would be ready for their arrival, and last night, she'd notified Caraway of the skating plans for today.

However, Caraway hadn't skated since she was a little girl. She wondered if she even remembered how.

It's too bad Peter and Owen's mother aren't here. Jonathan's younger brother and the dowager countess had both decided to spend the holiday with friends.

With everyone bundled up for the cold and each holding a pair of skates in hand, they trekked out to the frozen pond. Owen tested the firmness of the ice first, citing if he felt any give they were turning back around. But the ice held and soon they ventured onto the smooth surface.

"Have you ever skated before?" she asked Sılas as he struggled with putting the skates on. Puffs of hot air shot from him with each grunt of frustration.

Shaking his head, he gave a short, "No," before cursing the strap that kept escaping the clasp. Smiling at his ineptness, she knelt in front of him. "Here, hand it to me."

Her hand reached for the troublesome skate, and he placed it in her palm, careful that the blade didn't catch on her glove. Aligning the skate with the bottom of his foot, she strapped it securely over the top of his shoe and around the ankle. With one done, she switched to the other side.

"It looks like you've had some practice doing this."

Shrugging, she stood back up and held her hands out to help him stand. A gust of wind brought a whiff of his scent, the pine aroma she adored finally mixing with the natural smell of the woods he always reminded her of.

"When you're the eldest child, you learn quickly that it's your responsibility to fix your siblings' problems." Together, they awkwardly waddled to the edge of the pond where the rest of the couples already twirled around like a scene from a painting. Calloway and Trent noticeably stayed close to their pregnant wives, protective hands around each woman's waist.

Stepping backward onto the pond, Caraway encouraged Silas to take his first tentative step forward. A wobble almost brought them crashing down after both feet met the ice, but they managed to right themselves before falling.

"Now, I'm going to pull you along at first, so you get a feel for the ice. Then we can work on teaching you how to skate," she explained as she began shifting backwards.

"I feel like this should be the other way around with me pulling you. Instead, I'm like a child who needs babysitting." His disgruntled statement echoed that of a childish tantrum which caused her to duck her head to hide an amused smile.

A brisk breeze blew giving a helpful push as they moved around the pond. Winter birds chirped as they passed by as if upset at having their morning interrupted.

"Don't worry, soon you'll be skating around the pond like a seasoned sportsman, and I'll be happy to have you drag me along," she placated.

Indeed, it made a romantic scene with couples skating in circles, arms locked around each other. She almost wished they were alone even though they weren't back to being intimate yet. The truce struck the day before was still fresh and only one step toward returning to a normal place in their relationship.

Spotting a deer staring at them, Caraway slowed her pace and brought them to a stop. "Look," she whispered, pointing to a tree the animal stood behind. "It's a deer."

Silas turned his head to find the graceful creature. Its brown eyes refused to blink as it tried to determine what these people were doing in its home, disturbing the quiet peace of the woods. Tan spots covered the tawny fur along with a few flakes of snow from a branch above. A moment later, it bolted out of sight, seeking refuge from the crowded area.

Silas smiled down at her, the first genuine expression of happiness she'd seen from him in a while, a fact that bothered her, she realized. "That's the first time I've ever seen such an animal in real life."

"What? How is that possible?"

"My father never had a use for the country. It's not exactly a business hub. I grew up in London before deciding to build my company in Manchester." The matter-of-fact retelling of his childhood belied any disappointment with the upbringing, but she didn't fall for it.

"Surely, you had a holiday or visited a friend in the country." It was unfathomable to her that someone could go most of their life insulated from nature. Growing up here and with parents intent on the glories of everything botanical, nature was ingrained in her blood. That's part of what made living in Manchester so abysmal sometimes.

She thought she'd adjusted well enough, but every once in a while the overwhelming crowds of people and buildings became too much.

"Never." He let go of her hands to try to skate on his own. "A friend from university invited me once, but my father insisted I come home. He wanted my help in the office."

Once again, he gave her another reason to dislike Elias Riverton. Her annoyance brought a welcome rush of heat to her cold limbs. Caraway swore to herself from now on she'd help Silas enjoy life more. Embarrassment at her own contribution to his latest unhappiness washed away some of the frustration at his father.

They were both to blame for how they'd treated Silas. The difference between them would be how she changed her behavior.

"Well, you don't have to worry about him anymore. As your wife, I take precedence, and I say we're spending every Christmas here. You'll see so many deer and squirrels that you'll wonder why you went so long without seeing one," she promised, following Silas as he quickly figured out how the skates worked.

"I never said I haven't seen a squirrel. We do have parks in London and Manchester, you know." His eyes crinkled at the edges as he teased her. As she started to respond, his skate caught on a divot in the ice, pitching him forward. Throwing her arms out, she grabbed his coat, attempting to re-balance him. Instead her efforts backfired, sending her careening into his body until they landed in a heap on the hard ice.

"Are you okay?" Trent's tense question pierced her jarred mind. Sliding off Silas's back, she struggled to a sitting position while Silas slowly pushed up to his knees.

"I'm fine, but shaken. What about you? You took the brunt of the fall. You didn't injure yourself, did you?" She tried to pat his shoulders and down his arms, but his thick coat prevented her from feeling anything of consequence.

"No worse for wear. My pride took a hit, though. I'm sorry I dragged you down with me."

Owen helped her to her feet while Jonathan assisted Silas.

"Maybe we should take a break," Jonathan suggested. Everyone agreed as they slowly made their way to the bank of the pond. Back on solid ground, they rested on blankets, which provided little protection from the wet snow seeping in underneath. Caraway tried to warm her frozen cheeks with her gloves to no avail.

"Come here." Silas pulled her closer, cushioning her cheek with his open jacket so his heat filtered through the fabric. Shivering, she huddled deeper into him, inhaling the new mix of sweat with his cologne. Eventually, however, the chill became too much to bear as they sat open to the elements.

"I'd like to suggest heading back for hot cider instead of trying to skate again. Iris is tiring, and I don't fancy freezing my arse off," Clarke called out to the group. His wife punched his arm at the expletive but asserted her own need for something to warm her. The walk back to the mansion took longer than the journey earlier as exhaustion set in.

Once they entered the warm halls of the Trent Estate, a tacit agreement to adjourn to individual rooms for cider and rest was made. Silas and Caraway walked to their guest room and collapsed on the bed.

"I didn't think I was as tired as I apparently am." Silas covered a yawn.

"This is how it always is. Once the energizing fun fades, fatigue sets in."

Nodding, he closed his eyes until a soft snore reached her ears. Chuckling at how quickly he fell asleep, Caraway adjusted the blanket until it could cover both of them as she laid down next to him. Sighing, she admitted to herself how much she'd missed this.

They've been sleeping separately, but being able to wrap her arm around him and rest on his shoulder brought a deep satisfaction to her as she drifted off.

She'd missed this.

CHAPTER THIRTY-FOUR

"This one's from me." Lily offered a haphazardly wrapped package five days later for Caraway's birthday. The entire family was gathered around to celebrate, and the sheer amount of love imbuing the room caused Silas to fidget in his seat. It was at once endearing and uncomfortable—an intimate setting where it didn't feel like he belonged.

"I'm sure she could tell from the lack of wrapping skill," Owen teased. According to her sisters, Lily had never mastered the more delicate refinements such as embroidery or painting. Apparently, gift wrapping also made the list.

Everyone laughed as Lily raised her hands in a 'guilty' gesture as Caraway unraveled the twine bow before tearing the butcher paper away to reveal a jagged phrase. Tilting her head to the right, she studied the embroidered sign, attempting to decipher its meaning.

"It says 'Love is patient, love is kind' then the bible verse location at the bottom." Lily sighed, knowing it wasn't perfect but she'd really tried.

"Well, of course, I see it now," Caraway blatantly lied. Silas leaned over her shoulder to read the words and only saw squiggly lines in red and black thread. He'd never seen a worse iteration of the verse than this, and a choke of laughter caught in his throat.

At least she'd tried, though. It was more than he could say of Elias Riverton on Silas's birthdays.

After Caraway added the gift to the pile of books she received from the Traverses and satin gloves from the Calloways, half a dozen expectant expressions turned to him. Taking his cue, Silas retrieved the velvet box sitting next to him.

"Happy birthday, little Venus." His words sent a flush over her skin, since the endearment was usually confined to their private moments. Firelight painted a warm glow on her pink skin as if she really were a goddess lit from within.

Biting her bottom lip, Caraway opened the box to showcase pearl earrings along with a pearl bracelet—perfect matches to her engagement ring and the necklace he'd given her.

"I thought you should have the complete set," he murmured as she ran a finger over the opalescent jewelry. The pink deepened to red, and he wondered if she was recalling the last time she wore the pearl necklace.

Although the night had ended badly, the explicit use of the pearls lingered in his own mind. She'd been so receptive to him and their game, surprising and arousing him at the same time with her willingness to participate.

Licking her lips, Caraway shyly met his darkened gaze before looking back down at the set in her hands. "Thank you, Mars." The whisper barely reached his ears, but he knew he heard her correctly.

All of a sudden it seemed like the heat in the room congregated around them as his cock hardened in desire. It had been too long since they'd made love.

Perhaps tonight that will change.

Silas could only hope.

The party ended early when Lady Trent and Mrs. Calloway began yawning—their pregnancies clearly taking its toll—though Silas and Caraway stayed downstairs a little longer to talk with Hazel and Travers, eventually everyone adjourned to their bedchambers.

Following his wife to their room, Silas couldn't keep his eyes from the swaying of her hips or his mind from conjuring all sorts of ways to initiate love play. A niggling piece of doubt made him question whether she'd accept him yet, but he squashed the thought immediately.

He was desperate for her, and tonight seemed as good as any to try his luck. It could be his private birthday gift to her and an early Christmas present for himself.

The plush carpet dulled their footsteps, only the swish of her gowns and a chiming clock ringing through the home. Reaching for the doorknob, he let Caraway in before himself then made sure to turn the lock—not wanting any interruptions tonight or in the morning.

"Did you enjoy the evening?"

He watched her set the gifts on a side table near the window. Moonlight filtered in, bathing her in a softer glow than the fire from earlier. Instead of the fiery goddess, she'd become an ethereal one.

"Yes, the whole day has been lovely. My sisters and I don't get to spend much time alone together anymore—which is as it should be since we all have husbands and families to attend to. But it felt nice pretending like we were the same four girls who grew up here." A wistful note caught his attention.

"Do you wish to live here again? Return to your family cottage?" They'd talked briefly and mostly hypothetically about Silas taking a less active role at the factory and hiring someone to handle day to day tasks. It would allow him to live farther away from Manchester, but Silas hadn't thought they were at that point in their relationship yet.

Removing the pins from her hair, Caraway gently shook her head. "No, that's not necessary. It would bring me closer to Lily, but I'm just as close to Hazel in Manchester. I'm just glad that when I am longing for a visit to Hampshire, we have the cottage to reside in. We almost lost it, you know." Her nose wrinkled at the reminder.

She'd told him the story that had precipitated Lily and Owen reuniting, how a Mr. Laramie threatened to steal their home out from under them because of a contract their father had signed. It had been one of their conversations after marrying, when they'd spent dinners getting to know one another. So much had been shared in those early days despite the unconventional circumstances.

Coming up behind her, Silas retrieved the brush sitting in front of her and when her curls were free—cascading down her back in a shining waterfall—he drew the soft bristles down its length. A satisfied hum vibrated through Caraway, the soothing movements lulling her into a dreamlike state.

Brought back to his course of action for the night, Silas gathered her hair to one side and placed a lingering kiss on her bare neck. A gasp escaped as her closed eyes popped open. Meeting her sleepy gaze, Silas took his shot.

"Your birthday isn't over... I was hoping to give you a more... *private* gift. I realize it's been awhile..."

"Yes," she blurted out. "I accept... um, your gift." The words stuttered out quickly, her acquiescence warming him. Maybe she'd missed him as much as he'd missed her. When he'd woken with her in his arms after their skating afternoon, he'd realized exactly how much their distance had bothered him.

Setting the brush down, Silas took her hand and led her to the bed. Carefully, he unbuttoned her gown, letting it fall to the floor in a heap of gold fabric. Her thin drawers came next before he untied the laces holding her chemise together, and soon Caraway stood naked before him—shivering slightly from a chill or in anticipation, he didn't know.

"Lie back on the bed." The gentle command scraped against his dry throat. He rapidly removed his own clothing as he watched her lay back crosswise on the bed, bringing her knees up to display the treasure between her thighs. The bold move shook him.

His wife had definitely grown more forthright with her sexual needs since their wedding night. He appreciated her willingness to learn and participate in her own pleasure. So many Englishwomen grew up believing sex was a necessary evil, but his Caraway had obviously given up on that lie.

The fire dimmed, casting her in shadow as Silas stood over her. Stepping to the side, he let the light from the windows illuminated her body, highlighting the hills and valleys he longed to explore.

Kneeling before her, he started at her toes then kissed up to her ankle, the delicate bones causing a slight dip that he licked playfully before continuing north. From firm calves to the ticklish skin behind her knee, Silas adored every part of his wife as she squirmed beneath him, trying to entice him into going where she really wanted his attention.

"Stop teasing...," she begged, but he ignored her pleas. Too much time had passed since they'd last been together. He wasn't going to rush this.

Crackles from the fire mixed with her heavy breathing, and he imagined he could hear her heartbeat, too. The rushing pulse at her throat drew his gaze and mouth. He lightly licked along the vein before tracing the line of her jaw, scratching his beard against the soft skin until he finally reached her swollen lips. Plump from her biting them in frustration.

"Does my goddess need a kiss?"

A whimper tumbled from her lips as she arched her body to get closer to him. Lowering his head, Silas claimed her mouth with his as he allowed his hovering body to sink into her—his heavy weight pressing her deeper into the mattress—and a needy groan of his own caught in his throat at the taste of her again.

What was meant to be slow and sensual erupted into a passionate duel, each fighting to rebuild their former connection. Kissing had never been a favorite of his, preferring other methods of foreplay. Perhaps his heart had recognized how important such an act could be between two lovers and protected him from sullying it with nameless women.

The romantic idea should have repulsed him, yet Silas found himself grateful if that was the truth. Sharing the intimate act with Caraway eclipsed all past engagements.

Rearing back, he buried his head in her neck, his breathing unsteady as he attempted to gather his wits. What she did to him... without even realizing it.

When a modicum of restraint was restored, Silas continued his exploration, determined to create a birthday to remember. A trail of love bites on her neck, breasts, and stomach pointed toward the most intimate part of her—leading Silas to his prize. Reaching the apex of her thighs, the musky sweetness of her desire tickled his nose. Heat greeted him as he parted the dark curls to expose wet, pink flesh.

His knees hit the floor as he shuffled backwards, dragging Caraway with him until he could settle himself between her legs, his shoulders ensuring they remained wide open. Dipping his tongue into her center, he intimated how he'd soon take her with his cock—a slow plunge filling her again and again.

"Silas, please..." Her fingernails dug into his scalp as she tugged on his hair to move him closer to the glistening bud throbbing for his attention. Giving into her, he dragged his tongue higher to lave her sensitive clitoris, causing Caraway to jerk at the contact, so primed for him that the slightest touch was too much.

Silas loved the taste of her. It was a battle to not lose himself in fulfilling his thirst and instead focus on bringing her to climax. Keeping steady suction on her clitoris, he inserted two fingers inside her hot channel to reach the special spot that would push her over the edge.

"Come for me... Sweet little Venus..." Rumbled encouragement whispered across giving flesh until she tightened around him, her body going rigid with the power of her release. Wild curls haloed her head, darker near her scalp where a sheen of sweat gleamed in the dim light.

Nuzzling her, his beard grazed her clitoris, eliciting a soft cry at the over stimulation. "Are you ready for more, my love?" He barely registered the endearment, too focused on her response as he rose to adjust his cock at her entrance.

Nodding, Caraway wrapped her hands around his waist and whispered, "Come to me, Silas."

Arms shaking with quickly dissolving control, he burrowed deep, feeling the echoes of her last orgasm twitch around him. Her eyes dilated as he began thrusting in earnest, and he wondered what she saw in his face as they stayed connected—body and soul. Something was building between them, more than just physical pleasure. It felt monumental like the world ceased to exist as their individual selves twined together into a tight bond.

Disturbed by such intense emotions, Silas broke their eye contact.

"No, don't..." Caraway cried, but he focused on the bouncing of her breasts beneath him, leaning down to capture a hard nipple and suck as he increased his speed. This he could handle—knew what to do here.

The burn of her nails scratching down his sides preceded the squeeze of her walls on his cock as she orgasmed, and the combination shot him into his own release. A harsh groan rolled out of him as he collapsed to her side, careful not to crush her with his weight. The smell of sex hung heavy in the air as they tried catching their breaths.

Caraway tangled her fingers in the hair on his chest before eventually resting over his rapidly beating heart. Pushing up slightly, she brought her mouth to his ear. "Thank you, dear husband, for my gift." A gentle kiss feathered over his cheek then she lay her head down, cuddling into the crook of his neck.

Stroking her hair, Silas closed his eyes, ignoring the maelstrom of feelings swarming in his gut. "You're welcome, my dearest Caraway."

CHAPTER THIRTY-FIVE

The rest of their visit flew by in a blur. Christmas came full of merriment, food, and gifts. It would be the last Christmas before next year's brought more children to tend to, Which may have been a good thing considering the enormous spoiling Callum and Benjamin received. As the new year began, Caraway and Silas packed their belongings and stood with the rest of the couples leaving for their homes.

"We'll be back when the baby arrives," Caraway promised as she gave Lily one last hug. Her husband and brother-in-law shook hands before she and him left for the train station. This time they would ride with Hazel, Jonathan, and Callum.

The trip passed quickly, and it felt odd walking into their home. So much had changed in the fortnight—she remembered the tension between her and Silas when they'd left, and now things seemed to finally be good between them. The time together out of town away from Brandon and the mill allowing them to bond in a deeper way.

She kept busy during the day organizing the new school and daycare the mill would provide its workers once the storage room Silas had designated as its home was cleared and outfitted. He'd set workers to remove the wooden crates stacked in neat rows to another room after they'd returned from Hampshire.

Walking into the space, the smell of wood permeated the building, and Caraway turned to her guests and explained how things would change to accommodate children and a teacher. Hazel had recommended getting in touch with the newly formed school board, and a few members had agreed to hear her plans that afternoon. Mr. Blake and Mrs. Henley had spent a considerable amount of time promoting the educational reform movement, pushing for new laws that required children of a certain age to be in school.

"What a revolutionary idea. However, did you think of it, Mrs. Riverton?" Mrs. Henley asked as they stopped in the center of the room.

"I can't take credit," Caraway answered modestly. "An employee of the mill mentioned something to me about the workers worried about missing shifts due to sick children, and it snowballed from there." She waved her hands in a helpless gesture. The idea had grown in scope with hardly any encouragement from her.

"How marvelous!" The older woman exclaimed. "I'm certain the board would be happy to assist in any way we can. This can be an example for all factories."

Mr. Blake nodded as he agreed. Clearly such an undertaking from a profitable business would be a boon for their cause.

"We would appreciate any guidance since this is quite out of our area of expertise. However, we are up for the challenge—the health and happiness of our employees are foremost in our minds."

Relief flowed through her at their approval and offer to help. If they'd refused Caraway, she wasn't sure what her next step would have been.

"Of course it is very progressive of you. And your husband, Mr. Riverton, holds the same sentiment?" Mr. Blake asked curiously. His gray mustache twitched in a distracting way every time he spoke.

Directing her gaze upward, she met his light eyes. "Oh, yes. None of this would be possible without his support. He is fully behind whatever we decide is the best course of action for the school."

She knew how fortunate she was to have such a husband. It warmed her that he trusted her so much to give her full rein of this project along with the mess hall conversion. His faith in her abilities built her own confidence. She could accomplish beneficial tasks for the community—didn't need to sequester herself to the house or social calls.

"Well, I think we've seen all we need to for now. Mr. Blake and I will relay what extraordinary steps you are taking here, Mrs. Riverton. I'm sure we'll be in contact again very soon."

They exited the room to the main courtyard of the mill. Workers walked back and forth hauling products out to be shipped to their buyers all over the country. The neighing of horses hung in the air as they waited patiently for their wagons to be filled with goods.

"Thank you again for agreeing to meet with me. I look forward to working with you both." Caraway dipped her chin in farewell as they left. The last of her to do list done for the day, she wondered if Silas would be free to celebrate this small victory with her.

Biting her lip, she looked up at his office window before deciding that she could at least check. If she wanted to have an honest marriage, it would start with her treating him the way she wanted to be treated as his life partner. Sharing wins and openly communicating would be the beginning.

Determined, she took the first step forward.

LYMAN KNOCKED ON THE office door as Silas prepared to leave for the day. It was his first day back at the mill after returning from the holiday break in Hampshire, and he wasn't quite ready to leave the idyllic memories behind. But it seemed Ashley Mill had other plans.

"Pardon me, sir, but a few men from the floor wish to speak with you. Shall I tell them to come back tomorrow?"

Silas caught a glimpse of the two men behind his assistant, hats in their grease-covered hands. If they wanted to quit like so many of their former colleagues, he saw no reason to delay them. The sooner he knew, the quicker he could find replacements. Waving his hand forward, he said, "Let them in. I can't spare much time because I want to escort Mrs. Riverton home after her school board meeting, but I'll see what's so important."

His well-kept assistant retreated to be replaced by rougher counterparts, the smell of sweat and metal clinging to them from their work with the machines downstairs.

"Welcome, gentlemen. How can I help you?" he asked, cutting straight to the point. No use wasting any more time than necessary when his wife expected him home soon.

"Thank ye, fer seeing us, sir," the taller one began. "I'm Jasper, and this is 'arry. We've come on be'alf of the rest of the mill workers. We've all 'eard the rumors about ye going belly up soon 'nuf." The shorter man next to him nodded emphatically. "Now's some 'as seen the papers wiv somefing about 'ow much money you 'ave, makin' us wonder what's what, ye ken?"

"I assure you the financial statements published in the Manchester Gazette are completely factual. The mill will not be going bankrupt anytime soon. No one will be losing their jobs. It was a vicious lie started out of ignorance and vengeance," Silas explained. He'd tried to allay fears before but still ended up losing workers. Hopefully, this time would be different.

"That's what Joan said," Harry piped up. His short nails scrubbed at the scruff around his chin while Silas tried to understand the significance of that name. The man must have read his confusion because he prompted, "She's yer mizzus' friend, Mrs. Riverton."

"Ah..." He remembered now—the woman who'd regaled Caraway with the mill's problems, encouraging his wife into a life of bettering the Ashley Mill employees' working conditions. "Yes, Joan. Well, then trust her when she tells you that your jobs are safe. What can I do to satisfy your worries?"

"Maybe ye can tell everyone together?" Jasper suggested, "Most of us take lunch at the mess 'all. Ye can tell each shift."

"I've tried informing everyone already. No one believed me." And it irked him still. He'd always been an honest master; he didn't lie.

"Not altogether like, though. 'Sides that was before the paper."

Silas considered the proposition then nodded. "Alright. I'll address everyone together in hopes it will make a difference. Can I count on your support to sway the men and women? If more cling to the lie of our bankruptcy, it may eventually come true. As it is, I can't prove its falsity until more time passes and nothing's changed."

The two men agreed, bowing quickly before exiting. Rubbing his hands down his face, Silas sighed. He prayed this would work. This whole business exhausted him, and he longed to return to life before Cannon decided to interfere. Longed to return to everything except being alone, that is. He wouldn't go back if he couldn't still have Caraway.

On cue, his wife entered his office.

"What a nice surprise. I was about to head your way to see how your meeting went," he said, shrugging on his jacket.

"It went well. They seem receptive to our plans, which is a huge step in the right direction." Caraway glanced behind her at the retreating backs of his employees. "Who were those men? Please tell me they didn't quit like the others."

"Thankfully, no." He told her about the men's visit and the plan they'd devised.

"Oh good! I pray they take your words to heart. Joan is doing her best to talk sense into people, but another statement from you couldn't hurt."

Caraway rested her hand on his, and he gave her fingers a quick squeeze of gratitude. *What a change from when I demanded she take my hand all those months ago.*

Silas enjoyed discussing the company with Caraway. Though unorthodox, it was a huge part of his life that he was used to keeping to himself. Relief eased his mind at the ability to share some of the burden with his wife.

"Yes, it seems your relationship with Joan may prove even more invaluable." While he'd prided himself on maintaining a good work atmosphere, he hadn't thought to build personal relationships with his employees, opening the lines of communication for issues to be resolved before they had time to gain momentum. However, Caraway had accomplished such a thing without even meaning to as he recalled the day she told him about meeting Joan.

"Let's hope so... I know how frustrating this mess has been for you. And I hate knowing I had a small part in it."

His eyes narrowed in confusion. "What part are you speaking of? None of this is your fault."

Clearing her throat, she met his eyes with a resigned look on her face. "Hazel told me what Brandon did. I'm so sorry."

While he'd been angry at her directly after the incident, lamenting all the ways she'd brought discord to his life, underneath it all he'd known she wasn't to blame.

"Brandon's actions aren't your responsibility. He made his choice, and I won't have you burdening yourself with this," he commanded, voice brooking no refusal.

Caraway nodded but focused on her footsteps during their journey home, obviously not taking his words to heart.

It concerned him—he loathed seeing her upset—but apparently, this was something she'd have to work through on her own. He doubted she'd listen to him any further on the subject, so he switched to a different topic.

Anything to raise her spirits again.

THE MORNING SILAS WAS set to meet with his employees dawned overcast and dreary, a sign he didn't take to heart as most days in Manchester looked that way. With Brandon finally behind him and Caraway, he wanted to settle this problem as well. Maybe his luck had changed, and things were finally starting to turn around.

Walking into the office, he confirmed with Lyman, "Make sure I have a clear schedule from eleven to two today. I'll be in the mess hall for any emergencies, but don't disturb me unless the building's on fire or someone's dying."

"Yes, sir." The thin man nodded vigorously. Lyman had worked for him for five years, starting out in accounting before moving up to Silas's personal assistant. To date, he handled Silas's affairs efficiently, better than any previous assistant.

At a quarter of an hour before eleven, Lyman knocked, then entered to remind him that it was time to head downstairs before the first lunch shift arrived at the mess hall. Thanking the man, Silas straightened his clothing before leaving.

He rubbed his palms down the front of his trousers, fidgeting once he stood in the large empty room. Slowly, men and women began to trickle inside, forming a line to grab their lunch. A few stole quick glances at him which he tried to catch and nod in acknowledgment. That caused a stir as groups began whispering as they moved through the line.

Flicking an imaginary speck off his sleeve, Silas cleared his throat once everyone was seated. The loud din drowned out his attempt at gaining everyone's attention. Realizing he'd need to shout, he yelled, "Excuse me! Can I have a moment, please?"

It took a few minutes, but eventually everyone's eyes landed on him at the front of the room. Feeling like a bug under a microscope, he tried to smile but feared it appeared closer to a grimace.

"A lot of rumors have been flying around the mill about our financial situation and the security of your jobs." Their attention zeroed in on him as he noticed a few people turn to face him more squarely. "I want to assure you these rumors are a pack of vicious lies concocted by a fellow mill owner who disapproves of my bringing some progressive innovations to the industry, alongside my business partner Jonathan Travers." He paused to read the crowd before pushing on, "This man doesn't approve of improving workers' environments such as the new ventilation system we put in or this mess hall my wife spearheaded along with Joan McCormack."

The name of one of their own seemed to soften their stances, more relaxing shoulders and nodding heads traveled through the room. Encouraged, Silas went on to describe the newspaper article outlining their financial records along with assuring them again their jobs were safe.

After he finished he offered to answer any questions which helped to allay more fears. Overall, by the time the second lunch shift came in, Silas felt good about the prospect of putting this behind them.

Each shift responded well to his speech, and he discovered talking with the men and women one on one to answer questions proved more beneficial than he could have imagined. So much so that he decided it would become a regular occurrence. Caraway was right—speaking with the employees and learning of their issues was an integral part of improving Ashley Mill.

CHAPTER THIRTY-SIX

The winter chill permeated the parlor windows as Caraway pulled her hand back from the cold glass. Her breath fogged the surface, briefly obstructing her view of the street. People raced to their destination in a bid to escape the bitter weather, and she was thankful for the warm blaze behind her.

Returning to her seat by the fire, Caraway picked up the discarded booties she knitted for her future nieces or nephews. The first pair already sat complete in yellow next to her knitting basket, and now she hoped to finish the green set before moving onto hats.

A light tap on the door notified her of Giles's entrance. "My lady, a letter just arrived for you." The folded missive rested on a silver platter he held out to her. Thanking him, she set the booties aside and retrieved the letter.

"I wonder who it could be from," she mused aloud. It was too early for either Lily or Iris to have given birth, and Hazel usually preferred to drop by unannounced.

Cracking the seal, she read the letter, her lips puckering at its contents. Her teeth ground together as she reached the end and saw "Love, Miles." Crumpling the sheet, she tossed it angrily on the floor. How dare he try contacting her again after their last interaction. And to so brazenly address her. The nerve!

He wanted to meet to apologize. His letter outlined the regret he felt at how they'd left things and set a time and place to fix his error. Caraway shouldn't go, yet if she didn't, things would remain unsettled when they both needed closure.

I need to settle this once and for all.

With her mind made up, she rang for a maid to return her knitting to her room and asked Giles to ready a carriage as she put on her cloak. A quarter of an hour later, she sat huddled under a woolen blanket as the driver navigated through the streets of Manchester. The letter listed the Botanical Gardens as their meeting place. Ironically, it had been on her list of places to visit upon her arrival to town. But after marrying Silas, she hadn't managed to find the time.

Stopping at the entrance, Caraway told the driver to meet back here in one hour. She hoped this wouldn't take even that long, but perhaps if they finished early she could explore a little before returning with Silas at a later date.

Purchasing a ticket, she followed signs leading to the herb gardens. The Botanical Gardens encompassed every type of garden ranging from exotic flowers to the humble vegetable patch, teaching each visitor the differences between growing methods, soils, and plant natures. Her parents would have loved it.

The further she walked, the less crowded it became as it became obvious guests weren't as interested in basic herbs when they could see vivid roses or orchids. Finding herself alone, Caraway reached her destination, wandering around the various patches of herbs until she found Brandon.

"Mr. Brandon," she stated briskly, her tone business-like. The young man in front of her smiled and raised his arms for an embrace. Immediately stepping back to avoid his touch, she scolded, "Have you learned nothing? I didn't come to give you false hope or say I've changed my mind. I want to stay with Silas."

His arms dropped back to his sides as a frown marred his handsome face. "Don't be like that, Cara. I don't want to fight." He returned to the plot of plants he'd been studying on her arrival. "I found your namesake—Caraway, also known as *Caraway Carum Carvi*, meridian fennel, or Persian cumin. Quite a plain flower by the looks of it."

He pointed to the delicate white blooms clustered together. A biting note edged his voice, making her feel as if he was talking about her lack of beauty as well.

"It may be plain, but it's a spice—very useful." She didn't come to be insulted because she refused to play along with his scheme. "Can we get on with it? Say your piece, and we can be done."

"In such a hurry? Does your husband have you on such a short leash?" Brandon stalked closer, backing her into a marble fountain that served as one of the many fountains watering the gardens. "He must know that left alone for too long, you'd succumb to me—finally having the love you dreamed of."

Her knees knocked against the lip of the fountain, halting her movement. Swaying backward, she feared falling into the water, but Brandon gripped her arms in a tight lock.

The bruising contact elicited a pained gasp from Caraway as she struggled to get away.

"Let me go!" She tried to sound firm, but fear caused a slight wobble to enter her voice. Logically, they weren't alone—dozens of people populated the gardens. Surely, Brandon wouldn't commit any truly dire act, yet no one was around at the moment, and the fact worried her.

"Listen to me, Cara!" A wild look took over as his pupils dilated, encapsulating the light blue color. "We can finally be together. We can move back to Hampshire if you'd like—whatever you want. Just agree to an annulment, and you'll be mine."

He sealed the delusional tirade by forcing his lips onto hers. Grimacing, she kept her mouth tightly closed as she attempted to turn away to no avail. He'd shifted one hand to the back of her head, crushing it to his and ruining her coiffure.

When he finally pulled back, she mustered enough strength to raise a fist and punch him in the jaw. The jarring impact traveled up her arm as pain exploded in her knuckles. Although they stood close, she still managed enough impact to surprise him as she disentangled from him.

Wiping the back of her hand over her lips, Caraway spat, "Don't ever touch me again or my husband will make you pay. Don't doubt it." She imagined Silas at the boxing ring and knew he could easily flatten Brandon—he'd already done it once. "As far as our acquaintance, it is over. If you ever contact me again, the authorities will be notified. As for your reputation, be grateful that I want this to end, so I won't be telling my brothers-in-law who will end any chance you have of a decent life in the whole of England. As for my husband, well, he still might hunt you down for your actions today, so I'd run while you still can."

Throughout her monologue, Brandon became paler and paler, the blood draining from his face. A tremble wrought his body, and satisfaction settled inside Caraway at the reversal of roles. Her task completed, she left him standing where she found him, the only Caraway he'd ever have lay in front of him in the dirt.

The ride home passed in a blur. She'd waited in an alcove for her driver to arrive then sat in a haze. When she entered the foyer, Silas stood talking with Giles, and they both stared at her as if she was garbage dragged up from the gutter.

"You're back," Silas said tonelessly. He held a piece of paper in his hand before shoving it in his pocket.

Meeting his now blank stare, she repeated, "Yes, I'm back... You're home early."

"I thought I'd see if you wanted to visit the bookshop. I know you were excited to discover if your sister's latest release was on display yet. But when I got here, I learned you'd already gone out."

Giles discreetly excused himself as Silas led her to a side room. His fingers landed on the same place on her arm as Brandon from earlier, causing her to flinch, and immediately, he drew back, creating space between them.

※

SILAS CLENCHED HIS hand at her rejection of his touch—hated her flinching reaction at his hold. Shoving a hand in his pocket, the crumpled edges of the note he'd found earlier hit his palm. When he'd come home, the thought of spending a carefree afternoon with his wife had filled him with happiness. It was to be short-lived, though, as a sheet of paper on the carpet caught his attention.

Once he'd read the letter from Brandon asking to see Caraway and learning of her immediate departure, a sense of dread eclipsed his joy. Despite their efforts to move forward, she'd still gone back to Brandon. He poured a glass of whisky and quickly downed it—desperately requiring the numbing effects of the alcohol.

"I went to the Botanical Gardens," Caraway explained, walking closer to him. Needing space from her, he retreated. He couldn't take her news of leaving him while being surrounded by her lavender scent.

"I figured... I read the letter" He motioned to his pocket where the offending paper sat like a rock.

"I see..." She stared at her feet, no doubt ashamed over her actions. "I—"

"I'll have my lawyers draw up the documents," he cut her off. Though she'd no longer be his wife, Silas would make sure she was well taken care of. "I only ask that you wait to... consummate..." The word stuck in his throat, the idea of any man but him touching her abhorrent. "Wait to consummate your relationship until any chance of you bearing a child of mine has passed." For the first time, he prayed she wasn't with child, then they would be well and truly stuck together.

"Wait, what are you talking about?" She tried to touch his arm, but he sidestepped her. Running a shaky hand through his hair, Silas faced the window overlooking the street below. The coldness emanating from the glass seeped into him, slowing his rushing blood, bringing a much-needed numbness.

"Don't pretend ignorance. I know you went to see Brandon. If it is your wish for an annulment, then I won't stop you." He only wanted her happiness, and he could give this to her no matter how much it pained him. Rubbing a spot on his chest, he continued, resignation heavy in his tone, "You can finally have what you've always wanted. You've tried to make things work with me; I can't fault your efforts. But your heart lies elsewhere—no need to waste your life spending it with me when you can be with him."

Leaning his forehead against the cool pane, he closed his eyes, waiting for her acceptance. He'd stay at the mill tonight, unwilling to sleep in the same house as her as she slept in their bed before leaving him for Brandon. Perhaps, he wouldn't have to see her again until they signed the annulment papers.

Feminine hands reached around his waist to hug him from behind, causing him to stiffen. "While you're correct I went to see Brandon, you've clearly been under the wrong impression. I didn't go to Brandon to declare my undying love. I went to end things."

Eyes flashing open, he asked in disbelief, "What are you saying?"

"I'm saying I choose you. I told Brandon I never want to see him again which he didn't take well, but it's done. I don't want an annulment, I don't want Miles Brandon... I want to stay with you." Caraway buried her head in his back as her confession rang through the room like a shot blast. A rough breath pushed past his gritted teeth. Could he truly believe her?

"Why?" The whispered question reverberated through his mind. All this time her feelings for Brandon had been on display, no matter how they tried to ignore them, to move past them. The man always remained a ghost in their marriage.

"Look at me, Silas." She leaned back and tried to turn him around. Resisting her, he stood firm, not ready to face her, in case this wasn't real. "Silas, please."

A silence settled, only broken by their breathing. Realizing she refused to answer him until he complied, he sighed and turned. Her smooth palms cupped his face as she made sure he listened.

"What I felt for Brandon was born of a girl's childhood fantasy. I yearned to be wanted, to be desired, so I concocted a whole story of our unrequited love. It wasn't real, and I don't need the illusion anymore. I'm a grown woman who prefers the husband who has made me feel desired and trusted. Worthy of being given the responsibility of improving your company. Not many men would accept their wives' interference. Besides, if it's your vanity that needs stroking, I find you immensely more attractive than Brandon. Does that satisfy you?"

Finished with her long tirade, Caraway peered up at him speculatively, waiting for his response. The ice inside him began to thaw as he read the truth in her eyes. Somehow, he'd won her over. She was his and his alone.

Relaxing his shoulders, a rueful smile played with the corners of his mouth. "So, you prefer a mature man to that dandified pup?" The flippant comment served as a cover for the deeper feelings coursing through him, ones he didn't dare name, let alone make her aware of.

Rolling her eyes, a huff of mock annoyance blew in his face. "It would seem so, but don't get too full of yourself, sir."

A few curls fell from the haphazard bun on her head, and for the first time, Silas realized she wasn't put together as neatly as usual. "What happened to your hair? It's barely staying contained." He fingered an errant strand to confirm his statement.

Pink splashed her cheeks as she tried moving away, patting the multitude of loose pins on her head, "Oh, I hadn't realized... I've been in a fog since Brandon, and then you accused me of leaving... Is it terrible?" She rushed to an oval mirror overhanging the mantel. An upset gasp flew out of her open mouth, gaping at her disheveled appearance. "It's a good thing I'm not seeing Brandon again, or I'd..."

"He did this to you?" Quick anger infused him. The thought hadn't occurred to him that Brandon would try to touch her in such a public place. Coming up behind her, he held his hand out as was their ritual, and she filled it with removed pins.

"He kissed me," she mumbled as she ducked her head to reach some errant pins hiding in the back. "And he wasn't exactly gentle about it. This must've happened during the struggle."

Bracing a hand on Caraway's shoulder, he stopped her ministrations, urging her to meet his furious stare in the mirror. "He dared to force himself on you in broad daylight? In a museum full of people? I'm going to kill him." Seeing his seriousness, Caraway forgot about fixing her hair and whirled around.

"No, Silas. I told him to leave. You're not going to find him and prolong his presence in our lives. I already dealt with him."

"He can't touch you and expect to get away with no consequences. Travers will find him, then I'll send Brandon to hell." The vehemence in his voice shocked her, but Brandon couldn't be allowed to assault his wife without facing repercussions. And, oh how he wanted Brandon's blood.

"I said no." She met his gaze with a stubbornness of her own. Deciding to placate her, he acquiesced but privately knew he'd get his revenge. Her pointed look said she didn't quite believe him, but she let it go, refocusing on her appearance.

"I know it seems anti-climactic after our day so far, but would you still like to go to the bookstore? It might be nice to do something normal today," Caraway asked as she put the finishing touches on her newly restrained curls. Tilting her head this way and that to make sure she hadn't missed any wayward strands, she then faced him.

"I think that sounds like a capital idea. We both could use some normal."

And finally let the past go.

CHAPTER THIRTY-SEVEN

Hours later, Caraway watched him as he shrugged off his jacket. Since the end of dinner, he'd caught her staring at him with an odd look on her face as if she wanted to say something but wasn't sure how to broach the topic.

Catching her eye again, he asked, "Something on your mind?"

She bit her lip at being caught and shook her head in denial before flashing him a quick smile. His brows quirked in confusion at the obvious lie, but he decided to let her keep her secrets.

"I'm going to take a bath to wash this dust from the bookshop off... unless you'd prefer to go first?" He wished he could ask her to join him but wasn't sure they were at that point yet, since they only put Brandon behind them that afternoon.

"You go on ahead." Caraway shooed him toward the washroom as she began unlacing her dress. Hesitating, he longed to see her bare curves again, but she stopped when she noticed his appraisal. Chuckling, she pushed, "Go on."

Sighing, Silas left her to undress alone. The brass handles at the top of the claw foot tub twisted easily as hot water poured out. His rumpled clothing dropped into a messy pile on the floor, and he dipped a hand into the tub to test the water temperature, jerking back at the swift burn. Adjusting the handles, he waited a moment before settling into the tub with his head resting on the raised lip. Steam wafted over him as the heated water relaxed his tense muscles.

The day had been long and mentally taxing.

Pattering feet broke the silent reverie a minute later. Opening his eyes, Silas saw Caraway standing beside him in a chemise with her braided hair over one shoulder.

"What are you doing?"

Kneeling beside the tub, she grabbed a rag and submerged it in the water, before rubbing a cake of soap into it. Suds formed on the damp fabric to form a molehill of bubbles.

"I'm bathing you. Just relax." Her calm voice soothed him, yet he placed a hand over hers, halting her progress on his chest.

"You don't have to do this." He flashed back to all the times he forced her to touch him or make a loving gesture and how badly that had backfired.

Meeting his eyes, hers soft and his vulnerable, Caraway simply said, "I know. I want to do this for you."

Slowly, he lifted his hand from hers, so she could continue. He felt like they were floating in a bubble secluded away from the outside world.

A contented haze settled over the room. Closing his eyes, every stroke from Caraway became magnified as the soft fabric rasped over sensitized skin, raising goosebumps along its path. Soon, she reached under the water, brushing against his engorged sex as she traveled down each leg, making sure to clean every inch of him.

A grunt rumbled from his chest when she returned to his cock, wrapping the cloth around him and stroking it up and down a few times. "Careful, little Venus," he warned as his eyes slitted open. He didn't want to ruin the moment by spilling his seed like a youth with his first woman.

She ignored the warning and leaned further over the side of the tub. Steam caused the thin linen of her chemise to cling and turn transparent. The pale valley of her breasts glistened with the moisture as they swayed in front of him—the dusky tips calling for his touch. Raising a hand, he cupped her, circling the hardening bud.

"No... this isn't about me," she retreated, separating them. Silas prepared to object, but she moved to a spot behind him. The heat of her scalded the back of his neck as her hot breath tickled his ear. "Lean forward. I need to wash your back."

How such a simple request could sound seductive, he didn't know, but he complied, and she made quick work with the wash rag, before abandoning it and kneading his muscles with bare hands. Hanging his head forward, Silas surrendered to the comforting touch. Emotions whirled within him—desire, peace, fear.

No one had ever treated him with such care. As if he mattered to them. Was something precious. A tremble shuddered through him at the foreign feeling. He realized now how empty his past attempts to force affection from Caraway had been. None of those superficial things compared to this. His eyes squeezed shut and he clenched his fists, overcome by a wave of vulnerability.

Oblivious to his revelation, Caraway ran her hands up his back, massaging his scalp before rubbing soap into the strands and emptying cups of water over his head to cleanse it free of soap. Task completed, she returned to his line of sight, picked up a drying towel, and motioned for him to get up.

"Come now, husband, before you wrinkle beyond recognition."

Carefully pulling himself up to a standing position, he watched her eye the water sluicing down his body, pausing on his cock before raising her gaze to his with a blush.

"Let's dry you off," she stated, briskly running the towel over him, a much quicker exploration than when she'd washed him.

"Am I going to get to bathe you next?" he asked, eagerness suffusing his tone. He'd shown remarkable restraint so far but was reaching his breaking point—he needed to touch her.

"No, you're going to get into bed next," she ordered, pushing him towards the door. Lips thinning in disappointment, Silas lay down in the center of the bedding.

"You've spent a considerable amount of time making sure I enjoyed our lovemaking, and it's time I returned the favor." Caraway crawled up his body until her thighs straddled his waist, the hem of her chemise riding high, exposing soft skin. He tried resting his hands on the enticing spot, but she gently grabbed him, pushing his hands to either side of his head until her face hovered over his.

"Am I to be your prisoner, then?" he asked at the dominant display. This new Caraway intrigued as well as aroused him. They'd never explored power dynamics before—his mind wavered on how he felt about it now.

"For the time being." Her lips brushed his cheek then his mouth, and he could've sworn he felt the whisper of her tongue before she moved further down his neck and chest. Light fingers traced up one arm over his shoulder and down to the ridges of his stomach, her curious mouth following along and leaving a wet trail of kisses behind.

Locks of curls tickled as they dragged across his hot skin. Raising his head slightly, he silently urged her to take him in her mouth—imagining the warm slickness encircling him.

When her chin bumped his standing erection, he jumped at the contact then moaned as she nuzzled up and down the length with her downy cheek. Breathing harsh, every muscle tensed, he waited for her next move, until finally her pink tongue darted out to lick the mushroom head. She caught a drop of his essence before shaping her mouth around him and lightly sucking.

Panting, he fell back onto the pillow behind him and groaned, "Cara..."

"Is this alright?" she asked, pulling back from him. "I figured since it feels so good when you kiss me down—"

"Yes," he cut her off. "God, yes... Don't stop, please." The added plea spurred her on as she returned to take more of him in her mouth. His fingernails dug into the cover beneath him, determined to follow her rules—no touching. But the feel of her wet mouth around him with her suckling sounds surrounding him were quickly becoming too much.

Afraid of frightening her, he reached down to tenderly grip her hair. "Caraway, sweetheart... You need to stop or else I'll spend in this pretty mouth of yours."

She released him long enough to say, "I thought that was the point," before continuing her ministrations.

Tightening his hold on her, Silas found himself urging her to take him deeper down her throat even as he tried to explain, "Yes, but you don't need to... It doesn't have to be..." He groaned in sexual frustration, wondering how to delicately phrase such a primal event. "I can spend on the bed instead of your mouth," he settled with. He'd never had to explain the concept before. Previous women were unwilling to perform such an intimate task as swallowing his seed.

However, Caraway ignored his direction or refused to understand his meaning because she just increased her actions, adding her hand to the base she couldn't reach with her mouth, and the combined stimulation brought him roaring to release. Jets of his seed shot down her throat until finally his tremors subsided as he collapsed beneath her.

Sexual euphoria filled him along with a fierce possessiveness. Only his wife had ever known that part of him, only *she* had wanted to. And she'd reversed roles on him. Men usually used a woman sucking him off as a means to show domination and power, yet she's the one who exhibited those traits tonight. It attracted him to her all the more—her growing confidence in the bedroom pleasing him to no end.

A long lick up his stomach sent a shiver down his spine, rekindling his need for her. "I think you enjoyed that, Mr.

Riverton. And I must say I did, too," she purred as she finally let her body rest on top of his.

Stroking her hair, he rumbled an agreement. They lay there quiet and content, until Silas mustered enough strength to flip them over, so she lay beneath him.

"Now, it's my turn," he promised darkly, a growl of anticipation vibrating through him. With a gasp, Caraway gave in as he reminded her *exactly* who she belonged to.

CHAPTER THIRTY-EIGHT

Caraway finished her letter to Mrs. Henley with an update about the mill's school. Desks, books, and a board of slate had arrived the day before and sat ready for students. The last task to be completed before opening was hiring a teacher along with a few nannies for the children too young to attend class. A satisfied smile twitched at the corners of her lips as she sealed the letter then left it on the front table to be picked up with the post.

Life seemed to be righting itself after the debacle with Brandon. She thought back to when she first arrived in Manchester, prepared to change herself to catch his eye. And now months later, she had everything she'd ever wanted along with a few things she didn't know she needed, and it turned out Brandon wasn't one of them, after all.

No, she needed a man like Silas Riverton, who accepted her as she was and trusted her opinions.

Despite their rocky start, it felt like they were finally in a good place.

Silas met her in the foyer, returning early from work again. He was making a habit of coming home earlier in the afternoon, so they spent time together visiting museums, shops, or staying home chatting about the day.

"Sending a letter?" He hung his hat before leaning in to kiss her cheek. The smell of the factory clung to him overpowering his usual woodsy scent.

"I thought I should notify Mrs. Henley about our progress with the school so far. We still need a teacher which I think she'll be able to help us find," she answered, wrapping her arms around his waist and looking up into his dark brown eyes.

"What are you going to do once the daycare and classes are up and running? What's next on the list of improvements for Ashley Mill?"

"I'm not sure yet. I've been talking with Joan about the list, and we're trying to prioritize issues. Perhaps we can look it over together, and I can get your input on what's feasible at the moment." She liked the idea of working together with him. It allowed her into his world, offering a different perspective on who he was as a person.

"If you'd like, but for now, I've been looking forward to viewing your namesake. I admit I had no idea you were named after a plant until Trent called all of you the Garden Girls." Caraway playfully punched his arm at repeating Owen's moniker for their group. Ever since he'd first learned their names, he'd teased them.

"Unfortunately, I fear I have the least interesting floral name. Lily and Iris are beautiful flowers while Hazel's has its no unique beauty. Mine is quite plain." Her disappointment in her namesake was written on her face. From the first time her father had shown her what the caraway plant looked like, she'd held a certain frustration as if her parents naming her after a nondescript flower doomed her to the same fate. And for the first thirty years of her life it held true.

"I doubt that very much." His voice dropped lower as he gently pressed his lips to hers, before murmuring, "I'm rather partial to my little Caraway."

A blush heated her skin, heat coursing down her body. He always made her feel desirable even when she couldn't see it. Breaking their contact, she waved a flustered hand towards the door. "We should leave, so we have time to look around before they close."

A satisfied smirk appeared as if he enjoyed making her so blustery. "Alright, lead the way, my lady." He gave a short bow before following her outside.

Although she felt strange returning to the scene of her showdown with Brandon, Caraway decided not to let it affect her enjoyment with Silas. That day closed a chapter of her life while this one started another.

"I don't think these are plain at all." Silas bent down to examine the white lacy wisps of caraway petals, tenderly cupping a floral head in his palm. "We should plant some in our garden at home."

"If you'd like," she demurred, warmed by his suggestion. "It's too bad we can't have more trees."

He glanced up at her, a brow raised in confusion. "That's an odd jump. Why trees?"

"Because you remind me of the woods around our old family cottage. It would be a piece of home here while holding a piece of each of us within it. Silly sentiment, I suppose."

She expected him to laugh at the romantic idea, instead he sat back on his haunches, contemplating the array of plants in front of him before responding, "Would you like to start spending more time at your family's cottage in Hampshire? Then you can have as many trees and flowers as you desire."

Standing, he dusted his hands off and waited for her reaction. The suggestion of living in Hampshire part of the year appealed to her. It could be their secret hideaway when they needed a break from the stresses of their world.

"You would agree to live in the country? You hardly have any experience living in the wilds outside the city," she teased, remembering his fascination with the deer at Christmas.

"I'd agree to whatever made you happy," he said simply, the sincere confession darting an arrow straight to her heart. Shy, she toed a bit of dirt fallen on the walkway. "And that would make you happy, as well? Your opinion counts, too."

"As I said, whatever makes you happy." Silas moved in front of her to tilt her down-turned head until her blue eyes met his darker ones, and she read the truth in his clear gaze.

"Then I guess we should plan our schedule for residing in Hampshire."

"Agreed. Let's seal it with a kiss." She opened her mouth to object—they were in public, after all—but he quickly covered her mouth with his. Once fully occupied with his kiss, Silas pulled back to her disappointment and smiled. "Looks like I'm moving to Hampshire."

SILAS STROLLED INTO Travers's office at the mill, a certain lightness carrying his steps. Ever since he and Caraway had put their problems to bed, literally, it was as if his life had turned into a fucking fairytale.

Fucking being the key word as he remembered their lovemaking from the night before when he'd finally been able to claim her in their large bathtub before eating her out on the wet tile floor—unable to wait until he had her in bed. His cock started to rise at the memory, but he tamped it down. Focus was needed for his meeting with Travers

Knocking on the open door, Silas stepped inside. "Afternoon, Travers. I trust everything's in order for our opening next week?"

The day they'd been planning for months would finally be here. The true test to see if their engineering improvements would really make a difference in the industry or if they'd wasted a ton of money for nothing. He grimaced as he imagined his father relishing such news.

"Yes, everything's on schedule. We have our last inspection Friday, then we're cleared to open. I'm just reviewing the employee records." He gestured for Silas to take a seat in front of his desk. Accepting the invitation, he relaxed in the leather chair and crossed his legs in front of him.

"Good, good. I'm glad things are finally on track. It's been a hell of a few months," he remarked, recalling their past issues.

"For you, it has. You got married, invested in this new mill, and all the while staved off a mutiny in your own factory," Travers studied him carefully. "That is staved off, isn't it?"

Nodding, Silas confirmed, "Yes, I believe the men and women of Ashley Mill finally understand we're doing fine, and the rumor was nothing but that—a rumor. I've even had a few of the men who quit approach me about returning to their former jobs."

"How'd you respond?" Travers asked, opening another folder which held the next employee's information.

"I rehired them. No use in punishing them when they thought they had a rightful cause to leave. They have families they're trying to take care of." Silas shrugged, understanding the need to protect the ones you care for.

Travers barked in amusement. "What's gotten into you? Since when are you so forgiving? There was a time when you would have slammed the door on those men. It wasn't your fault they didn't think things through before they quit." He lowered his voice in a mocking portrayal of Silas.

"You make me sound unfeeling." Though he knew very well that was exactly how he'd been. He'd emulated his father to an extent, not allowing personal feelings to interfere with business affairs.

"You were," Travers said point blank. "But ever since you became a married man, you've changed. Which is just as well, because if you'd remained so heartless with Caraway in your life, I might have been forced to save her from you."

Silas sat straighter at the nonchalant threat. "And how exactly would you have accomplished that?" Anger rested on a razor thin edge.

"Calm down. I'm not saying I'll do it now. Caraway's made you soft." At Silas's huff of denial, Travers explained, "It's a good thing. A wife *should* change you. She's the better half you never knew you needed but now can't live without."

Clearly, the man thought of his own wife now, judging by the lovesick look in his eyes. Silas envied the man's relationship with Hazel. Perhaps one day soon, he and Caraway would reach a similar point in their marriage. They'd already grown by leaps and bounds.

"Caraway's been a real help," Silas agreed. "Her ideas for improving the mill have gone over well, and I'm sure we'll see the benefits here, too." After seeing the success of the on-site mess hall, they'd outfitted a building at the new factory for the same purpose, along with creating a space for daycare and a school. At this rate, they'd be single-handedly responsible for educating a quarter of the city's children.

"I wasn't talking about her business acumen..." Travers replied, but let Silas redirect the conversation. "Though you're right. Her ideas of improvement will revolutionize the way we do business."

With that, he handed half the stack of folders in front of him to Silas with instructions to sort out any people he thought they should reconsider. A separate manager had hired all of the new employees, but they were intent on starting off on the right foot which meant having the right group of workers.

Beginning his inspection, Silas scanned person after person as the image of Caraway floated in the back of his mind, encouraging him to finish quickly, so he could return to her.

CHAPTER THIRTY-NINE

The opening day of Travers Mill presented an uncharacteristically cheery visage for a February day in Manchester. Silas left early to meet Travers and welcome the men and women for the first shift while Caraway would arrive later for the celebratory lunch they were providing for all employees.

Although he'd heard rumblings of continued discontent from Cannon at board meetings, the old man seemed to have backed off from actively trying to ruin him. It still surprised Silas that Cannon had taken such a bizarre dislike to him in the first place—having never shown animosity to him before the modern building plans.

The carriage approached Travers Mill, and he waited for the vehicle to stop before hopping out and searching for Travers among the crowd gathered in front of the iron gates. The younger man stood to the side of the entrance speaking with a group of men dressed in common work attire.

Weaving through the mass of people waiting to be let inside the mill, Silas caught Travers's attention who excused himself from his conversation.

"Ready for our official opening?" Excitement exuded from Travers. His eyes held a twinkle of eagerness as he placed two fingers in his mouth to release a piercing whistle, and the din of chattering voices quieted as focus turned to them.

"Welcome everyone to the first day of business for Travers Mill. My partner Mr. Riverton and I would like to thank everyone for being here today, and we look forward to working with all of you to make this mill the most profitable in all of England!" Travers shouted exuberantly, the confident statement bringing a smile to Silas's face. *Oh, the arrogance of youth.* But knowing Travers, he would make it happen.

He'd have to step up his game at Ashley Mill to compete, and the prospect amused him, looking forward to the competition.

"Without further ado, Travers Mill is officially open!" Travers extracted a key with a flourish from the inside of his jacket, unlocking the black gate and pushing it open to allow people through. In the center courtyard of the mill stood the mill managers ready to direct people to their stations and handing out pamphlets explaining the mill amenities such as free meals in the mess hall and childcare along with schooling for older children due to Caraway's influence.

Once the last straggler passed through the gate, Travers turned to him with a satisfied smile. "Well, we did it. Despite the push back and propaganda against us, we managed to get this thing off the ground."

"That remains to be seen," Silas cautioned, although he, too, felt they would do well. "It's only the first day. Many businesses succeed or fail within the first year. Let's see what the next three hundred and sixty-four days hold."

"Don't be so cynical," Travers scolded as he crossed his arms over his chest. "This will work. We have state of the art machinery, pay fair wages, and provide employee benefits no other mill is offering."

Silas nodded in agreement but a part of him would always hang onto the possibility of things turning south. He liked to view it as realistic instead of cynical.

The morning passed in a flurry of activities, trying to field first day snags that cropped up and make sure everything ran smoothly. Before he knew it, he saw Caraway wander onto the ground floor. She turned in a slow circle, observing the workings of the mill, before noticing him watching her from the upper level offices. A bright smile replaced her curious expression, and she waved at him as she moved to the exposed stairwell leading upstairs.

He followed her movements, tracking the green cotton of her skirts sweep across the floor. A matching hat sat at an angle on her head, allowing for a gathering of curls to cascade over one shoulder, and a pleasant rush of adrenaline coursed through his veins as she neared.

"How are things going? Well, I hope?" she asked as he took her hand and interlaced their fingers, his bare skin scratching against her lacy glove.

"As well as could be. We've had the usual hiccups, but we've managed to control them. Did your sister ride with you?" He knew Mrs. Travers wouldn't miss such an important day in her husband's life. Frankly, with her curious personality, he'd been surprised not to see her roaming around already, poking her nose in every facet of the factory line to understand how it worked.

"Yes, she sent me on ahead. Callum decided to throw a tantrum once we arrived, so she's trying to curb his temper at the moment." The loud machines nearly drowned her out before she raised her voice to be heard. Guiding her away from the noisy floor below, they headed toward Travers's office which offered a barrier from the bustle outside.

"Your ward is determined to harangue your poor wife, Jonathan," Caraway teased with a mock frown. Raising her arms, she embraced her brother-in-law who squeezed her tight.

"Hazel is definitely a saint," he agreed wisely. "I'll have to explain to Callum that we don't cause mama trouble or else she'll withhold her favors." Caraway shot him a shocked look.

"Such as new toys or an extra biscuit for dessert," he tacked on with a wink.

"Yes, those are only a few of the things I have power over," Hazel's weary voice floated into the room as she held Callum in her arms. Tear streaks marked the boy's red face, evidence of his earlier fit.

"Come here, Cal." Travers relieved his wife of her burden which she seemed profoundly grateful for as she sank into a nearby chair. With the boy securely in his arms, he went to his wife and began massaging the back of her neck. Continuing on as if nothing was amiss, Travers said, "We can all use a bit of a pick me up. Lunch begins in a few minutes. After Riverton and I give our speeches to everyone, we can enjoy the delicious meal prepared for us."

Everyone nodded their heads in agreement before leaving the office and making their way to the mess hall.

Settling their families at one table, Silas and Travers proceeded to thank the workers for their hard work and trust in the new company then returned with meals for Mrs. Travers, Callum, and Caraway before grabbing their own.

The afternoon was spent laughing and chatting, soaking in family time, and celebrating their accomplishment. Silas absorbed the conversations around him, a contentment settling over him as he recalled a time not long ago when he was alone. Caraway and her family had invaded his life and made it all the better for it.

He'd never be able to thank them enough for showing him what a true family looked like.

CHAPTER FORTY

Caraway glanced at the clock in the hallway—eleven o'clock. Sighing, she walked towards the windows facing the street. Silas had come home for dinner but left promptly after stating he was meeting Jonathan at the boxing club. She'd almost asked if she could go with him but stopped herself. Remembering her reaction to him after a fight flushed her hot with desire, an occurrence she didn't wish her brother-in-law to witness. So, Silas could have his men's night with Jonathan while she focused on knitting hats.

The finished baby booties for Iris and Lily's children had been a bear to tackle, but now she'd moved on to matching caps which were proving much easier. About to turn and pick up where she last left off, Caraway noticed movement behind the window of Silas's office at the mill. Wondering if it was a trick of the light, she leaned closer to the glass and squinted when she saw it again.

Annoyance and exasperation flashed through her in equal parts. If Silas needed to return to the mill to finish work, why lie to her? And, for goodness's sake, it was nearing midnight. He hadn't worked such long hours since the beginning of their marriage when they'd fought.

Deciding to persuade him to come home, she grabbed her cloak in the foyer and turned the handle of the door when someone cleared their throat behind her.

"Mrs. Riverton, may I ask what you are doing? It's not safe to go out alone at this time of night," Giles said, concern coloring his tone. His wrinkled hands settled on his waist, mimicking the stance of a father catching a child escaping to the kitchen for a sweet.

"I'll be fine. No need to worry. I'm just going to fetch Mr. Riverton. I saw him in his office from the parlor." She pointed back to the windows with an outlook to the mill across the street.

"But Mr. Riverton is at his gentleman's club," the butler explained, clearly confused. She almost grinned at the elevated term for Silas's underground boxing ring but controlled herself.

"I thought so, too, but I just saw him in his office. I'm not sure why he'd lie, but I'm going to find out. I'll be back soon." With that, she scampered out the door before the graying butler could object again. The distance between Ashley Mill and their home hardly warranted a carriage ride since it was so close. Surely, a quick walk wouldn't end so badly. It's not like they lived in Jonathan's old rookery—Devil's Haven. This was a respectable street.

Pulling the cloak closer around her to ward off the cold and her sudden misgivings, Caraway hurried down the pavement underneath intermittent gas lamps lighting the way. When she reached the gate to the mill, she noticed the lock firmly closed. Reaching into a pocket, she withdrew the spare, figuring Silas would keep the mill secure while he worked.

Easing the gate open, she re-latched the lock before hurrying to the front entrance and unlocking that door as well. The empty factory unnerved her at its unusual silence. Her muscles tightened in paranoia, preparing for some ghost to appear out of thin air. Not usually prone to such gothic fantasies, she tried to shake off the bad feeling sitting like a boulder in her stomach. When she saw Silas, he was going to get an earful for causing her such trouble.

A curious orange glow emitted beneath his office door as Caraway reached the upper floor. As she got closer, the smell of smoke assaulted her. Worry skittered down her spine, blooming into panic when she touched the hot door handle. Wrapping a hand in the woolen cloak for protection, she turned the handle, releasing a cloud of smoke and heated air. A coughing fit wracked her body at the sudden attack.

Desperately, she searched the room for Silas. How did the room catch fire? Where was he? Questions swirled in her brain as all she could find were burning flames crawling up the walls and engulfing shelving and Silas's desk. Unable to find him, she stumbled back into the hallway to escape the epicenter of the fire. Perhaps he'd left a candle burning when he'd left, but why hadn't she run into him on her way here?

Placing a hand in front of her, she tried maneuvering through the row of desks being quickly devoured by the fire. Someone needed to warn the fire brigade before the mill burned to the ground and took the neighboring buildings with it. Her vision became hazy as she tried to retrace her steps from memory. She'd walked this hall many times.

Surely, she could make it downstairs without trouble despite a raging fire around her.

Finding the stairs, Caraway grabbed the metal railing to guide her path before reeling back with a hiss. Pain rocketed from her palm at the contact of heated metal. Berating herself for such a stupid move even after the door handle incident earlier, she tried to take fast but measured steps down.

The heat at her back warned of the approaching flames traveling to the lower level of the building. Fear left an acrid taste in her mouth as she struggled to remain calm. Suddenly, a loud explosion shook the building, shoving her off balance and down the last few steps.

Landing hard on her side, Caraway's temple smacked into the concrete floor, eliciting a short moan before a wave of unconsciousness took her.

CHAPTER FORTY-ONE

Silas dragged the rough rag over his sweaty face. He hadn't meant to stay so late at The Warehouse, but he'd gotten to sparring with Travers, and they'd lost track of time. Travers always gave him a run for his money when they faced off. He was one of the only men who could manage to beat Silas.

The man held no compunction when it came to using dirty tricks he'd learned from growing up in the rookery. Silas adapted to the moves and used them himself when he fought other opponents.

"Good bout today," Travers remarked as he tugged a clean shirt over his head.

"For you." Silas joked, rubbing a sore spot on his rib. "Next time, you'll pay for this." Tomorrow, he'd be sporting a large bruise along his torso from Travers's jab. But maybe Caraway would kiss and make it better, he thought, eager to return home to his wife's tender care. At this point, she probably wondered what was taking him so long, since he rarely stayed out so late now that he had someone waiting at home for him.

Travers laughed as they passed through the crowd of men huddled around ongoing fights. Separating on the street, Silas raced home, eager to see Caraway. But as he turned onto the street, a plume of smoke rose in the air as bright yellow light filled the road. Upon closer inspection, he realized men gathered in a line leading to the mill, trying to halt its burning path before it brought down the buildings around it. Silas ran forward until a constable barred him from getting any closer.

"That's far enough. Let the men work." The man held his arms up, wielding a stick in warning.

"That's my mill. I'm Silas Riverton. Let me through!"

The constable hesitated, unsure of the veracity of Silas's statement, when Giles separated from the crowd and called out, "Mr. Riverton, thank goodness you're here!"

Identity confirmed, the constable stepped back with a nod to let him pass before moving forward again to stop curious onlookers from getting too close.

"Giles, what happened?" Silas stared in horror as his life's work literally tumbled to ashes in front of him. The overwhelming haze of smoke burned his nose and eyes as he watched the fire brigade try to staunch the flames.

"I'm not sure, but Mrs. Riverton thought she saw you in your office and went to bring you home. The next thing I hear is shouting that the mill's on fire," Giles rushed out, worried lines creasing his forehead, hands waving in despair towards the burning mill.

"Where's Caraway now?" Silas asked, a fear like he'd never known washing over him like an icy blast of water. He swallowed the bile rising in his throat at the thought of losing her.

"I don't know. I've tried to warn the brigade that someone might be inside the building, but they waved me off saying no one could survive in there this long. I'm afraid she might've succumbed to the fire..." His normally placid butler wrung anxious hands, distinct fear in his tone.

"No..." Silas snapped widened eyes to the blazing inferno. He would not lose her. "I've got to find her." Giles tried to grab his arm, but he shook the man off and ran towards the front of the building.

A line of men pelted the inferno with water, blocking the usual entrance. Jogging to the side of the building he noticed a stack of crates below one of the windows. Silas found a brick and tossed it to the top of the stack before climbing up the precarious formation and tearing off his jacket, wrapping it around the brick in his hand before punching the window. Shards of glass fell onto him causing pricks of pain to bloom over his exposed skin. Released smoke blinded him for a moment as he tried to clear out sharp edges by running the brick over the sides of the windowpane. Once he determined it was clear enough, he hauled himself through the opening.

Hunching over to the cooler air near the floor, Silas yelled, "Caraway!"

Hearing nothing, he shouted her name again as he searched the row of machines, making his way towards the stairwell leading to the upper floor. He covered his nose and mouth with an arm as a coughing fit overtook him. Salty tears tracked down his cheeks as the smoke burned his eyes while rubbing them only made it burn more.

Struggling to see, Silas tried to get his bearings by reaching a hand out and feeling the way, and long minutes dragged by as a sense of slogging through mud flashed through his head. Sparks hit his shoulders when part of the roof fell down. He wasn't sure how much longer the building would stay upright. He needed to find Caraway and get them out while it was still possible.

The closer he moved to the front of the building the louder the roar of the fire became. Clearly, whatever started the fire originated up here. And he would discover what happened after all was said and done.

Assuming I come out of this alive.

Something bumped into his leg before he realized it was the bottom step leading upstairs. Crawling upward, he prepared to shout for Caraway again when he felt an arm.

"Caraway, sweetheart?" He patted her arm until he reached her cheek. Terror shot through him like a bolt of lightning when she didn't respond. Shaking her lightly, he tried waking her before noticing something wet touch the back of his hand. A pool of blood reflected the fiery light surrounding them. "No, god, no," he pleaded as he carefully pulled her into his arms and maneuvered down the stairs.

Visibility became non-existent as he straightened to his full height to carry her. Retracing his steps, Silas stumbled over a newly fallen wood beam and crashed to the concrete. A grunt of pain expelled from his chest as he twisted to take the brunt of the impact, bracing Caraway against his chest.

He lay there for a moment trying to catch his breath in the oxygen-deprived space. A wave of eerie calm settled over him as he considered how this might be the end. How unfair that he would finally have a life worth living, and it would be ripped away from him through a fluke accident.

After all these years, life had finally seen fit to gift him a woman like Caraway. A woman he loved when he never thought he would feel the emotion. Hell, he'd never even told her how he felt. Just accepted her affection without giving her anything in return.

A sudden movement followed by a groan brought Silas back to the present. Caraway twitched above him. Rolling over, he stroked her face. "Caraway, can you hear me? Wake up, love."

Her unfocused gaze met his, and he breathed a sigh of relief. "I'm going to get us out of here. Hold onto me." He helped her stand and with an arm around her waist, guided her to the broken window. Her nails dug into his arm as she struggled to stay upright.

"Just a little further, sweetheart," he urged as he hopped through the window onto the precarious stack of crates. Turning around, he reached back through for her, and she wrapped her arms around his neck as he pulled her over the ledge, praying she wouldn't get cut by any stray glass.

The empty wooden crates wobbled under the added weight of two people. Gingerly, they climbed down to solid ground. Silas kept them moving forward, away from the rapidly deteriorating building. Flames burst through the remaining windows, shooting out dangerous shards of glass and metal.

They erupted into a crowd of people outside of the mill who quickly formed a circle around them. Giles pushed through, creating a space for them to breathe as they collapsed to the cobblestoned street.

"Sir, my lady! Thank goodness you're alive!" The older man dropped to his knees in front of them, examining their soot-covered faces. Smoke clung to them as they each struggled to inhale clean air. "We must go somewhere and call the doctor at once. The staff has already found lodgings elsewhere in case the flames reach the home, and your carriage is ready to take you to St. James Hotel since it's not far away."

Agreeing, Silas slowly moved to all fours, hanging his head as he gathered enough strength to walk the short distance to the carriage. Steeling his will, he pushed up, swayed, then righted himself as he took Caraway's hands and pulled her up into him. He hugged her tightly before they both followed Giles as he cut a swath through the curious onlookers.

At the hotel, servants fretted and called for baths to be drawn and fresh clothes as someone was sent for the resident doctor. By the time Caraway and Silas were clean and resting on their bed, Dr. Forrester, a friend of Travers's, had arrived.

He moved to Silas first, bag in hand, but Silas waved him off. "My wife first. She was in there the longest, and I think she hit her head."

Nodding, the serious gentleman removed a stethoscope and carefully examined Caraway. Finding burns on her hand and a gash on the back of her scalp, he clucked his tongue before pulling out supplies for bandaging her wounds.

When it was Silas's turn to be looked over, the doctor commented, "You were very fortunate. You'll escape with some minor burns that should clear up within a few days." Reaching back into his leather bag, he removed a small bottle of liquid. "Use these eye drops twice a day to help with the dryness from all the smoke, but you shouldn't have any eye damage. I'm also leaving some laudanum for any pain

Mrs. Riverton experiences. I'll return tomorrow to check on her bandages." Setting a second bottle down by the first, Dr. Forrester took his leave.

Sitting up to take a dose of the medicine for his eyes, Silas blinked a few times before facing Caraway who lay next to him. Exhaustion had won as her breathing evened, her lashes resting against her cheek. Adjusting himself closer to her, Silas draped an arm over her torso before his own battered body fell into a deep sleep.

CHAPTER FORTY-TWO

The next morning a flurry of activity sounded outside the bedroom door before it flew open to reveal the Travers family. Hazel rushed to Caraway's side. "Cara! We heard about the fire and came straight over. Are you alright?" Jonathan stood behind his wife holding Callum who played with a stuffed bunny.

"I'm fine, just a few burns and a scratch on my head."

"It's more than a scratch," Silas interjected. "She fell down the stairs after an explosion on the upper level. When I found her, she was unconscious—hardly the consequence of a minor scratch." Frown lines marked his face at the reminder. Only twelve hours had passed since they'd arrived at the hotel, so the memory remained fresh.

"Thank you for saving my sister, Silas." Hazel shot him a grateful smile as she reached over to squeeze his hand.

"Yes, we're indebted to you," Jonathan added as he set Callum down to play on the carpet. "I've put out feelers to try to figure out what happened. It's odd that the building would randomly combust."

"Maybe someone left a candle burning..." Caraway suggested but trailed off at Silas and Jonathan's twin looks of disbelief.

"No, I believe it was intentional," Silas said, his hands tightening into fists. "We've had nothing but trouble since beginning work on Travers Mill. After the rumors of bankruptcy failed to stop us, they stooped to arson in pure retaliation. Especially since the mill opened without trouble."

Caraway knew they'd been having issues, but to commit such a heinous act seemed a big leap. It didn't make sense to her how a person could feel so strongly about the modern mill that they felt the need to destroy Silas's livelihood.

"I still had a man on Cannon, so we'll see what he finds out. In the meantime, I'll start organizing some kind of clean up crew for the wreckage. Thankfully, your home survived. You can return once you're fit for travel," Jonathan commented as a look passed between him and her husband.

"Thank you. I'll be sticking close to Caraway as she recovers, so that will be a relief. And I'm glad to hear we still have a home." Silas's soft gaze met hers causing Caraway to look away from the intensity of emotion in his eyes.

Something had shifted since last night, but she wasn't sure what. In her own heart, she realized how much Silas cared for her, willing to risk his own life to save hers. Everything had come into focus last night, highlighting the deep emotions that had been building in her for quite some time. Caraway loved him, plain and simple. Against all odds, he'd reached past her doubts and fears and embedded himself in her heart.

Hazel, Jonathan, and Callum stayed for another hour before leaving so Caraway could rest. While she hadn't felt tired talking with them, as soon as they left, a yawn escaped her and she wanted to sink into the bedding.

"I think it's time for you to take a nap, little Venus," Silas murmured, his low voice lulling her into a peaceful dream state. Snuggling closer to his side where he lay stretched out next to her, she sighed, breathing in his familiar scent and relaxing into a deep sleep.

SILAS SAT BY CARAWAY'S side as he read from her favorite book. With her injured hand wrapped for protection, she had trouble turning pages and laying in bed was quickly becoming boring.

After a knock on the door, Mary entered the room. "Beggin' your pardon, but there's a detective downstairs who would like to talk with you about the fire. Should I tell him to return another day?"

Silas shot Caraway a questioning glance. "It's up to you, love. We just returned home yesterday. Do you feel well enough to describe what happened?" Only a few days had passed since the fire, her wounds still rang fresh. But she nodded her head anyway.

"Might as well get it over with. We'll be down shortly, Mary."

Pulling the cover back, Silas helped her stand. "Can you grab the lavender dress from the wardrobe, please? That's the easiest one to put on," she requested, holding her injured hand to her chest. A dull headache radiated from the gash at the back of her head, but she refused to take any medication yet. Her mind needed to be clear when she gave her statement to the detective.

With the cotton dress in hand, Silas gently tugged it over her head, careful of her injuries before buttoning up the front, and together they walked downstairs.

The detective stood by the fireplace in the parlor studying the painting of a bird above the mantel. He looked to be around Silas's age with a head full of silver. Noticing their arrival, he bowed. "Mr. And Mrs. Riverton, I'm Detective Lucian Hawthorne. I promise this won't take up too much of your time." He flipped open a small notebook and pulled a pencil out of his jacket pocket. "I just want to ask a few questions to determine if any foul play caused the mill fire."

He proceeded to ask question after question as Caraway tried to remember details of that night. Unfortunately, she didn't think her information would be very helpful—all she'd seen was a shadow in Silas's office. And nothing seemed amiss in his office when she'd visited except for the fire, which she wasn't able to ascertain how it started. The detective thanked them for their time before promising to report back with any updates and leaving.

"How are you feeling?" Silas asked, placing a comforting hand on her healthy one. Nicks from the broken window decorated the back of his hand.

Bringing it to her lips, she brushed a soft kiss over them before answering, "As well as can be expected, I suppose. My head hurts a little, and my palm stings. But it could be worse."

"I'll get the laudanum for you." He moved to run upstairs, but she stopped him.

"Ring for Mrs. Frost or somebody else to retrieve it."

Reaching for the small bell on the side table, he summoned a maid who fetched the medicine. After taking a dose, Caraway returned to the safe harbor of Silas's arms, gratitude swelling in her chest for their survival.

"I'm sorry to disturb you, but a note just arrived from Mr. Travers. The messenger said it was urgent." Giles entered the room and brandished the letter with reluctant aplomb.

Brows furrowing, he tried to figure out what could be so significant that he'd need to leave Caraway. While she improved every day, he still didn't like leaving her alone for any extended amount of time, especially since she'd just gave her statement to the detective, draining what little energy she had.

"What's it say?"

"He wants to meet me at this address." Silas showed the scribbling to her as she covered a yawn.

Scanning the sheet, she puckered her lips. "What's at that address?"

"I don't know, but I guess I'll find out. Hopefully, it won't take long though, and I'll be back soon."

"Don't worry so much. I think I can survive without you for a few hours. In fact, our bed is calling my name." She joked, shooing him away before heading upstairs.

Smiling, he grabbed his coat and decided to take a single horse. It felt good to be outside instead of the enclosed space of a carriage. He enjoyed being able to breathe freely ever since the night of the fire when air had become such a rare commodity.

Silas headed towards the southern part of town where the wealthy elite lived. Manchester had a clear divide—the upper class and nobility stayed in the maintained parks of the south, businessmen and merchants stayed in midtown close to the city center and shopping, while the lower working class lived in the rundown northern part of Manchester.

Currently, he and Caraway lived in midtown as did the Travers, so he wondered what business Jonathan had in this neighborhood. Perhaps he and Hazel were considering moving further outside the hustle of the city since they had Callum?

Reining his gelding in front of a massive iron gate, he spied Travers's carriage further down the lane. The younger man exited the vehicle and waved to Silas. Disembarking himself, he took the horse's reins and led him forward to meet Travers halfway.

"What are we doing here? You know I don't want to leave Caraway for too long," Silas immediately launched into his tirade, annoyed.

"I thought you'd be interested to know they caught the arsonist who lit your mill on fire," Travers cut in, a satisfied smirk on his face as Silas shut his mouth. "They got a tip that a man was bragging about coming into a large sum of money in exchange for a small task... You can imagine what the task was." He raised an eyebrow, his meaning explicit. Turning to his driver, Travers instructed the man to take charge of Silas's horse before leading him closer to the gated entrance of the mansion set back from the street.

"Detective Hawthorne hasn't informed us of the arrest yet. But what does that have to do with why we're here? Did the man confess to who paid him?" Silas shot the questions in quick succession. He wanted to interrogate the man himself along with beating him to a bloody pulp for what happened to Caraway.

"Indeed, he did," Travers confirmed. "One Horace Cannon who lives at 53 Cherry Street which just so happens to be this address." A wave of his arm encompassed the estate in front of them. Their purpose clicking into place, Silas cracked his knuckles in preparation for what he'd do to Cannon when he got his hands on him.

"I see I've got your attention now. No doubt constables will be here soon to apprehend Cannon, but I managed to get my contact on the force to delay proceedings for the next hour. You'll get to say your piece..." He glanced down at Silas's clenched fists, "And do whatever else you want. Just make sure he stays alive—can't have you going up on murder charges."

Nodding, Silas followed Travers back to his carriage as they went through the gates down the long gravel driveway. Bare trees lined the lane leading to a grand Georgian home. Silas wondered if someone had notified their master that company was coming—if Travers's carriage would be recognized.

As they reached the entrance and banged on the front door, it took a moment before a balding gentleman answered.

"I'm sorry. We're not accepting visitors at this time. Please call on another day." He tried to shut the barely opened door in their faces, but Silas pushed through, his broad shoulders shoving past the smaller man.

"This isn't a social call. Where's Cannon?" he growled, advancing on the butler. A hand gripped his arm, trying to hold him back.

"Calm down. We'll find him," Travers said, loosening his grip as Silas stopped stalking the other man.

"He... he's in the... library," the butler stuttered out before scurrying away. Silas didn't know where that was but figured he'd tear the place apart stone by stone to find it if he had to.

Stalking down the hallway, he and Travers looked into each room before finding the library at the back of the home. Massive shelves wrapped around the walls, home to thousands of books. The smell of old leather and smoke filled the atmosphere.

Silas discovered Cannon in a leather chair behind a writing desk, a cigar hanging from his hand. Clearly, he'd heard the commotion making its way toward him as they'd sought him out. His clothes lay wrinkled and undone, hardly the put together man Silas had met before.

"You know why we're here," Silas stated, rounding the table to pull Cannon out of his seat and shove him against the wall. "We know you're behind the mill burning down. I almost lost my wife in that fire, and now you're going to suffer like she had to."

Drawing back a fist, he slammed a punch into the man's left cheek, deflecting the weak attempt to block the blow. A satisfying groan emitted from Cannon as he spit blood out of his mouth.

"Why'd you do it? I don't understand why you'd risk yourself in such a way," Travers interjected before Silas knocked Cannon out. Reeling in his erratic emotions, Silas waited for an answer.

That part had confused him as well. Cannon was a respected member of the community and the owner of a successful business. Why jeopardize all of that because he didn't agree with their progressive way of doing things?

"Rumblings of dissent started to travel through my factory. People started thinking they deserved more because you decided to pay outrageously high wages... among *other* ridiculous things. Manchester has thrived the past fifty years doing things the same way, then you came along to ruin things," Cannon spat out, contempt in his voice.

"Why focus on me? I've worked alongside you for the past fifteen years, doing it your way. Why punish me so harshly instead of Travers?" The obvious target on him instead of Travers had always confused him. It didn't make sense for him to become the scapegoat when he was known around town already as a successful businessman.

"Because you should have known better. You should have stuck with your fellow neighbors here. Instead you went in with this interloper." Cannon gestured to Travers who stood off to the right, observing the exchange with keen interest. "You turned your back on tradition and stirred up trouble with all of these progressive changes. And as if Travers Mill wasn't enough, you provided free food to workers along with a school and daycare at Ashley Mill, too? Intolerable!"

"Yes, I can see that," Silas sneered, his hold on Cannon tightening, yanking the man further up the wall. "Treating people fairly and offering needed resources would be intolerable to such an old, privileged windbag."

He tossed the older man to the side in disgust, and Cannon slid to the ground, clutching his bleeding face.

"Are you finished?" Travers calmly asked, leaning against a chair.

Exhaling a heavy breath, Silas nodded. Cannon would get what he deserved in prison. Besides, he'd rather not get caught bloodying the man in his own home.

"The authorities will be here soon enough. Good luck trying to buy your way out of this," Travers tossed out as the man attempted to pull himself to his feet. Leaving him behind, the two men exited the room to the frightened gazes of servants in the hallway. Quickly, they scattered back to their jobs, no doubt afraid of what would happen to them.

Stepping into the light outside, Silas breathed in a deep well of cool air. The brisk breeze washed away the last of the heaviness clinging to him from his past. He felt reborn on the winter day. Eager to return home to Caraway, Silas knew he couldn't keep his feelings secret anymore. Despite his reluctance, somehow he'd fallen for his wife.

Fear had stopped him from telling her, unsure of her reaction, but he'd almost lost her. And he couldn't live life hiding from her. The journey back home passed quickly as he debated how to broach the subject. Such a sensitive thing warranted a romantic gesture or so he thought. It's not like he'd ever declared his love for anyone before. He didn't think he'd even told his father that he loved him—of course, there was a reason for that.

Stopping by a shop, Silas bought Caraway's favorite candies, wondering briefly if he should get flowers, too. Realizing he was stalling, he pushed his horse faster towards home. Instead of finding his wife resting in bed, she sat knitting mittens by the window in their room. Her nose crinkled in concentration as she moved the needle through a stitch, and the vision she made floored him.

How had he gotten so lucky?

Catching sight of him, Caraway grinned. "See that didn't take long at all. You've hardly been gone for an hour. What did Jonathan want?"

"He found the one responsible for having the mill burned down," he replied, not bothering to lie to her. She deserved to know that the man responsible for her injuries would pay the consequences of his actions.

"Really? Who was it? Did he notify Detective Hawthorne?" Setting the knitting aside, she rose to pace around the room.

"It was Horace Cannon, a fellow board member. He didn't agree with the improvements we were making to the mill. Apparently, it caused his own employees to question their workplace which he didn't care for. Don't worry the law was right behind us when we arrived. We just wanted a word alone with him first to learn his motives."

"Thank goodness. I'm glad it's officially over then." Noticing the hand behind his back, she asked, "What are you hiding?"

Backing away from her, so she wouldn't ruin the surprise, he deflected, "I may have roughed him up a little, but nothing too serious."

An awkward pause fell between them, and he realized now was the time. Running a hand through his air, he stumbled over his words. "There's actually... um, something... I wanted to talk to you about." Embarrassment and annoyance flushed red on his face at his inability to form a coherent sentence. "I bought these for you." He removed the box from behind his back, practically shoving them in her face.

Jerking at the sudden movement, her eyes narrowed as she studied him. "Thank you?" She took the box from him before setting it aside on the table. "Are you alright?"

Sweat formed on his skin, the fabric of his shirt scratching against his skin as nervousness overtook him. Taking a deep breath to calm down, he started again, trying to speak clearly this time. "Yes, I'm just doing a terrible job at saying I love you." The words blurted out without much preamble, and a groan of frustration rumbled through his chest at the most unromantic declaration possible.

He was supposed to tell her how much she made him happy and that he couldn't live his life without her before ending with his love for her.

"What did you say?" Amazement teased her round features, the blue in her eyes shining brightly.

Licking his lips, he repeated himself, "I love you, Caraway. I realize you may not feel the same, but—" She cut him off with a kiss as she pulled his head closer.

Silas raised a hand to her cheek, stroking the soft skin as he said more firmly, "I adore you—your loyal nature, how you care about those less fortunate, your brilliant mind. I am in love with everything about you."

Caraway's eyes twinkled with a sheen of wetness. Glancing down, she wiped a shaking hand under her eyes, catching fallen tears. "I love you, too, Silas. I have for a while, but I was afraid to say anything. We didn't start out on a great foot, and I know I had a part in that, but somehow we've managed to make it through the past few months of struggles."

A tremulous smile formed on her mouth, filling him with hope and elation. The pounding of his heart doubled its pace as he absorbed the softly-spoken words like a parched man in the desert needing water to survive.

Reassuring his guarded heart, he asked, "Are you sure? Don't feel like you have to admit to feelings you don't have just to placate me. I told you how I felt because I wanted you to know, not because I expect anything in return." Her familiar lavender scent drifted over him as she moved closer to him. For the rest of his life, he'd associate the delicate flower with this moment.

"I'm sure," she confirmed, twining her arms around him for a hug. "You see me. You trust me with important decisions. You don't view me as some trophy to only be taken out during parties, who should only speak when spoken to. Do you know how rare that is? My sisters were able to find such husbands, but I figured the luck would run out with them. Even with Brandon I knew not to expect such treatment."

"He never deserved you. Hell, I don't deserve you, but I'm grateful you're mine." Bending his head, he poured every ounce of love he had for her into a kiss as her curves melted into his firm body, providing the softness he craved, and a shiver of excitement shocked him with its intensity.

Caraway loved him.

Really, truly loved him.

Finally.

CHAPTER FORTY-THREE

As Silas read from Caraway's favorite book the next day, the clip clop of horse hooves drifted into the parlor. Once news had spread of the fire and their injuries, people had inundated them with cards of well wishes, but thankfully people had stayed away, allowing them to recuperate in peace. However, it seemed that at least one person had no compunction about interrupting their day.

Spotting a familiar figure, Silas cursed under his breath.

"Who is it?" Caraway asked from her spot by the fireplace. Her injured arm lay in a sling across her chest while her long curls lay loose so as not to irritate the cut on the back of her head.

"It's my father. He must've heard what happened and came to gloat," he sneered, imagining the glee with which his father would eviscerate him. The burning down of the factory would only serve to prove that his father had been right. If Silas had stayed focused on his own mill instead of Travers's or his wife, he'd probably still have a working factory.

Resigning himself to an uncomfortable next few minutes, he waited for Giles to introduce Elias Riverton, steeling himself for a fight. He wouldn't tolerate more insults directed towards Caraway, especially not in her condition.

Elias strutted into the room, swinging his mahogany walking stick in hand. Glancing over at Caraway with hardly a pause on her injured arm, he faced his son. "So, Ashley Mill is gone."

The simple statement hung in the air as if Silas could offer some reasonable explanation as to why. "Yes, and I believe you know the party responsible: Mr. Horace Cannon. It seems he was none too happy about the changes we were making."

While Silas didn't think his father would condone such behavior, after all it was bad business to commit a crime, the fact that his father and Cannon had been in contact rankled him.

Elias harrumphed at the comment. "Horace always let emotion get the best of him. He should have known better than to get so worked up he'd resort to such a petty crime."

"It's hardly petty. My wife and I almost died. Caraway still bears the marks of that night." Blistering sparks exploded inside him at the use of such a cavalier term to describe the horrors of the incident.

"But you're both still here, alive and well," his father pointed out, sweeping a hand over a chair by the window before sitting. His coattails fanned out around him as he leaned both hands on the walking stick between his legs. "Besides, that's in the past. What are your plans moving forward?"

Of course his only concern would be the state of the business. Silas wasn't even sure why it mattered. Elias had never financially backed him or invested in the company even after it had grown successful. He had no stake in the business.

"We plan to rebuild. Travers is going over plans with our architect from Travers Mill. While I'm not exactly thrilled about the ashes of Ashley Mill, it does allow for us to start again and add needed upgrades and additions."

Honestly, it would be easier to make some of the changes starting from scratch. It would have been a pain having construction going at the same time as production. His only concern was for his employees who would be out of a job for the next few months.

Perhaps he and Caraway could come up with a plan to take care of them in the time being. Looking over at her, he knew she would appreciate the idea.

"You mean adding cafeterias and schools. You're not running a charity, boy. No matter what sort of ideas this one puts in your head." He shot a nod in Caraway's direction, derision clear in his tone.

"This one, as you so lovingly put it, is my wife and your daughter-in-law. You will treat her with the appropriate respect. And what we decide to do with Ashley Mill is none of your business. I don't even know why you've come all this way. To gloat? To see for yourself how far I've fallen? Well, I hate to disappoint you, Father, but I'm better than ever. I have a loving wife. Friends and a family that are more than I can ever say I had with you!" The diatribe ended with a shout.

Heavy breaths filled his lungs as he tried to regain composure. A calm hand settled on his forearm. Caraway stood beside him, her eyes soft with understanding.

Covering her hand with his, an unspoken moment of gratitude passed between them.

Oblivious to the exchange, Elias scoffed, "You act like you had it so bad. Look around, boy. Does this look like the poorhouse to you? I gave you the tools you needed to survive in this world. You wouldn't be a success without me, so don't start crying about what a sad childhood you had or what a horrible father I am."

His puffed out chest and smug look were a testament to his belief in the veracity of every word he spoke. It was clear he'd never take responsibility for any wrongdoing in his son's life or change his harsh ways.

Shifting Caraway's hand down to his palm for a gentle squeeze, they faced his father together, side by side.

"Sir, while I appreciate the fact that you believe you did what was right at the time, Silas is telling you that it was very hard for him growing up without any word of affection from you. But the both of you don't have to stay stuck in the past; you can forgive and learn to build a proper father-son relationship," Caraway entreated, the plaintive plea in her voice hopeful that Elias would want such a thing, but Silas knew better.

"It's of no use, my love."

"Listen to your husband, girl. Our family is of no concern to you. You're just the wench he got caught fucking at a ball. No better than a harlot off the street."

That was the last straw.

Freeing himself of Caraway's suddenly tight hold on him, Silas punched his father directly in the nose. Blood sprayed everywhere as a howl of pain exploded from the older man.

"Get the hell out of our home, and don't ever come back. I'd hoped our last meeting would have been clear enough, but since it wasn't, let me spell it out for you: you are not welcome here. I don't want you in mine or my family's life. Any future grandchildren will be lucky not to know they have such a bastard for a grandfather." Rubbing his sore knuckles, Silas called for Giles, who must have been standing right outside the door, as he entered a second later.

"Yes, sir?"

"Please see to it that my father is escorted back to his carriage and is not allowed entrance into this home anymore." Elias tried protesting the decree, espousing all sorts of epithets, but Silas ignored him. Turning his back on the man who'd been like an anchor weighing him down all these years, he finally felt free.

Once the commotion from outside died down and his father was well and truly gone, Silas collapsed onto the settee. All of the previous energy and anger evaporated, leaving him feeling curiously exhausted.

Settling beside him, Caraway wrapped an arm around his head, pulling him into her neck. The smell of lavender soothed him as he breathed her in.

"I'm so proud of you," she whispered. "I'm sorry you were forced to make such a declaration, but I truly believe it's what is best for you. And you'll never be lacking for love or family." Her gentle strokes through his short hair brought a sense of comfort to him.

No... He'd never lack for love again.

CHAPTER FORTY-FOUR

Madame Fleur had impeccable timing.

Yesterday, Caraway had finally gotten the all clear by the doctor. Her burns were healed and the gash on her head completely closed. It had been a few weeks since the fire, and today was the first day Silas had left her alone.

She appreciated his care, but his over-protectiveness was becoming suffocating. Though, she couldn't be too upset—Silas had told her he loved her, freeing her enough so she could share the secret she'd been holding onto for weeks: that she was in love with him as well.

They'd spent the rest of that fateful day and evening talking and sharing more about each other than they'd ever had before. It filled her with a flush of happiness remembering the intimacy, but tonight she wanted a different sort of intimacy.

It would be the first time they'd make love since their declarations and the fire. And she wanted it to be as special as could be, hence her excitement about Madame Fleur's special delivery. Boxes full of undergarments direct from Paris littered the bed as Caraway tried on one scandalous piece after another.

Lace, silk, chiffon, the variety of soft, transparent fabrics surprised her. And the designs! She had no idea such items were available, since she mostly stuck to respectable white cotton underthings. But this was a whole new world she was excited to explore to entice her husband.

A secret smile peeked out as she studied herself in the full length mirror.

Caraway skimmed her hands down the see-through negligee. Before she would've looked in the mirror and seen only flaws. But now she knew her husband adored every hill and valley.

She blushed at the thought. Yes, he most definitely enjoyed her curves as their past sexual exploits floated through her mind. And now that part of their lives would be deeper and more meaningful as their feelings grew deeper.

How ridiculous I'd been to favor Brandon over Silas.

It embarrassed her to remember those tense months, of how she'd struggled to fully accept her husband because of a childhood fantasy. He'd saved her from a terrible mistake following her into that room at the Gibbons' ball!

A letter from Hazel a few days ago had outlined Brandon's true reason for his sudden interest in Caraway—his family had cut him off after years of dissolute behavior and marrying Miss Bradshaw had been his attempt at securing an influx of wealth through her dowry.

Unfortunately, once the girl's father learned of Brandon's reduced status, he'd rescinded his approval of the courtship, so Brandon had approached Caraway with his annulment plan to capture the trust fund Owen set up for her years ago.

"*He's penniless,*" Hazel had written. "*There was a clause in the contracts he signed to join Jonathan and Riverton that he legally broke when they found proof of him sharing financial secrets with competitors. Even if his information* was *false. Guess Jonathan made sure to add a loophole in case they needed to rid themselves of Brandon. Isn't my husband so wise?"*

Caraway had rolled her eyes at that last bit of wifely gushing, but she admitted it was a smart move by her brother-in-law. To think, she could've married Brandon only to have him steal the fortune Owen bestowed upon her and watch him gallivant around town with other women—because she'd received a separate letter from Lily stating the exploits that had precipitated Brandon's visit to Manchester in the first place.

Hearing the door open and close behind her, Caraway dismissed the past with a firm shake. There were more important matters to attend to rather than musing about the past. She was done with that way of living. It only led to trouble.

Whipping around to find Silas silently observing her, she pretended to scold, "You're early."

She thought she had another hour before he'd retire. With having to figure out how to rebuild Ashley Mill along with his work at Jonathan's factory, a pile of things was surely built up since he'd done minimal work these past few weeks.

Silas stood frozen, taking her in from head to toe. "I'm sorry, little Venus. Am I interrupting something?"

"Well, I had planned to be waiting for you in our bed. However, I suppose this works as well." She strolled up to him, gently tugging away his loose necktie.

"I received a new order from Madame Fleur this afternoon. I'm wearing one of her new designs." Her hand followed the path of revealed skin down his neck to his hair-covered chest.

"Does it please you?"

"It pleases me greatly, wife."

Smiling in victory, Caraway continued, "Then I believe you're overdressed, dear husband."

Relieving him of his jacket, she watched as he tugged his linen shirt overhead, muscles shifting beneath his skin. Once again, wonder at his strong body flitted through her.

Despite her worry for him when he fought, Caraway couldn't deny her appreciation of the results of such physical labor. His toned body was so different from hers.

"Is this better, my love?"

She leaned in to place a kiss in the center of his chest, feeling the soft curls there tickle her lips. "Almost." Her fingers unbuttoned his trousers to reveal his hard erection.

Holding his dark gaze, she sank down and pulled the fabric away from his body. Fully exposed to her gaze, he stood proud, waiting for her next move.

"Now, go lay on the bed, Mars of mine," she ordered breathily, excited to have him laid out like a feast in front of her. His nostrils flared at the endearment before complying.

"As you wish, little Venus." Walking to the massive bed in the center of the room, he swept an arm over the strewn boxes leftover from her try-on session. Swaths of translucent fabric floated through the air like butterfly wings. "I see I have more to look forward to."

"Mmm... yes, you do," she agreed, climbing over him to rest on his lower stomach. Lowering herself to him, she brushed a kiss over his mouth, his beard scratching pleasantly against her lips. "Have I mentioned how much I love your beard?"

"Not in so many words," he drawled as a hand grasped her exposed thigh by his side. "Why don't you tell me?"

"I thought I just did."

"You're no fun," he pretended to pout before she shifted back to rub against his cock—the thickness a pleasurable distraction.

"Really? Then perhaps we should just go to sleep..." She acted like she was about to climb off of him before his grip on her thighs tightened, pushing her back to where he wanted her. The ridged skin of his abdomen met her bottom as she retook her seat.

The flickering light from the fire dimmed as it slowly went out, casting more shadows over their prone bodies. A waft of ash floated through the room, briefly reminding her of the terrible night in the fire before she shook her mind of those sobering thoughts. Returning her attention to the man beneath her, she slid a palm up his chest, teasing, "So, I guess I am fun, then, hmm?"

"Yes, just too proper and polite," he smiled, not seeming too bothered by the assessment. Caraway knew he enjoyed pushing her past her comfort zone to new heights of sexuality. And she loved it, too. It made her feel like a desirable woman when for so long she'd never felt that way. Men never noticed her, and they certainly had never elicited such responses from her before.

"I have to be those things when you insist on being their complete opposite," she asserted, knowing their individual strengths complemented the other's weaknesses. Somehow without their knowledge, they'd managed to form a fairly balanced marriage when it came to temperament and personality.

She feathered a kiss over his lips before pressing for more. His kisses always transported her to another realm, full of heat and passion. Long minutes felt like lifetimes passing as they got lost in each other's taste.

Her hands slid along the silky sheets beneath him until her body lay flush against his—every curve held by his firm frame. Warmth emanated from him, pervading past the thin fabric of her nightgown to sink into her own overheated skin. The sense of having nothing between them was only refuted by the sensual tugging of the fabric along her over-sensitized skin. Baby fine hair caught on the light chiffon while her nipples were rubbed into hard peaks.

Breaking their kiss, she followed the line of his bearded chin to the cords in his neck, gently sucking on the distended muscles. Another groan erupted from him at her soft touches, careful not to go too hard too fast. She wanted the night to be drawn out, an expression of their love for one another.

"I see you're in a playful mood tonight. May I ask what brought this on? Not that I'm complaining." Silas's deep voice vibrated from his chest, creating a soft hum beneath her.

"Since the doctor signed off on my injuries being completely healed, I figured I'd take the next step because I wasn't sure you would. You've been very protective these past few weeks." She huffed, knowing he'd felt her annoyance a few times, "Besides, Madame Fleur's new designs were the perfect excuse to seduce you."

"Believe me, sweetheart, you don't need an excuse." The rumbled words were followed by him rolling them over to pin her underneath him. His weight crushed her back into the mattress, the soft bedding cradling her body. "And if I'd known my wife needed my touch, I would have found a way around your injuries... Shall I show you?"

He moved down her body, his hot breath scorching her through the light nightgown, until his shoulders rested between her open thighs. A shiver of anticipation shot through her core as he separated her folds. Such exposure to his view brought a wave of uncertainty mixed with desire. It felt naughty for him to see her so open despite their past liaisons, and she knew she had nothing to fear from him, yet the sliver of self-doubt tried to overpower the desire.

As if understanding her distracted thoughts, he brought her back to focus with a stabbing motion straight to her core—the sudden act shocking her. Usually, he preferred to build up the moment before thrusting inside her, but clearly tonight he'd reached his limit which she couldn't help but feel smug over.

She'd hardly started her planned seduction before he'd been moved to take over. The hungry sounds coming from him spurred on her own pleasure as she arched up into his greedy mouth. Her peak crashed through her in time with his licks before he reared back and thrust inside her, filling her up in a way that would never get old.

Bringing his hand between them, he cupped her throat, the pressure heightening the vulnerability between them. It brought her back to that night at the ball when he'd used the pearls to lightly restrain her before moving onto more daring uses. Reaching up to him, she gripped his disheveled hair and pulled him down for a brutal kiss—their tongues dueling as he moved inside her.

Digging her nails into his scalp, she cried out as another, stronger orgasm rocked through her, setting off his own release. Shuddering, he slowly collapsed on top of her, resting his head in the crook of her neck. Gentling her touch, she stroked his hair and neck, soothing him as pulses of pleasure wracked his body.

"I love you," he whispered, the words bringing tears to her eyes. This is what she'd always wanted—this feeling of completion body and soul with a man who truly loved her.

"I love you, too." She turned her head to place a kiss on his sweaty forehead, then licked the salty taste from her lips. Closing her eyes, a hum of pleasure buzzed through her veins.

All these months of pain and distrust had finally led them here. To this place of love-filled intimacy. A place she'd never imagined she'd reach after the rocky way their marriage started. But they persevered and came out the other side winners.

A satisfied smile tilted her mouth. Yes, they'd both won hard-fought victories. And now they could enjoy the spoils—starting tonight and continuing for the rest of their lives.

Thinking back to that first day in Manchester, she thanked God and even Brandon for bringing her here, to a town so different from what she'd grown up in. However, as she considered her circumstances, she also knew she'd never felt the way she did now in Hampshire.

No, she'd felt displaced after her parents died and her sisters had all married. But finally, *finally*, she was home.

EPILOGUE ONE

Hampshire, England, April 1876

The smell of freshly baked bread tantalized Silas as he dropped off the last of the cut logs he'd finished splitting for the stove, and he brought the side of his open collar up to wipe away some of the sweat coating his face. Walking inside the small cottage at the edge of the forest, he watched as Caraway took a loaf of bread out of the hot oven. Here in the country, they lived as simple village folk—seeing to their own needs without servants. It was always a welcome relief when they were able to escape Manchester to unwind in this little oasis.

A cry erupted from the bassinet under the window, drawing his attention. Catching his wife's eye, he motioned for her to continue what she was doing as he went to the baby girl fussing in her bed.

"What is it, little darling?" he asked as he carefully lifted the baby up and into his arms, cradling her head against his shoulder. Miss Harmony Winter Riverton had been born that spring, a sweet charmer who took after her name and mother. Fine curls covered her tiny head as navy-blue eyes peered at him.

"She must be feeling needy today; I only set her down a few minutes before you came in," Caraway explained with a slight smile as she prepared the rest of dinner. The loaf of bread cooled on the table as she stirred the pot of stew bubbling over the fire.

"Hmm... sounds like her mother," he teased Caraway as he rocked his daughter until she stopped fussing and began cooing playfully. "She just needed daddy's touch." He sent a significant look to his wife which she rolled her eyes at, though a flush reddened her skin, more so than the heat of the kitchen warranted.

Sighing, exasperated, Caraway lamented, "You are going to be such a bad influence on our children. I can't imagine the things that will come out of their mouths as they get older."

"Then they'll fit right in with their cousins," he reasoned. Heaven knew, Travers and Clarke were worse than he was when it came to inappropriate comments. Their children were sure to be hellions.

Laughing as she shook her head in surrender, she doled out two bowls of the steaming soup, setting them next to the place settings on the small wooden dining table. "I'm glad they'll be able to grow up so close to their cousins, though. They'll have Callum and Clem in Manchester, then Lily and Owen's children here in Hampshire. Not to mention their cousins in London."

"They won't be able to step too far outside before they run into a relative," he joked, thinking of the profligacy of children running around England. Her sisters' families were booming; they needed to catch up, he thought with eagerness.

Joining Caraway, he took a seat, turning Harmony so she'd face the table as he attempted to spoon some of the soup into his mouth, which proved impossible with a bouncing baby in his lap.

"Here," Caraway chuckled, shifting her chair closer to him, so she could feed him. "It's almost like I have two children..." She tilted her head with raised eyebrows as she teased and fed him a slice of the freshly baked bread.

"Well, I wouldn't be opposed to having another child." The desire that flared in his eyes sent a shiver through her, his meaning clear—he'd enjoy making a baby as much as caring for one.

"You're relentless," she replied, carefully holding up a spoonful of the hot liquid. "Don't you want to enjoy this time with the three of us before adding another? You know it'll only make our lives crazier."

She made a valid point. The new Ashley Mills had finally finished being rebuilt and was bigger than ever with an enlarged mess hall to hold more employees and a separate wing for the daycare and school along with some other spaces Caraway had recommended.

It took most of their time fielding questions and requests for the various mill businesses. Plus, he still stayed involved with Travers's Mill to make sure it stayed on track although after these past few years Jonathan seemed to have a good handle on things. He'd learned quickly what needed to be done and how to accomplish it.

That was another reason they needed this cottage besides Caraway's love for her childhood home: they needed a place to take much needed breaks from the hustle and bustle of Manchester.

"True," he conceded, "But don't you want Harmony to grow up with siblings close to her age like you did? I know I don't want her to grow up an only child like I was." Memories of his childhood cast a pall over him. No, his child wouldn't know such loneliness or neglect.

"That will be impossible. You're nothing like your father, and you both have me now." Once Silas was finished with his dinner, she turned her attention to her own meal. "I'm not saying I don't want more children; I just thought we might want to wait a little longer. But honestly either way, I know we'll make it work, and we'll love the child."

This he knew for a fact. No matter his own shortcomings when it came to parenting, Caraway would make sure their children were loved and cared for. She exuded a warmth that had only magnified with the birth of their daughter. And he was relieved when he needn't have worried about the dangers of pregnancy: Caraway had given birth with flying colors. Granted, the hours of seeing her in pain still haunted him, but the doctor assured him it was all normal and nothing out of the ordinary.

"Besides, you'll want a son, of course," she teased, a twinkle in her smiling eyes. "We have a lot to live up to... I believe Venus and Mars had at least four children."

Holding Harmony up as she batted her arms and legs in excitement, he added, "Perhaps after you give me another one of her; she needs a sweet little sister to play with."

"I swear she has you wrapped around her little finger," Caraway laughed, reaching out so Harmony could clutch one of her own fingers. "The way our family's formed in the past and your propensity towards girls, we'll have four daughters to carry on the Garden Girls line."

"I wouldn't mind." He and Caraway had carried on the tradition by giving Harmony a shortened version of wintergreen as her middle name. All of the previously Taylor sisters named their daughters in the family tradition, the males of the group missing out on that honor.

Finished with her meal, Caraway grabbed their empty bowls and brought them to the wash tub.

"I can do that, sweetheart. Why don't you take Harmony? I think she might be getting hungry." The baby reached for her mama, her rosebud mouth opening and closing in an eating gesture.

"I think you're right." They switched places with him beginning to clean the dishes while she sat in a rocking chair and unbuttoned the front of her dress for Harmony's feeding.

A contented feeling drifted over him at such a domestic scene. Never before would he have imagined himself living a life like this, especially one that included him doing simple household tasks, but he found it suited him. It provided a comfort he'd never known before Caraway, and he planned on making sure his family stayed safe and happy for the rest of their lives in gratitude.

EPILOGUE TWO

Hampshire, England, July 1876

Caraway shifted the picnic basket in her arms as they made their way across the field to Owen and Lily's pond.

"Are you sure you don't want me to carry that for you," her husband asked as he cradled their daughter against his shoulder. Waving him off, she pointed out, "You already have your hands full; besides I can handle a picnic basket. I may not box everyday like you, but I'm stronger than I look."

Today, they were celebrating Lily, Clarke, and Callum's birthdays. With such a growing family, they found it easier to group close birthdays together in order to celebrate with everyone. The beautiful summer day boasted clear blue skies while a light breeze drifted over them—a perfect day to spend outside with family.

The rest of their family resembled a beehive as Lily and Iris set out a variety of food courses while their husbands played with some of the children in the pond, the bottoms of their pants rolled up to expose bare legs.

Caraway felt a wave of tears rise up unexpectedly at the happy scene before her. After their parents' deaths years ago, she'd worried about what would become of them.

Concerned they'd be forced into either a workhouse or bad marriages in order to avoid such a fate. And while some of their marriages hadn't risen out of a love match, they turned out to be exactly what each woman needed.

She could finally lay her mantle of responsibility down and allow their husbands to take care of her younger sisters from now on. And she could focus on loving them and building strong bonds of friendship.

The weight of it all finally lifted off her chest, after all these years, being replaced by a light and joyful spirit. They were all going to be okay. With loving husbands and children to come alongside them, the Garden Girls had finally found home.

THE END

THANK YOU FOR READING!

Please consider leaving a rating/review. Ratings & reviews are the #1 way to support an indie author like me.

To stay up-to-date on new releases and more, join my newsletter here[1] and follow me on Instagram: @authorjemmafrost[2]!

I appreciate your support!

Happy Reading,

Jemma

---

1. https://www.thearrowedheart.com/jemma-frost
2. https://www.instagram.com/authorjemmafrost/

ALSO BY JEMMA FROST

Charming Dr. Forrester[1]
All Rogues Lead to Ruin[2]
An Earl Like Any Other[3]
The Scoundrel Seeks a Wife[4]
A Gentleman Never Surrenders[5]
Earls Prize Curves[6]
Barons Adore Curves[7]
Princes Crave Curves

---

1. https://books2read.com/charmingdrforrester
2. https://books2read.com/u/md7vyQ
3. https://books2read.com/u/38yYMr
4. https://books2read.com/u/38eenr
5. https://books2read.com/u/4EJ9pM
6. https://mybook.to/EarlsPrizeCurves
7. https://mybook.to/BaronsAdoreCurves

ABOUT THE AUTHOR

Jemma Frost grew up in the Midwest where she visited the library every day and read romance novels voraciously! Now, she lives in North Carolina with her cat, Spencer, and dreams of stories to be written!

FOLLOW JEMMA FROST on social media: @authorjemmafrost

Made in the USA
Monee, IL
07 November 2024